MURDERS ON PIGEON MOUNTAIN

Also by Tony Spallone

Murder at Breeze Canyon

Within a span of weeks, three cyclists are killed along remote Santa Fe roadways. Assistant District Attorney Hank Kincaid, an avid cyclist and long-time member of the Canyon Cycling Club, believes their deaths are more than coincidence. He convinces ill-tempered Detective "Deeg" DeGarzia to examine possible clues and motives to confirm the deaths are not accidental. When prominent artist Carlotta Smith is also killed, evidence points to the beautiful and licentious Heather Dorell and her friend Stacey Keenan—also members of the Cycling Club—as prime suspects. The two women, minted by the media as the new "Thelma and Louise," criss-cross New Mexico to evade capture. In their wake, new suspects emerge in a twisted series of events and motives.

Murders in the High Desert

For three years, a serial killer has been targeting employees of Santa Fe's Indian Bend Hotel and Casino by first abducting them and then burying them alive in the vast high desert of New Mexico's Yiqua Indian Reservation. That's the conclusion of Detective Clay Bryce of the Santa Fe Criminal Investigation Unit and Chief Jacoby Johnstone of the Yiqua Pueblo Tribal Police. The two combine forces and expertise to solve the murders. Among the suspects are Denver Stennet, roommate of two of the victims, and John Grainger, Operations VP at the Indian Bend. Still others emerge with motives of their own in this perverse tale of death in the desert.

Reviews of *MURDER AT BREEZE CANYON*

"Thought at least six different times that I was absolutely sure 'who done it,' but I was wrong every time, and stunned by the plot twist at the end."

"Terrific in its development of characters, relationships and plot."

"... an exciting crime novel. The writing was so clear and real that I could easily picture each crime and the progressive investigation."

"The threads Spallone weaves! You will get to know each character well. You will think them interesting. You will just notice the hints of loose threads and not see the cloth until the very end."

"What a ride! When I got to the end, breathing hard, I found myself doubling back, looking for clues I had missed. They were there, skillfully planted in a plot so fast paced it virtually compels the reader to, well, breeze by them."

"I can't wait for the next books. Spallone is a fantastic writer. What a page turner."

"Wow—What a thriller. It had me fooled!!!!"

"Spallone's book spins a racing tale of the wheel of life, friends, family and tragedy. Who is friend and who is shadenfreude?"

"What a ride! *Murder at Breeze Canyon* is a great blend of surprise and suspense."

"This book is so suspenseful and the character development is fantastic. This would make an excellent addition to your summer reading list or a fun vacation book. LOVED IT!"

Reviews of *MURDERS IN THE HIGH DESERT*

"Hints, suspicions, clues, accusations and deceptions flash through the pages of *Murders in the High Desert*. Spallone takes us on another ride as breathless and bumpy as the twisting trip through Breeze Canyon in his first novel."

"From the beginning, the tone of this crime thriller is well established. It's diabolical."

"A closer read reveals that Spallone writes from a solid psychological background, and the careful reader is left with a lot more to think about than all the red herrings that make this suspense novel so much fun."

"Each time I thought I knew who the murderer was, there was another twist in the plot, leading me to re-think my first, second, third, fourth and fifth opinions as to "who dunnit. A fun read."

"As with Spallone's first book I had trouble putting it down. There was always something at the end of each chapter that caused me to want to read more, to find out what happened next."

"Fabulous! This book is an A+. It's as good as famous authors like Baldacci, Connelly and Deighton."

"Another great mystery from Spallone! It has an interesting plot with many twists and turns. It is easy reading which I highly recommend to anyone who enjoys mystery novels."

"A quarter of the way through, I knew who the killer was... except I was completely wrong. Then about half way through, I figured it out... and I was wrong again. Near the end, I nailed it! But no, I was wrong."

MURDERS ON PIGEON MOUNTAIN

by
Tony Spallone

MURDERS ON PIGEON MOUNTAIN

Published in the United States of America by Long Walk
Publishing.
www.TonySpallone.com / Tony@tonyspallone.com

ISBN-13: 978-0-9864271-4-5

Edited by Stephanie J. Beavers Communications
www.StephanieJBeavers.com / 610-247-9494

Cover design by Cover Book Designs
www.coverbookdesigns.com

To Leigh

You brought kindness, beauty, and grace to this world.

ACKNOWLEDGEMENTS

At the publishing of this, my third book, I once again thank my wife Patti for her unfailing support and encouragement.

My editor, Stephanie J. Beavers, of Stephanie J. Beavers Communications, has taught me much and reminds me how glad she is we both have a sense of humor. She has burnished my stories and helped them become appealing mysteries.

To my friend Gary Boegershausen, a former cop and pilot, who helped in the development of several scenes.

To Steve McNally, another former cop, who went above and beyond what I asked in research to provide extensive background information on key elements of this story.

To Rose Williams, my little sister who, true to Italian brother-sister loyalties, willingly (maybe unwillingly) pores over every draft of my stories and gives cogent grammatical and punctuation advice before I present my novel to my editor.

Thanks also to my son Mark, my daughter-in-law Sheri, and my friend Terry Work for their enthusiasm and advice.

Finally, my thanks to everyone who has enjoyed my novels and offered wonderful reviews on the internet and social media. I hope you enjoy Murders on Pigeon Mountain just as much.

Part I

PROLOGUE

Two men coasted up Catherine Street in a dark green Ford sedan. They stopped and double-parked a dozen yards from Vincent Vendetti's row house, exited the car, and walked casually toward the mob boss as he climbed the three steps to his front porch. Vincent should have noticed his assailants, but he did not. As he reached for the door knob, the men pulled out revolvers and fired.

The shots drove Vincent against his front door. Blood splattered onto his house like Rorschach inkblots. Four rounds hit him. One penetrated his left side, missed his heart by two centimeters, then veered off to embed in a rib. One went through the fleshy part of his shoulder and two others grazed his left arm.

The shooters ran back to their car and sped erratically down the street, sideswiping one car and barely missing another.

* * *

Three days later, Vendetti was moved from Saint Elizabeth Hospital's ICU to a private room guarded by one of his men who ensured no one other than doctors or nurses entered. Vincent's seven-month-pregnant wife Concetta sat in a chair in the corner of the room. She used a white lace handkerchief in one hand to dab tears from her eyes and worked the beads of a black and gold rosary in the other. Her lips moved in cadence to her silent prayers.

Vincent was propped up in bed reading the two-day-old Philadelphia Bulletin newspaper account of his attempted murder.

MOB BOSS SHOT!

June 17, 1953: Vincent Vendetti, 41, reputed leader of the Philadelphia Mafia, was shot four times in front of his South Philadelphia home on Catherine Street. A spokesman for Saint Elizabeth's Hospital reported that Vendetti's condition has been termed serious but stable and says he is expected to survive. Detective Robert O'Hara, who is heading the investigation into the attempted murder, announced there were no witnesses to the event. O'Hara expressed concern that the shooting might be the start of an all-out war over control of the Mob's lucrative Philadelphia/South Jersey territory and involve one of the five New York crime families (continued on page A2).

* * *

A doctor dressed in a green surgical gown approached the guard outside Vincent's room. A surgical mask covered the man's face up to his eyes. He nodded to the guard, who did not challenge him, and entered Vincent's room. Vincent looked at the doctor over his newspaper.

The doctor asked, "How are you feeling?"

"I'm good," Vincent said, and set the newspaper aside.

"Good. You'll be able to go home in a couple of days." The doctor nodded to Concetta then opened the door to beckon Vincent's guard into the room. "Please come in for a second."

The guard entered the room and flipped his chin to the doctor. "What do you want?"

In a swift, deft motion, the doctor pulled a .45 from the pocket of his scrubs and shot the guard once between his eyes. The red hole on his forehead, twice the size of a Hindu's bindi, oozed surprisingly little blood. The guard fell backward against the wall and slid to the floor in a sitting position. His right hand was inside his suit jacket—he had been a split second too late reaching for his weapon.

The doctor turned his .45 to Vincent, but without warning, Vincent emptied his Colt .37 in rapid-fire succession from underneath the thin blanket that covered him.

From underneath his mask, the doctor opened his mouth, but no words or screams came out. He crumbled to the floor, dead. Blood quickly soaked his scrubs.

Concetta did not move from her chair. She worked her rosary faster than before and stared at Vincent in disbelief and horror. *What just happened?*

Vincent shrugged, lifted his newspaper and turned to page A2. Within five minutes, two policemen entered his room with revolvers drawn. Vincent lowered his newspaper and exhaled loudly to show his impatience.

"Keep your hands where we can see them!" The cops looked at the bloodied doctor and the dead Vendetti guard. "What the hell happened here?"

"That doctor killed one of my men and then tried to shoot me. Had to defend myself." Vincent's response was matter of fact. "Had to protect my wife, too. She's pregnant."

The cops glanced at Concetta who remained focused on her rosary.

Vincent continued, "The doctor came in with an operating mask covering his face. I ain't never seen a doctor wear a mask over his face when they ain't doin' any operating, so I knew he was a player. He was gonna try to get me next so I shot him first."

"Where's your weapon?"

Vincent nodded toward the tattered blanket. "Under here."

One cop holstered his weapon and pulled the blanket down to expose Vincent's revolver. He removed it by its barrel.

The other cop asked Concetta, "Mrs. Vendetti, you okay?"

She looked at him blankly and did not answer. After five years in the United States, cloistered in Philadelphia's Little Italy neighborhood where most people spoke only Italian, Concetta still did not understand or speak English.

"She can't speak no American. She's from Italy."

Vincent asked his wife how she was, *"Come stai?"*

"Come pensi che io sono?" she said. "How do you think I am?"

Vincent translated for the cops. "She says she's good, couldn't be better."

* * *

Playing off the fact that Vincent had shot his attacker with a revolver he had hidden underneath his bed covers, the tabloid Daily News headlined the shootings "Mob Boss Goes Undercover to Kill Attacker!"

The Philadelphia District Attorney wanted to charge Vincent with murder, but Vendetti's lawyer argued that his client's shooting of a fake doctor was nothing more than an act of self-defense. No charges were filed.

Two days later, Vincent exited Saint Elizabeth's in a wheelchair accompanied by his wife and his Mafia lawyer. He was immediately confronted by a half-dozen reporters who shouted questions at him, none of which he or his lawyer answered. With cops guarding Vincent's departure, his lawyer whisked him back home to Catherine Street in a black Ford sedan.

Over the following two months, Vendetti's leadership role in the Mafia came under increased police and media scrutiny. Philip Giambroli, who had split with Vendetti a year earlier and was thought to be allied with either the Anastasia or Lucchese families in New York, was himself killed by a single shot to the back of his head. His chest had been etched with the letter *V* and his body dumped along the Delaware River near the Tacony-Palmyra Bridge. Three other men associated with Giambroli also were executed, and the internecine war for control of the Philadelphia mob was quickly over.

CHAPTER 1

In the early 1900s, seventy-five percent of Italian immigrants came from the hill towns and mountain villages in the impoverished southern portion of the country.

* * *

Vincenzo Antonio Vendetti was born in 1912 in San Bartolomeo, one of the many picturesque mountain villages in the Province of Benevento, northeast of Naples. His parents, Dominic and Maria, lived a simple existence and enjoyed the warmth of their close-knit family and friends. They struggled to overcome the poverty that eventually drove hundreds of thousands of their fellow countrymen to emigrate from villages in the rural south to the United States and other countries. Letters from immigrants told how the United States offered a new beginning and bright future, with jobs available for artisans and untold educational opportunities for their children.

With hearts full of optimism, yet fearful of the unknown, Dominic and Maria Vendetti, along with their infant son, left their beloved San Bartolomeo, immigrated to the United States, and settled in Philadelphia.

A stone mason by trade, Dominic prospered immediately. He hired out to contractors who built stone mansions in the wealthy western suburbs of Philadelphia. Ironically, the architectural style of these houses that were celebrated for their classic use of stone was often reminiscent of the style and design of buildings in poor Italian villages like San Bartolomeo.

In Italy, male children at eight or nine years of age were considered old enough to become apprenticed to their fathers or other artisans. For generations, sons born into the Vendetti family had been destined to be stonemasons, skilled and proud craftsmen. But Dominic vowed his son would not suffer the trials of the poor workingman in their new country. Vincenzo would become an educated professional, someone people would respect for his mind, someone who did not work with his hands, but with his brains. That was Dominic's wish.

But the hopes of a father for his son are not always realized.

To ensure his son's brightest future, Dominic wanted to extract every ounce of potential from him. But nothing Vincenzo did was good enough for his father—not his school grades, his mannerisms, or his ability to speak Italian. When Vincenzo stopped growing at the age of thirteen, his father ridiculed him and called him *brutto nano*—ugly dwarf.

Dominic's harping and stifling control over every aspect of his son's life made Vincenzo grow surly and short-tempered. He became an outcast among the neighborhood kids who bullied him, and was ready to fight at any slight. Kids called him Shorty, a nickname he despised. Although innately intelligent, Vincent, as he was called by the nuns in parochial school, grew to be an indifferent student who showed neither remarkable skill nor any ambition to learn.

CHAPTER 2

The Eighteenth Amendment to the United States Constitution established a nationwide ban on the production, importation, transportation, and sale of alcoholic beverages—otherwise known as Prohibition. The ban remained in effect from 1920 to 1933.

* * *

Growing up, Vincent's only friend was Frankie Impolito, an odd-looking boy with permanent dark circles under his eyes and deep lines in his face that stretched from the sides of his nose to the outer edges of his mouth. His resemblance to a puppet earned him the nickname Dummy.

From their earliest years, Vincent and Frankie were inseparable, spending most waking hours together doing what the kids in Little Italy did when there was nothing else to do—roaming the streets of South Philadelphia, stealing apples from fruit merchants' sidewalk displays, pitching pennies against the stoop to Vincent's front porch, or playing stickball on normally empty Catherine Street.

Frankie and his older sister Elaine—nicknamed Pansie—lived with their mother Dolores and father Eddie in an apartment above the tavern Eddie owned.

Eddie Impolito was a slight man, with thinning hair, skittery eyes, and a demeanor to match. Eddie's Tavern, located directly across the street from the Vendetti's house, was a typical South Philly neighborhood saloon with its windowless brick facade, half dozen plain-top tables, eight stools lined up along a polished mahogany bar, and a waxed shuffleboard table along the back wall. Eddie had placed two large potted plants in the far corners of the room in an attempt to spruce up the dimly lit tavern. Sawdust on the wood floor absorbed spilled beer and whiskey. The pungent-sweet smells of smoke from cheap stogies and sawdust combined to linger on patrons' clothes and in their nostrils for hours after they left the tavern.

In January 1920, Eddie had to close his thriving bar when the Eighteenth Amendment to the U.S. Constitution became law. Whereas prohibition was disastrous for saloon-keepers such as Eddie, the law proved to be a boon to the Mafia. It ushered in thirteen years of bootlegging, speakeasies, and a rise in crime in Chicago, New York, and most other major cities. The Philadelphia Mafia, which was getting its start under mob boss, Salvatore Sabella, saw its influence swell.

Eight months after Eddie had shuttered his tavern as mandated by the new law, Nunzio and Angelo Spatola, Sicilian immigrant cousins and Mafia soldiers, visited him to speak about a "business proposition" they had in mind for him.

By outward appearances, no one would ever guess the two cousins were related. Nunzio was tall, thin, and balding, and his face pockmarked from years of acne as a teenager. Angelo was a short, muscular weightlifter with a full head of black hair.

Nunzio rang the doorbell to Eddie's apartment above the tavern.

Eddie leaned out the second-floor living room window. An oppressive August heatwave had made the temperature in the apartment soar. Eddie's muscle t-shirt was soaked with sweat. He shouted down, "Whaddayawant?"

"We want to talk to you."

"About what?" Eddie knew of the growing influence the crime family was having in Little Italy since Prohibition had been enacted. He also knew of the cousins' reputation for assault, intimidation, and violence. "I'm busy. Talk to me from there."

"Who's that?" asked Eddie's wife Dolores. She stood behind him and away from the window, dressed only in her slip.

Eddie pulled back from the window to answer her. "It's those two Sicilians."

Nunzio yelled from the street. "We can't talk to you from down here. We want to come up. What are you afraid of? We ain't gonna bite you."

"I don't want them up here," said Dolores.

He stuck his head out the window again. "My wife ain't feeling too good. Tell me from there."

"I said we can't talk to you from down here. Listen, why don't you come down and open the bar."

"Shit," Eddie said under his breath. He knew he had to talk to the men. "Yeah, all right. I'll come down."

Minutes later, Eddie went downstairs to unlock the door for the cousins who, in spite of the heat, were dressed in suits. Inside the stifling tavern, chairs were upside down on the tables and stools leaned against the bar. Eddie walked behind the bar and casually ensured the revolver he had for protection was within easy reach if he needed it. The cousins straightened up two stools to sit on.

"Smells like vomit in here," said Nunzio.

"Yeah, whaddya expect? I been closed a while."

Angelo nodded toward an old pile of sawdust that had been swept up and left in the middle of the floor. In the searing heat, the odor was oppressive. "Why don't you get rid of the sawdust?"

Eddie shrugged in response.

Nunzio removed his suit jacket and hung it on the back of his stool. He used his handkerchief to wipe sweat from the brim of his Panama, wiped his forehead with the same handkerchief, and set his hat on the bar. Angelo also removed his jacket, making sure Eddie saw the revolver tucked into his shoulder holster.

Eddie's face glistened as much from the heat as from the anxiety of having the two mobsters in his tavern. "What do you guys want?"

Angelo lit a Camel cigarette, snuffed out the match between his thumb and forefinger, and flung the spent match close to the pile of sawdust.

Eddie shouted, "Hey, watch out. You're gonna set the place on fire." He set an ashtray in front of Angelo.

Angelo smirked and said, "Now, why would I do that?"

"With all this heat, I'm kinda thirsty," said Nunzio. "You got any whiskey behind there, Eddie?"

"Yeah, I got a couple of bottles."

"How about a shot for us?"

Eddie filled two shot glasses and set them in front of the boys.

"You ain't drinking?" Angelo asked.

Eddie looked back and forth at the two, waiting to hear the reason for their visit. "What do you want with me?"

Nunzio spoke first. "Eddie, we know you've been hurting because of this Prohibition thing, but we know how we can make things better for you. We have an idea."

Eddie eyed Nunzio with suspicion.

"How about working for us—for Angelo and me? You work for us, and get back on your feet again."

"Doing what?"

Nunzio explained, "We got to thinking that maybe you can run a little business for us here in the tavern. Nothing big, a little numbers thing. You know, we'd be your bankers, and you can be one of our *office* workers. We got a couple dozen other businesses in the same bad shape as you, so we thought, let's see if Eddie wants to try it too. You know what I mean?"

"In other words, you want me to run a betting parlor."

"Think about it, Eddie," continued Nunzio. "What harm is there in people betting a few cents? Everybody likes to gamble. Who's gonna care?"

"Hey, boys, listen. I ain't gonna do that."

"Why not? You got another way to make money for yourself?"

"No, but goin' to jail ain't worth a couple of dollars I'd make."

"You ain't gonna go to jail. We have an understanding with the cops, if you know what I mean. They ain't gonna bother you. You'll see. They'll come in here to place bets too."

Eddie tried to read the cousins to see if they were lying about cops being on the take.

"I swear to God, Eddie," said Nunzio.

"He's right," said Angelo.

"So how much is in it for me?"

"That's a good question. You can make a pretty good penny. We know things are tough for you now, but this way you'll have money so your wife can put food on the table. All you have to do is keep track of who bets and how much, and the numbers they bet. That's no big deal, is it? And, at the end of the day, we collect the money and take it to our bank."

"Yeah? Then what? How am I supposed to pay off the winners?"

"You don't have to worry about covering the bets. We take care of everything," said Nunzio.

"And that's it?"

"That's it, Eddie boy."

Eddie shook his head. "I don't know. Sounds too easy."

"Nothing to it," Angelo said. "A lot of businesses do this for us. Look at it this way. We give people a chance to make money when they ain't got any—people like yourself. *Capisce?*"

"Let me think about it."

"We like it better when people say yes to us, don't we Nunzio?" Angelo lit another match. This time, he flung it toward the sawdust while it was still lit. "You get what we're saying, don't you, Eddie?"

Eddie wiped the sweat from his forehead with a dish towel. He was well aware of Angelo's reputation and had heard stories of his use of a baseball bat against the knees of recalcitrant debtors. Thankfully, the match extinguished itself before hitting the sawdust. "Yeah, okay."

"Yeah, okay, *what?*" asked Nunzio.

"I'll run the betting parlor."

"And you'll get rid of the sawdust too?"

"Yeah."

"Good boy, Eddie."

CHAPTER 3

With three months remaining before Vincent and his pal Frankie were to graduate from Saint Theresa's Parochial High School, a chain of events occurred that would change their lives. The boys were seventeen years old.

In school, Vincent sat in front of Joey "Hammer" Caitano. Vincent and Joey were polar opposites in all respects. While Vincent was short and stocky, Joey towered over him at six-foot-three. Vincent's round face accentuated his closely clipped dark hair, while Joey, with his dark eyes and classic Italian good looks, sported wavy, jet black hair. Vincent looked at everyone and everything through an ever-present stern gaze, while Joey viewed the world through nothing more than a lock of hair that curled down the middle of his forehead. Popular with the nuns and students alike, Joey wore a constant grin and delighted in tormenting Vincent.

The period before Sister Beatrice arrived to start class was a normally raucous time—students threw spitballs, joked, flirted, and teased each other. Vincent dreaded this time and usually sat stoically, pretending to read his textbook, trying to control his anger from the barbs Joey threw his way, and occasionally sneaking peeks at the classroom door in anticipation of Sister Beatrice's arrival.

That morning, Joey reached over his desk to flick the back of Vincent's hair with a ruler. He turned to Frankie, who sat in the rear of the classroom. "Hey, Dummy, I just killed a cootie on the back of your friend's head. You better make sure he don't give you none."

The kids laughed.

Vincent ran his fingers through his coarse hair but did not turn around.

14

"Shorty, I'm serious," Joey said. "Did you know you got cooties?" He then pushed his teasing to another level. "Circle, circle. Square, square. Shorty's got cooties everywhere."

Frankie spoke up from the back, "Leave him alone, Hammer. He ain't done nothing to you."

Joey flicked his ruler at Vincent again.

Vincent turned and glared at his tormentor. He was now breathing in short bursts through his nose, his jaw muscles twitching and his heart racing. He was on the verge of displaying his notoriously short fuse.

"Oh, Shorty, I'm so scared of you. Look at me. I'm shaking." Joey pretended to be trembling in his seat, to the delight of the other students.

Vincent turned back to face the front of the room.

"And don't turn around again. I don't want to look at your ugly face." Joey slapped his ruler hard and flat against Vincent's head. "Look, everybody, I got another cootie."

"That does it!" Vincent jumped out of his chair, grabbed Joey's tie with his left hand, and used his beefy right hand to hit the bigger boy in the face with a half-dozen short, powerful punches. Joey fell to the floor, covering his head with his arms. Blood streamed from his nose.

Vincent stood over him, snorting like a wild animal, his face red as fire. He looked at the other students. "Anybody else wanna try me?" He stood there, his fists balled up at his hips, waiting for a challenge, but the boys shook their heads and the girls covered their mouths with their hands.

Frankie walked to the front and took Vincent by the elbow. "Vincent, c'mon. Let's get outta here." Once in the corridor, they kept walking until they were out of school.

Vincent would never set foot in Saint Theresa's again.

CHAPTER 4

Vincent's father returned from work that day at five o'clock. He removed his dusty boots on the porch and left them just inside the front door. Even on the hottest of summer days, Dominic wore khaki trousers, a long-sleeved shirt, and a felt hat to ward off the sun—all of which were dust laden and smelled of a hard day's work. He rinsed his callused hands at the kitchen sink, then dried them with a dishtowel. He sat at the kitchen table with a nod to Maria. As usual, she had dinner ready for her husband. She poured him a glass of homemade wine, hoping to calm and relax him before relating what had occurred that day with their son.

"Vincenzo," Maria called. "Mangia!"

Vincent shuffled out of his bedroom and down the hallway to the kitchen. He was still dressed in his school clothes, which showed traces of Joey's blood on his white shirt. To Vincent, the blood was a badge of honor he wanted his father to see. He sat quietly at his normal place to the left of Dominic and listened anxiously as Maria explained his fight with Joey and her meeting with the principal at Saint Theresa's, Sister Mary Katherine. The nun held Vincent responsible for the fight and announced that he was suspended from school for the remainder of the year. And to make matters worse, he would not graduate until he made up his classwork at summer school.

As his mother spoke, Vincent glanced at Dominic from time to time. Though uncertain how his father would react, Vincent was hopeful Dominic would approve of his whipping the bigger boy.

Dominic glared at his son. He did not say a word.

Vincent took his father's silence as a good sign. "That guy's been picking on me and Frankie for a long time. He was sitting behind me in class and kept smacking me in the head with a ruler, so I knocked him out. I didn't start it. Ask Frankie."

Without warning, Dominic struck Vincent across the face with the back of his stonemason's hand—a hand that was as hard as the stone he cut with chisel and mallet. A *serviette* he called the backhand slap.

The hit knocked Vincent off his chair and onto the linoleum floor. His cheek immediately flashed a red bruise. Vincent felt his face for blood and whimpered, "Papa, why did you do that? You almost knocked me out. I told you Joey started it."

Dominic was breathing hard. He did not answer, but instead spoke to his wife in Italian. "He will never amount to anything. Tomorrow he will come to work with me."

Dominic's tone and words saddened Maria. The relationship between father and son had always been fractured and without affection. This incident with Joey would make mending their relationship more difficult than ever, if not impossible. Dominic showed his son the back of his hand again. "And I warn you, do not embarrass me in front of the other workers."

* * *

The next morning, for the first time in Maria's memory, she did not have to wake her son to start the day. He was up before she knocked on his bedroom door. Vincent bounded out of his bedroom and burst into the kitchen where his mother was preparing a lunch pail of thick-crusted sandwiches for him and his father. The smell of fried peppers, onions, and garlic wafted through the house. Vincent surprised his mother with a slobbering kiss on her cheek and capped it with an exaggerated pop from his puckered lips. She had not seen him happy about anything for some time and smiled at his newfound enthusiasm. He was excited about going to work and about the things he could do with the wages his father would pay him. Best of all, being kicked out of school meant he didn't have to worry about payback from Joey or putting up with the taunts and giggles from classmates.

CHAPTER 5

After Vincent was expelled from school, Frankie became the new target of Joey's bullying. "You're gonna pay for what that crazy bastard friend of yours did to me."

"I ain't done nothing to you."

"Yeah, you did. You're his friend. That's enough for me to beat the shit out of you."

A week later, Joey and two of his friends yanked Frankie into the boys' room, shoved him into a stall, and tried to stuff his head in a toilet. Frankie fought back hard, but the stout Sister Beatrice, the morning hall monitor, heard the commotion and barreled into the boys' room. "What are you doing?" she yelled. "Who started this?"

Joey pointed at Frankie and said, "He did."

"I didn't do nothing," Frankie shouted. "He's a lying sonofabitch."

The nun said, "We'll see about that." She clutched Frankie and Joey each by the elbow and marched them and the other two boys to the principal's office.

Sister Mary Katherine was never surprised by the behavior of her students. She had seen the worst during her time as principal at Saint Theresa's and developed a constant bad-tempered expression that terrified most students. She looked over the top of her wire-framed glasses. "Yes? What is it?"

Sister Beatrice positioned the boys in front of Sister Mary Katherine's desk in a tight semicircle, and proceeded to give the principal the account of what she had seen in the boys' room.

The principal asked, "Joseph, what do you have to say about this?"

Tony Spallone

"Sister, we were in the boys' room when Frankie starts pickin' a fight with us. He said how he was gonna get even with me because Vincent was expelled."

"And you, Frankie. What do you have to say?"

"That ain't true. What Hammer just told you was pure bullshit."

The principal had long ago run out of patience with teenagers. She glared at Frankie and said, "Young man, don't you curse in my office. Do you understand me?"

"Yeah, yeah."

"Perhaps if you had not been friends with Vincent Vendetti, none of this would have occurred."

"But I didn't do nothin'."

"*Any*thing—you did not do *any*thing," she corrected.

"I know. That's what I've been telling you. I didn't do nothin'."

"It seems to me, Frankie, that you tried to extract retribution from this nice boy. Is that what occurred, Joseph?"

Joey had no idea what the principal had said but he nodded yes.

"Exactly as I suspected. Frankie, from today until graduation—and Lord knows I pray for graduation to come quickly—you will be spending an hour each day after school in the detention office."

Frankie stammered. "You mean to tell me that these assholes wanted to drown me in piss water on account of Vincent beatin' up on Joey and you're blaming me?"

"This is a hard-learned lesson for you to not pick on nice boys like Joseph."

20

Frankie bolted for the door, threw his fist into the air, and slapped the inside of his arm with his hand. "*Va fongool!*" he cursed in Italian.

Stunned, the nun bowed her head and made the sign of the cross.

Joey and his two pals hid their faces in the crooks of their elbows trying to stifle their laughter.

Frankie reached for the door handle.

Sister Mary Katherine shouted at him, "Young man, do not leave this office. If you do, you will never be allowed back in this school for as long as you live."

He shouted at her again. "Va fongool!" Then, to Joey, he added, "You sonofabitch. I'll get even with you some day. I promise. I'll get even if it takes a hundred years." On his way out, Frankie slammed the door so hard, the photo of Pope Pius XI that hung above a filing cabinet next to the door tilted.

* * *

When the denizens of South Philly saw Sister Mary Katherine walking resolutely down Broad Street during the middle of the school day, they knew another son was about to feel the wrath of one of God's servants. She walked ramrod straight and did not look one way or the other, did not acknowledge parishioners she passed on the street, and did not slow down until she reached Eddie's Tavern. She threw open the door to the betting parlor, paused long enough to make the sign of the cross, and stormed in to where Frankie's father stood next to two elderly Italians who had come in to place bets. The three men looked up in the mirror behind what had been the bar and were shocked to see the image of a nun in full habit standing behind them.

Eddie was unsure of her intent. "Do you want to place a bet, Sister?"

Sister Mary Katherine ignored his question. "*Mister* Impolito," she muttered. "Your son cursed at me today."

"What do you mean, he cursed at you, Sister?"

"He cursed at me—that's what I mean. And he made gestures of contempt toward me."

Eddie did not fully understand. "He *contempted* you, huh? Why, that little sonofabitch."

"Not once, but twice."

"No kidding. Twice?"

"Yes. Where is your son now?"

Eddie flicked his chin. "Upstairs. He came in a little while ago, said he wasn't feeling too good."

"That is a lie!"

Eddie opened the door to the stairwell that led to his family's apartment above the tavern. "Frankie! Come down here," he yelled. "Now!"

"What do you want?" Frankie yelled from the top of the steps. "I'm doing my homework."

"I said, come down here. *Subito!* Now!"

Frankie sauntered down to encounter Eddie and the nun waiting for him at the bottom of the steps. "Oh, Jesus," he said under his breath.

"The sister here says you swore at her. Is that true?"

"No. I didn't say nothing to her."

Eddie smacked Frankie on the back of his head. "Don't lie to me."

Frankie quickly raised his arm to defend himself from another slap, then admitted, "Yeah, okay, I did. But she made me do it."

Eddie asked, "What do you mean 'she made you do it?' You're telling me she asked you to swear?"

"No, she just pissed me off. She's in love with that asshole, Joey Caitano. She thinks he can't do nothin' wrong. I told her what happened, but she didn't believe what I said, so I got mad."

"Frankie, I'm telling you one time and one time only. You never swear at a nun again, or else. Understand?"

"Yeah, okay, Pop. I promise."

"Tell her you're sorry."

"Sorry," Frankie whispered.

"Sister, you hear him? My son apologizes. He won't swear no more."

The nun was not satisfied. She issued Frankie an edict. "You are not to return to Saint Theresa's until you are prepared to apologize to Joseph."

Frankie shook his head, "I ain't never apologizing to that asshole."

"See what I mean?" the nun said to Eddie. "He's cursing some more. Mr. Impolito, as of this moment, your son is expelled." Sister Mary Katherine turned on her heels and stormed out of the betting parlor.

Eddie watched the nun leave, then turned to his son and shrugged. He was neither surprised nor disappointed. Frankie was not the best of students, and Eddie realized his son was destined to work in his betting parlor after graduation anyway. "No more school for you, eh? So, you're not going be a doctor or nothing. Go change your clothes."

CHAPTER 6

Joey Caitano held a magnetic sway over the girls of Saint Theresa's. Despite the Catholic Church's teachings of guilt and sin, nearly every coed was willing to suffer eternal damnation to be with him—everyone except Angelica Marinelli.

Angelica was a brilliant, outspoken, serious, and religious student. She had earned a full scholarship to the Women's Medical College of Pennsylvania with the intention of becoming a physician—rare for women in what was essentially a male-only profession. Her empathetic nature made her one of the few students who had been friendly toward Vincent and Frankie and who thought Joey had gotten what he deserved when Vincent thrashed him.

Joey's nickname for Angelica was the Iceberg Madonna. She wore large, brown-framed glasses on her thin nose and pulled her black hair back into a tight bun—not the type of girl Joey would normally date—but he boasted to his buddies that he would make her another conquest before school ended.

One morning in late April, Joey approached Angelica in the school library. He took a seat next to her at a study table and looked her up and down. He wondered what her body was like underneath the folds of her long, navy blue uniform.

"What are you looking at?" Angelica asked.

"You." And without any concern that she might turn him down, he said, "I thought you should know, Angelica, that I'm taking you to the spring dance on Saturday night. I'll be at your house at seven."

She turned to face him with a look of disgust. "I'm not going to any dance with you."

"What do you mean?"

She didn't answer.

He whispered, "I said, what do you mean? *You* turning *me* down?"

She shook her head at his audacity. "Hard to believe someone actually said no to you. Plenty of girls would go to the dance with you. Ask someone else. I'm not interested—*at all!*" She stood and moved to another table.

Joey looked around to see if anyone had heard her refuse him.

The following day he approached her again in the library. "You change your mind?"

"About what?"

"Goin' to the dance with me."

"No. I told you I am not going to any dance with you. Now stop bothering me."

"I want to know why."

"Because I don't like you. Is that a good enough reason?"

"No, that's not good enough. There's something else, ain't there?"

Angelica was incredulous. "*I don't like you* is not good enough?"

"Why are you saying no? Because you don't know how to dance? I can teach you."

"Ha!" she laughed, then got up and walked away.

Joey slammed the tabletop in frustration.

The following Sunday morning Joey knocked on the door of Angelica's row house on Eleventh Street. In one hand, he carried a plain white cardboard box filled with pastries from Sarcone's Bakery. In the other, he held a small bouquet of cut flowers he had bought from a street vendor on Ninth.

25

Angelica's mother came to the door.

"Hi, Mrs. Marinelli, I'm Joey Caitano."

"I know who you are, Joseph. How are your parents?"

"They're okay. These pastries are for you." He held out the box.

She wiped her hands on her apron and accepted the gift with a smile, though she was confused about his intentions. "That is very sweet of you."

"And these are for Angelica." Joey held onto the bouquet of flowers. "Is she home? I came to see if she would let me walk her to church this morning."

"Yes, she is," Mrs. Marinelli said. She was pleased that a good-looking boy like Joey would come to court her daughter. "Angelica," she shouted over her shoulder. "There's someone here to see you."

"Who is it?" Angelica asked as she walked into the foyer. She was wearing a white dress, her black hair loose around her shoulders. In preparation for church, she was also wearing a white lace mantilla on her head.

"What do *you* want?"

Joey was embarrassed at first by her brusque question, but recovered quickly. He offered her the bouquet of flowers. "These are for you." He was surprised at the change in her looks from the tense, studious girl he knew at school. "Wow, Angelica, you look very pretty," he said.

She made no move to accept the flowers, leaving Joey with his arm extended for a few awkward seconds.

"Angelica," her mother said. "Did you hear him? The flowers are for you."

"Yes, Momma, I heard him." She took the flowers and instinctively sniffed their fragrance.

26

Mrs. Marinelli scolded her daughter. "And what do you say?"

"Yeah, thanks."

"Can I walk to church with you?" Joey asked.

Angelica shrugged and said, "It's a free country."

Mrs. Marinelli overlooked her daughter's iciness toward the handsome boy. "Joseph, after church, you come back and have some macaroni with us."

Angelica could not believe her ears. What was her mother thinking? "I don't think he wants to."

"Sounds great to me," he immediately countered.

"Okay, go to church, the both of you. When you get back, we eat."

Joey held the door open for Angelica.

"What a gentleman," Mrs. Marinelli said.

Angelica rolled her eyes.

On the two-block walk to Saint Theresa's, Angelica asked, "What do you think you're doing?"

"I'm walking you to church."

"You know what I mean, Joey. What are you doing at my house?"

"I wanted to see you—that's all. I'm not a bad guy, you know. I'm not like you think."

"You don't know what I think."

"You're right. But listen, I'm sorry you didn't go to the dance with me last night. It was a lot of fun."

"Listen to me, Joseph Caitano. I didn't want to go to the dance with you. I don't want to go to church with you. I don't want to go out with you. I don't even like you. So stop coming to my house and bothering me."

"Okay. I give up," he said with false exasperation. "I'll tell you what. I go to church with you now, then I have some macaroni with your family—because I promised your mother—and then I won't *bother* you again. Okay?"

"Fine," she said, and remained silent the rest of the way to church.

Afterward, Joey tried to break Angelica's silence on the walk back to her house. "What are you gonna do after graduation?"

"What do you care?"

"You know, Angelica, you don't have to be mean to me. I told you I won't bother you again. I just thought you'd tell me what you want to do after school."

"Why don't you tell me what you're going to do first?" she said, suspecting he would not have thought that far ahead.

"I'm going in the Army. I already signed up."

She was surprised by his response. "Really? Good for you. I didn't know that."

"Yeah, I always wanted to join the Army. So, what about you? What are you gonna do?"

"I'm going to college to study to be a doctor."

"A doctor?" Joey was in awe. "I didn't know girls could be doctors."

She looked at him, uncertain if he doubted her, "There are a few."

"You know, Angelica, I know you don't like me, but I always thought you were pretty smart, you know. How do you always get A's? I'm happy when I get a C."

"I study a lot, that's all."

"Well, I've always been impressed."

"That's nice of you. Thank you."

Sunday afternoon turned out to be a pleasant change for Angelica from the usual quiet supper with her mother and father and the hours of homework that followed. Joey proved to be charming. He helped Angelica set the table then chatted easily with her parents during the meal, all the while complimenting Mrs. Marinelli on her cooking. Angelica watched as Joey won her mother over just as he did so often with the nuns at school.

When it was time for Joey to leave, Angelica walked him to the front door. The normally confident boy who was never at a loss for words now found himself babbling as he tried to explain his feelings. "I know I told you I wouldn't bother you again, but I really enjoyed myself this afternoon. I know you don't want to go out with me, but if you change your mind, I would be very happy to go out with you—but you don't have to give me an answer right now. I'll see you at school, okay?"

Disarmed by Joey's change in demeanor, Angelica surprised even herself when she blurted out, "Okay. I'll go out with you."

* * *

Angelica and Joey dated over the two months leading up to graduation. Surprisingly, she reveled in the envy she saw in the eyes of the other girls. Contrary to her past impression of Joey, she found him to be kind and considerate in everything he did and said. He brought thoughtful gifts to her mother, surprised Angelica with chocolates and trinkets, carried her books, and walked her home after school every day.

The Iceberg Madonna was smitten.

At Saint Theresa's senior prom in June, the two were anointed king and queen. After he walked her home, she invited him into her living room. Mrs. Marinelli was waiting for them and, after setting out some pastries, bid them good night.

Angelica and Joey sat on the couch, and kissed for the longest time. Joey was aroused and moved his hand to her left breast. At first she thought he had accidentally brushed her. But then he cupped her breast with his large hand. She immediately pushed his hand away, got up from the couch, and slapped Joey's face hard. "What do you think you're doing? That's the kind of thing you save for marriage. Is that all you've ever wanted from me?"

Joey was taken aback. He had been so courteous, so thoughtful. He thought the time was right. Angelica's reaction took him by complete surprise. "I... I thought... I thought you, uh, wanted to..." His words stumbled out of his mouth. "I'm sorry. I mean... I didn't..."

"How dare you try something like that! And in my father's house? Is that what you thought you were going to do? Well, you know what? I'm not like your other girlfriends. Now get out of here!" Joey was afraid Angelica's parents would hear their daughter and come downstairs to kick him out of their house. "I said leave!"

He stood with shoulders slumped and shook his head, uncertain what to say or do next. "Angelica, you're not at all like any girl I've ever dated before. You're smart and funny and sweet. I know you're mad right now, and I'm sorry about what happened, but can I still see you?"

"No! I don't ever want to see you again." She opened the front door and stood aside as Joey walked out. With a flick of her hand, she slammed the door shut behind him.

* * *

At school the following week, Joey tried to explain to Angelica how he felt about her, but she refused to talk to him. Frustrated by her continued rejections, he went to her house that Saturday to enlist Mrs. Marinelli's help. He knocked on the front door and waited. No response. He knocked again, and there was still no answer. He tried the handle and found the door was unlocked. He opened it and called out, "Hello? Mrs. Marinelli? Anyone home? Can I come in?" No answer. "Mrs. Marinelli, it's Joey Caitano. Anybody home?" he asked again, even louder. Again, no answer.

He entered the house and went into the kitchen where he saw a note on the table for Angelica.

Your father and I will be down the shore until Sunday night. Don't study too hard. I left food for you in the icebox.

Joey heard water running on the second floor. *That has to be her upstairs.* He snuck up the steps and heard Angelica humming in the bathroom. He turned the doorknob to the bathroom slowly, cracked the door open, and saw her soaking in a bubble bath.

He pushed the door wide open.

Angelica screamed, crossed her arms over her breasts, and sank in the bath up to her chin. "Get out of here, or I'll yell for my parents!"

"I know they're not here. They're down the shore."

"Yes, but they'll be coming back any minute now," she lied. "So you'd better get out of here."

"All I want to do is talk to you," Joey said. He sat on the edge of the tub and saw the outline of her body through the white suds.

She insisted, "If you don't leave right now, I'm going to scream." He shrugged. "Okay, Joey, listen. I'll talk to you if you promise to leave. Let me get out of the bathroom and I'll talk to you downstairs, okay?"

Joey knew she was lying. She would kick him out of the house at her first opportunity. "Angelica, I want you, and I know you want me too."

"What do you mean want you? I do not want you!" She was no longer shouting at him. "My father and mother are coming home any minute, and I'll tell you what... My father will kill you if he finds you here."

Joey scooped his hand in the water and sent ripples toward Angelica. "I read the note your mother left in the kitchen. I know they won't be back until tomorrow night."

"Okay, Joey, you're right. But please go downstairs. I'll be right there."

He sensed her tone had softened. He got up to lock the door then returned to sit on the edge of the bath. He stroked her hair.

She turned her head away from him. "Don't touch me. Do you want me to scream?"

"Shh. It's okay," Joey said. He reached over and removed the bobby pins that held up her hair. Long black locks cascaded to her shoulders, the tips touching the bath water. She leaned away, still clutching her shoulders to conceal her breasts.

"Have you ever had sex before?"

"No!" She pouted, offended by his question.

"I want to be your first."

Angelica lifted her face and searched Joey's eyes for reassurance. The warm bath water and bubbles stirred her senses. She felt a surge of sexuality she had never before experienced. He reached down and gently pulled her wrists away from her breasts. She resisted slightly, but sat up higher in the tub, her nipples now visible through the bubbles. He reached into the water to stroke her breasts, the soapsuds lubricating his hands as they glided over her white skin. She was numbed by the sensation and half closed her eyes as she marveled at the rush. Joey knew the time was right.

Angelica watched as he took off his clothes and stood naked by the tub. She had never before seen a man aroused and was astonished at his erection. He leaned over to kiss her. Her lips parted, reluctantly at first, then willingly, to let him explore her tongue.

He pulled the plug to allow the water to drain then took her hand and directed it to him. She didn't know what he wanted her to do, but he showed her. "That's good," he said. After a few seconds, he pulled away to climb into the bath behind her. He leaned against the back of the tub and eased her onto his lap, stroking her breasts and the inside of her thighs. Angelica had never known such ecstasy. He was gentle with her as she moaned with pleasure. They climaxed together, her body quivering in rapture. "Oh, my God!"

Joey held her afterward and stroked her breasts as she leaned her head against his shoulder.

She climbed out and wrapped a towel around herself. "You'd better go now, Joey," she said, and began to cry.

"Don't cry. You were wonderful."

"I was?"

"Yeah, you were, Angelica. You really were."

"You won't tell anybody, will you, Joey?"

"For crying out loud, who am I gonna tell?"

"You promise?"

"Yeah, I promise." He got out of the tub and dried himself, then hugged her for a long while until she stopped crying.

She felt him getting aroused again and gently pushed him away. "You should go now," she said, and kissed him tenderly on the lips.

"I'll call you, okay?"

"Okay," she answered.

Within an hour, Joey had given his buddies all the details of his conquest of the Iceberg Madonna.

Two weeks after graduation, Joey was sworn into the Army and sent to Camp Dix in New Jersey. Three months later, Angelica's parents sent her to live with her aunt and uncle on their small farm in central Ohio. Six months later, Angelica gave birth to a baby girl. Her dreams of becoming a doctor were shattered.

CHAPTER 7

In October 1929, after six years of great prosperity, the stock market collapsed, marking the beginning of the Great Depression. Banks failed and millions of people lost their jobs and life savings. Companies shuttered their doors. Unemployment soared to 25% and thousands went homeless. People stood in bread lines for free food, and charitable organizations opened soup kitchens across the country to feed people who didn't have money to buy food for their families. Even the rich suffered.

* * *

One evening, Vincent and Frankie were sitting on the Vendetti's stoop, railing about the Depression and the financial suffering so many people were experiencing in the eight months since the Depression had started. Frankie said, "You should see the people who come into the tavern—people who can't even buy food for their table—and damn it if they don't bet the little money they got. They bet a couple of pennies, thinking they're gonna get rich if they win. And when they lose, they've got no money left to buy food for their family."

"What else are they gonna do? Most people ain't got a choice."

"Yeah, I know you're right. But you know, Vincent, I don't want to sit on my ass in that stinkin' tavern all day and watch those poor sonsofbitches give up their money and hope for a miracle. To me, it's guys like Angelo and Nunzio who are doing it right. I want to be like them. I want to have wads of money in my pocket like them. I want girls hanging all over me like they do. And I want to dress in fancy clothes like them."

"Yeah, you're right. I'd like that, too," said Vincent. "I mean, I have to get up at five-thirty every morning, work my ass off every day, and when I get home I'm too tired to do anything except eat and then fall asleep so I can do the same thing the next day and the next after that."

Frankie said, "You're lucky your father still gets work to do. He can put food on the table, and he don't gamble his money away."

Vincent's father was one of the fortunate few who had found steady employment working for the remaining wealthy families on the Philadelphia Main Line, but Vincent was struck by the disparity between the poor and the rich. "We're lucky all right. I know that, but I want to be like them rich people. You know what I mean? I want to be *like* them—not *work* for them. I want to buy a car someday. But I ain't gonna be able to do that as long as I keep working for my father."

"I know what you mean."

At that moment, Vincent spotted Angelo and Nunzio walking in their direction along Catherine Street. Their swagger was unmistakable. "Hey, talk about the devil. Look who's coming our way. I think maybe you're right—those guys have the right idea. You don't see them in soup lines, do you? Ever think maybe about getting a job working for them?"

"What are you talking about? I work for them now."

"You just told me you sit on your ass all day. Why don't you ask them if they've got something you could do for them—and me too."

"Like what? What could we do for them?"

"I don't know. Maybe help them collect. Hell, I don't know."

"Okay. But, Vincent, you can't tell them that you know what I do in the tavern."

"I ain't gonna say nothin'. You do the talking."

"When you think about it, I honest to God think they got the perfect jobs. They don't take no crap from nobody. I'm tellin' you what—people respect them because they're scared of them. I'd like to have that, too. And you know what else? I'd like to run into that Joey Caitano someday and have him look me in the eye and tell me he respects me. That's what I'd like. Respect. That's the most important thing."

Vincent disagreed. "Respect? Shit! For me, it's money."

Frankie thought about what Vincent had said, then nodded in agreement and laughed. "What am I saying? Yeah. You're right. It's money. If you got money, you get respect. Right? And you said it, for sure we ain't gonna get rich working for our fathers."

When the mobsters reached Vincent's house, Frankie stepped down from the stoop to greet them. "Hey, Angelo. Hey, Nunzio. You guys goin' to church?" He giggled. The cousins wore matching cream-colored suits with neatly pressed trousers, Panama hats, and wide ties.

"Yeah, very funny, Dummy. You wish you could dress like us." Nunzio bobbed his head toward Vincent who remained seated on the porch. "Who's the stoopie?"

"He's my friend. Vincent Vendetti."

Vincent stood on the middle step, but still had to look up at the much taller cousins. "How's it goin'?"

"You're really a short shit, ain't you?" Nunzio cackled. "You look like a fire hydrant with a face."

The two men laughed.

Vincent's breathing quickened but he managed to control his temper. "Yeah, I ain't much to look at, that's for sure. Not like both of you."

"Hey, guys," Frankie said, "Vincent and me, we'd like to work for you."

Angelo furrowed his brows and squinted at Frankie. "What have you been telling this stoopie, Dummy?"

"Ah, don't worry. I know about you guys," Vincent said. "Everybody does. Frankie didn't tell me nothin' everybody doesn't already know."

"What, exactly, does *every*body say about us?"

"They respect you," Vincent said. "And I know most people are afraid of you."

"That's good," Nunzio said with a grin. He was pleased by Vincent's comment. "Are you afraid of us too?"

"Nope. I ain't afraid of nobody."

"You're not, huh?"

"That's what I said."

"So... you want to work for us?"

"Yeah, we do."

"Doing what? Dummy already does."

"Frankie don't want to work in the tavern no more. And I don't want to work for my father no more. Me and Frankie, we thought, maybe you guys got jobs for us to do."

"Like what?"

"Be your assistants or something. Anything you want."

Frankie added, "Me and Vincent, we don't take crap from nobody. We could crack heads for you, maybe."

Angelo looked around and said, "Hey, keep it down."

Nunzio was less concerned about who might hear their conversation. "Let me ask you a pretend question, Dummy. What would you do for us if somebody owed us money, but they ain't paying us back?"

"Stop calling me Dummy. My name is Frankie."

The cousins looked at each other. "Where did you get *coglioni* all of a sudden?"

"I always had balls. And you know what? To answer your question, if someone wasn't paying you, maybe I'd break their legs, or smack 'em around for you—anything you asked us to do. Give us a test. Try us out. We'll show you."

Angelo turned to Vincent and sized him up. "You both think you're tough, huh?"

"We can take care of ourselves."

Nunzio wasn't convinced. "It don't look like you punks can take care of dog shit. Come on, Angelo. Let's get out of here."

Frankie was adamant. "I'm tellin' you. Try us out. We ain't lying."

Angelo said, "You stoopies are either full of crap or... I'll tell you what, me and Nunzio, we'll talk, and maybe we can get somebody to... Never mind. We'll let you know." He tapped Nunzio on the shoulder, jerked his head, and said, "Let's go."

Vincent and Frankie watched the cousins walk away.

"You know, Vincent, it'd be somethin' if we went to work for them and they told us Joey owed them a dime and that we had to collect from him. Could you imagine that?"

"Joey's in the Army, Frankie."

"He's gotta come home one of these days, right?"

"Yeah, you're right."

Frankie looked around to make sure no one was looking, then pulled a .38 caliber revolver from his pants pocket. He cupped it in his hands.

Vincent was shocked. "Where the hell did you get that?"

"I took it from behind the bar in the tavern. It's my father's."

"Is it real?"

"Yeah, it's real."

"Let me hold it. I ain't never held a real gun before."

"You gotta be careful you don't shoot yourself."

Vincent cradled the gun and lifted it up and down. "I like the way it feels. It's heavy. Maybe someday you and I could use it on Joey."

"Yeah, we could take turns shooting him."

CHAPTER 8

In the twentieth century, the American Mafia had given rise to twenty-six mob families. Members held dearly to their Mafia family and regarded their allegiance higher than even their allegiance to God.

Each family was headed by a boss with total say over anything that occurred within the family. Other members of the family had specific responsibilities understood by all.

The consigliere advised the boss, although not all families had such an advisor. The underboss was second in command, and usually the man to take over as head of the family when the boss died or retired.

Capos reported to the underboss. Each capo was given responsibility for a specific venture of the family—illegal drugs, gambling, loansharking, smuggling, robbery, or any other avenue of crime. Capos had a certain number of soldiers who reported to them. Soldiers were the men who did all the heavy lifting including collection of debts, murder, and intimidation.

Associates were on the lowest rung of the organization, but they were not members of the Mafia. They were business owners, politicians, union officials, rogue cops, small-time hoods—or young recruits willing to do whatever the family requested of them. Each family counted associates in the dozens.

* * *

The impact of the Great Depression was felt on the lives of most people and businesses—but not all. The Mafia was a notable exception. They continued to prosper from far-reaching gambling, prostitution, loan-sharking, and bootlegging operations.

Nunzio and Angelo Spatola worked directly for Danny Cardone, one of three capos in the Philadelphia mob. The forty-year-old Cardone was one of the family's brightest stars. His role was to build the mob's gambling and loan-sharking enterprises by linking the two operations—lending money to people and businesses at usurious rates, then gaining their fealty when they were unable to pay back the debt that compounded over time.

Cardone was self-educated, well read, and articulate, although he retained a slight accent from his native Sicilian roots. He was never without his briar pipe, puffing on it or alternately digging into his tobacco bowl to loosen or tighten the tobacco, patiently lighting and relighting the pipe dozens of times each day. Regardless of the weather or the occasion, he wore a bow tie and wrinkled tweed jacket, the fibers of which were imbued with the sweet smell of his pipe smoke. Cardone's wispy graying hair, seemingly impossible to train, gave him a slightly disheveled appearance. He resembled a prototypical college professor, especially when he peered over the top of his wire-framed glasses that sat low on his nose. Some felt he played up to the role. Angelo and Nunzio called him Professor, and he did not object.

Three years earlier, when the Professor was a soldier, he sponsored Nunzio and Angelo to be associates. The two turned out to be tenacious and ruthless—Nunzio was the brighter of the two, but Angelo, with the use of his signature baseball bat, was more adept at convincing obstinate debtors to pay up.

* * *

The cousins asked to meet with the Professor to talk about recruiting Vincent and Frankie to become associates. If the boys proved to be good hires, it would be feathers in the caps of both men. The meeting was arranged for the following Wednesday, in the living room of Cardone's row house at Eighth and Washington.

The Professor's wife set a small pot of espresso on the coffee table, along with a bottle of anisette, three shot glasses, coffee cups, and a plate of homemade biscotti. Matilda was slender and soft-spoken, with large brown eyes and naturally blushed cheeks on a porcelain-smooth round face. She nodded her greetings to the boys and left the room without saying a word. She knew not to linger when her husband attended to business—and to never intrude or question him about his work or the people who came to visit. She sealed her mind to any knowledge she gleaned from neighborhood whispers about her husband's ties to the Mafia and conveniently left clues uncategorized in her mind.

The Professor listened to the cousins without expression, puffing on his pipe and rarely looking at the two men while they took turns telling of their encounter with Vincent and Frankie. When they finished, the Professor turned to Nunzio but said nothing. His habit of staring at him without speaking always made Nunzio uncomfortable, and he looked away, trying not to squirm in his chair. After several seconds, the Professor asked Nunzio, "What do you think? Do you think these two boys are worthy?"

"Yes, Professor. They're pretty cocky, but I think they could work out. We know the one boy, Eddie Impolito's son Frankie. Nothing great, but he's okay."

The Professor turned his stare to Angelo. "What do you think?"

Angelo shrugged. "Yeah, we know Eddie's son, but I think he's full of crap. He talks a good game. The short guy, I could maybe believe he would do whatever we ask. But Eddie's son? I don't agree with Nunzio. I got reservations about him."

"Here's the thing, Professor," Nunzio said. "I think they're a package deal. Meaning, if we take one, we gotta take the other, or we won't get either."

After fifteen minutes, the Professor concluded the meeting. "Okay, boys. I will let you know. Have them meet me seven o'clock tomorrow night at Galante's."

CHAPTER 9

Galante's Funeral Home was one of the many quasi-legitimate businesses owned or controlled by the mob. Frank Galante, the funeral parlor's first—and now former—owner, learned the hard lesson that the mob did not deal in subtleties. Five years earlier, Galante had obtained a loan from Nunzio and Angelo. He did his best to make regular payments, but in time, the sum of the compounding debt owed became overwhelming. Galante begged for more time to pay, but Angelo's baseball bat convinced the funeral parlor owner to turn over stewardship of his business to the Professor. Cardone kept Galante on as undertaker while also using the business as a front to oversee the family's gambling and loansharking activities.

At five minutes before seven, Vincent and Frankie, wearing ill-fitting suits, walked into Galante's Funeral Home. The parlor was a traditional brownstone building, located on the corner of Seventh and Kroll. The two boys sat on a cushioned bench inside the vestibule and watched while Italian women dressed all in black grieved loudly over the death of a man from the neighborhood while men in dark suits and black ties sat stoically.

Frankie glanced at the clock on the vestibule wall. "They said seven o'clock, didn't they? It's ten past now, and they ain't here. Didn't they say seven? Let's find the guy we're supposed to talk to and tell him we're here."

Vincent said, "Hold your horses. We don't know who we're supposed to meet."

Another five minutes passed when Nunzio and Angelo finally rushed into the vestibule. They reeked of cigarette smoke.

Angelo got in Vincent's face. "Where've you guys been?"

"What do you mean? We've been here the whole time. You told us to meet here at seven, and we got here five minutes early."

"No, you didn't. We've been outside looking for you." Angelo was lying. They knew how much the Professor hated to wait for anyone, and they were prepared to place the blame squarely on the boys. "He ain't gonna be happy at the two of you."

Vincent looked at Frankie and got up to leave. "This is bullshit." Two mourners at the back of the room turned to shush them.

Frankie tugged on Vincent's sleeve. "It'll be okay. Calm down."

Nunzio said, "You want to leave? Leave. If you don't want to leave, come with us."

Vincent shrugged. "Yeah, okay."

They followed Nunzio and Angelo down the stairs to a large room containing a dozen coffins on display—a variety in bronze and wood, some decorated with ornate religious symbols, others with a simple cross on top. A card next to each coffin showed the price in stenciled numbers.

The air in the room was cold and heavy. Frankie shuddered from a sudden chill and put his hands in his pockets.

"Wait here." Nunzio and Angelo left the boys standing alone among the coffins and closed a heavy door behind them.

Vincent and Frankie looked around, unsure what to do next. "This place gives me the willies," Frankie said.

Vincent looked around and checked the cost of the closest coffins. "Whew, it costs a lot of money to die."

Neither Vincent nor Frankie saw the Professor at the far end of the room. When Cardone stepped out from behind a coffin, he frightened Frankie, who gave out a child-like shriek and took a step back toward the door. Vincent was startled, but stood his ground.

The Professor eyed the two boys and motioned for them to approach.

"*Buonasera*. I am Mr. Cardone."

"Buonasera, Mr. Cardone," the boys answered.

"You are late," Cardone said. "I don't like people who are late."

Frankie got defensive. "We're really not late. We were waiting upstairs since seven o'clock, but we must've gotten our signals crossed with Nunzio and Angelo because they said they were waiting for us outside, even though we didn't see them when we came in."

The Professor shook his head. "Do you always make excuses, young man? Do you have a name?"

Frankie looked down at the floor. "No."

"You don't have a name?" Cardone was playing with Frankie.

Frankie stammered, "Yeah, I have a name. I'm Frankie Impolito. I meant, I mean, no, I don't always make excuses."

"So you *do* make excuses, but not all the time? Is that what you mean?"

Frankie looked at Vincent for help. "I don't know what he wants me to say."

Vincent made no effort to help his friend.

The Professor turned to Vincent. "And you?"

Vincent was not intimidated by the Professor's stare. "What do you want me to tell you? Yes, I have a name," he replied. "Vincent Vendetti. And, no, I don't make excuses. And Frankie don't either. We were here since before seven like we were told, and those two assholes, they didn't show up when they said they did, and they blame us for being late. That's no excuse. That's a fact."

Cardone turned back to Frankie. "I understand you want to work for Nunzio and Angelo."

"Yes, sir," Frankie responded. "We both want to. We would do anything they want us to. We wouldn't let them down. I promise."

Cardone asked Vincent the same question. "And, you, Mr. Vendetti? Do you agree with your friend?"

"To tell you the truth, I'm not even sure I want the job now if it means we have to put up with more of the same crap from them two guys. I already got a job, but Frankie and me thought it would be good if we worked together because we want to make more money than we make now."

"And that is the only reason you want the job? Because you want to make more money?"

"Yeah. But it depends on a lot of things."

"Depends on what?"

Frankie sensed their opportunity to work for Nunzio and Angelo was quickly vanishing. He blurted out, "Mr. Cardone, I think there's been a little misunderstanding. Vincent would take the job. He's just a little pissed right now. He gets that way sometimes. He wants to work for—"

The Professor glared at Frankie over his glasses and interrupted. "Understand one thing, young man, if I ask your friend a question, I want *him* to answer. If I ask *you* a question, I want *you* to answer. You do not answer for him, and he does not answer for you. Is that clear?"

Frankie shuffled his feet. "Yes, sir. It's clear."

The Professor thrust his chin at Vincent and, "Continue with your explanation."

"Yeah, well, depends on how much money they pay us and what they want us to do. And if we're gonna be in a crap job forever, we don't want the job. We got that now working for our fathers."

"Mr. Vendetti, from what I know of your father, he's a good man, a hard worker, and a good stonemason. What's wrong with working for him?"

"Nothing. It's hard work and I work my ass off. But I ain't complaining about working hard. All I want to do is make enough money so I can buy a car. But I won't be able to buy one for another twenty years with what I make now."

"A slight exaggeration wouldn't you say? Shouldn't you consider yourself lucky that you have a job during these bad times when millions of others are out of work?"

"Yeah, I guess so. But I don't want to be no stonemason for the rest of my life. I'm sorry for all the people who ain't got jobs. Honest to God I am. I know my family is lucky we don't have to wait in a soup line for food. But, like I said, I don't want to be no stonemason forever."

"Then, what is it you want?"

"I ain't decided yet. Depends. All I know right now is I want a car. And I want to make a lot more money than I make now. And I want people to respect me."

The Professor was both irritated and intrigued by Vincent. The boy was irreverent, feisty, ambitious. "Respect? You want respect?"

"Yes, sir, that's what I want. I figure if I make enough money, people will respect me, like people probably respect you."

"Interesting answer. I understand you told Nunzio and Angelo that you would do whatever it takes to collect from someone who owed us money. Would you do that without hesitation?"

"Yes. Whatever it took."

The Professor was pleased with Vincent's responses. He then turned his attention back to Frankie. "Tell me about yourself."

"Me?" Frankie didn't know what the Professor wanted of him. He stammered, "I... I work for my father, Eddie... Eddie Impolito."

The Professor grew impatient. "I know who your father is and I know what you do. What else can you tell me about yourself?"

Frankie once again looked for direction from Vincent, who shrugged to let his friend know he was on his own. "Well, Vincent's my best friend in the whole world, and best friends are supposed to stick together, so we always stick up for each other. And I agree with Vincent. I'm sorry for all those poor people who can't afford to put food on the table. But I ain't sorry for them when they come into the tavern and gamble the little bit of money they got on numbers and think they're gonna hit it big. I don't like that about people."

"Well, young man, you're aware that if these people didn't go into your father's tavern to bet, you wouldn't have a job and your family would be like all the others who stand in a soup line?"

"I never thought about it that way. But yeah, I guess you're right."

"You think you could collect money from a debtor, like your friend Mr. Vendetti here says he could?"

"Oh, yeah. I even got a gun, and I would use it."

The Professor was surprised, "Where did you get a gun?"

"From my father's bar. Only, he don't know I took it."

"Does that mean you will take things from me without me knowing?"

"No, I would never do that," Frankie said. "If you hire us, we'd do anything in the world for you. I cross my heart—Catholic honor—I would never steal from you."

"You know, if you ever stole from me—even a nickel—it would be the last nickel you ever took from anyone."

Vincent spoke up. "Mr. Cardone, can I say something?"

Cardone nodded.

"Frankie and me, we want jobs working for Angelo and Nunzio. Like Frankie said, we're best friends and we want the job so we can work together. In fact, Frankie and me, we'd be the best damn workers you ever had. You wouldn't have nobody better."

Frankie nodded his agreement with Vincent and smiled, proud of the way his friend stuck up for him. He always had. Vincent defended him in high school. He defended him against the bullies in the neighborhood. Any kid who went after Frankie would have to contend with Vincent too.

The Professor liked that the boys stuck up for each other. Loyalty was one of the first things he looked for in a recruit. After all, the family was built on a tradition of loyalty. Cardone was satisfied. He looked at one, then the other. "Okay. I'm going to hire you both.

Frankie clapped his hands, punched the air, and whooped, "Yes!"

The Professor smiled at Frankie's exuberance. "We'll start you off slow, working part-time at night. You keep the jobs you have now. Then we'll see. If you work out, you will make more money in a month than you currently make in a year. But, two things. Once you agree to work for us, there's no going back. You don't just resign. You're with us for life, understand?" Frankie and Vincent looked at each other and nodded simultaneously.

Vincent asked, "What's the other thing?"

"You've got to keep quiet about your new jobs. You don't say anything to anyone. Ever. I don't like loudmouths. No one is to know what you're doing. I cannot emphasize that enough." The Professor raised an eyebrow and spoke in a low, slow tone. "I don't like people who shoot their mouths off. No one else is to know what you are doing—that includes your fathers. Capisce?"

"Capisce," they answered.

Frankie stepped forward to shake the Professor's hand. "Thank you, Mr. Cardone. You won't be sorry. I can't tell you how happy this makes me."

"And you, Mr. Vincent Vendetti, are you happy too?"

A rare smile creased Vincent's lips. "Yes, Mr. Cardone, I am."

CHAPTER 10

One week after their meeting with the Professor, Vincent and Frankie met Nunzio and Angelo at Galante's to begin their work for the mob. The cousins escorted the boys through a locked door in the coffin display room, down a flight of steps, and through a concrete-walled tunnel where they stopped outside another locked door. This door was made of steel and had a combination lock like that of a bank vault.

Nunzio explained, "This is what we call the tomb." Inside, two men were seated at a table with mounds of coins and stacks of dollars in front of them. They looked up briefly to see who had entered and, without acknowledging the visitors, turned back to their counting. They marked their tallies in an olive-green bookkeeping journal. Both wore visors to shade their eyes from the bright ceiling lights in the windowless room. A third man, seated on a stool in the corner of the room, was keeping watch over the two money-counters.

"You guys are gonna help count money," Nunzio advised. "Can you count, Frankie?"

"Yeah, Nunzio, I can count," Frankie mumbled. He was embarrassed not so much by the question but by the fact he had answered.

The job of money counter in the cold, claustrophobic room located twenty feet under the funeral home parking lot was unpleasant—a chore that was reserved for new associates. Heat was pumped into the room to take the edge off the cold, but the stifling closeness that was created when the heat came on caused the money counters to involuntarily take deep gulps of air to replenish their oxygen-depleted lungs. The walls and ceiling glistened with condensation.

Droplets of water dripped sporadically and pinged off the table and the shoulders of the workers. A droning exhaust fan drew off some of the heavy air from the room through a duct that ran along the inside of the access tunnel and up an exterior wall of the funeral home to be expelled through a vent in the roof.

Nunzio explained, "This is what you guys will be doing every night—counting money. And remember, if you ever take one dime, we'll know."

Angelo shot a quick glance toward his cousin. "He's right. We'll know, and you'll have to learn how to walk all over again, if you know what I mean."

"Somebody'll be here with you all the time—like Johnny over there. He don't count money. All he does is sit in that chair and watch to make sure you don't take nothing."

"We ain't gonna take nothin'," Frankie declared.

"We know you won't, even though you're gonna be tempted. All that money, and you figure who's gonna know, right? So you put a couple of coins in your pocket. Trust me, we will know. At the end of your shift, Johnny's gonna check you out, empty your pockets. No exceptions. He's even gonna check if you stuck anything in your mouth like one guy did a couple of months ago. The guy thought he was being smart, but he's learning how to walk again." Angelo laughed.

Frankie asked, "Is this money all from gambling, like from my father's tavern?"

"None of your business," Nunzio snapped. "All you need to do is count, not know where the money comes from." He looked at Vincent and added, "And you don't tell nobody—and I mean *nobody*—what you do here."

"Yeah, okay, fine. We understand. You don't have to keep telling us."

Frankie asked, "How long we got to do this down here?"

Angelo said, "Until we say to stop. You know what? This is your first night on the job and already you're bitching."

"I'm not bitching, Angelo. Honest. I'm just asking."

Vincent defended his friend. "He's not bitching. All he asked was how long we would be working down here so we know. But if you don't want us to ask no more, we won't. If this is what we do, that's okay with us. We know we ain't gonna do this forever, right?"

One of the workers got distracted in his count and had to recount a batch of coins. He looked up from his task to examine the two newcomers, and directed a comment to Vincent. "Hey, asshole, shut the hell up. You made me screw up my count!"

"Sorry."

"Well, how about this? Forget sorry. Just shut your trap."

Vincent's temper flared at the man's words, but he kept it under control. "I don't think you have any reason to talk to me like that. All we did was ask a couple of questions. I told you I was sorry."

"Sorry, my ass. Shut up so we can count, you ugly little midget."

No one was prepared for what followed. Vincent lowered his shoulder and charged at the money counter. He knocked him off his chair, toppled the cash-laden table, and sent bills and coins scattering across the room. The others were stunned as they watched the two wrestle on the floor. Though smaller, Vincent was stronger than the other man and quickly gained leverage. He rained punches on him, bloodying his nose before Angelo pulled him off.

Vincent shouted at the man, "Don't you ever talk to me like that again."

"What the hell is wrong with you?" Nunzio yelled. "Both of you, follow me." The cousins escorted the boys out of the tomb, back through the casket room, and up to the first floor.

Angelo said to Nunzio, "We've got to tell the Professor what happened. He's gonna want to know."

Nunzio pointed to a bench in the hallway outside the Professor's office and said to Vincent and Frankie. "Sit here, and don't say a word."

The office door was open and the Professor was at his desk. Nunzio leaned in and asked, "Can we see you for a minute? We had a little trouble here with the two new guys. The kid, Vincent, got into a fight with one of the counters."

"Where are they?"

"They're sitting out here in the hallway."

The Professor stepped into the hallway and stared at Vincent. He was mad. "You, get in my office. Just you." The Professor waited for Vincent to enter then closed the door behind him. He returned to his swivel chair and sat down. Vincent didn't say a word, but watched as the Professor sat and tapped his forehead. Finally, "Are you crazy, Mr. Vendetti? Did I hire a crazy person?"

"Mr. Cardone, the guy kept yelling at me and calling me names."

"You start today and already you have a fight. You cause problems with my men. In just one day. One day!"

"I'm sorry, Mr. Cardone. All we did was ask a couple of questions and the guy starts swearing at me and calling me names. That's what happened."

"You always fight when people call you names?"

"Yeah, well... sometimes. I know I don't look like everybody else. Kids in school always called me names. I can't help the way I look, but that's no reason why people have to say the things they do." Vincent's eyes welled up. Incredibly, he was discussing his feelings to this man he barely knew—about sensitivities he had never uttered to his father or even his mother. "That guy jumped all over me, for no reason. All we did was ask how long we were gonna have to work down there."

The Professor looked away until Vincent was able to regain his composure. He felt sorry for the boy. "Mr. Vendetti, I want you to come to my house on Sunday to have macaroni with my family."

The Professor's invitation took Vincent by surprise. "What did you say?"

"You heard me. You come to my house at two o'clock, Sunday, so we can talk some more. In the meantime, no more trouble. I want you to apologize to the men downstairs. Do you understand? No more trouble."

"I promise. No more trouble."

The Professor opened the office door and told the cousins, "He's going to apologize to the men downstairs. You tell them they will accept his apology—or else. Mr. Vendetti's going to be a good boy from now on. No more trouble." He put his arm around Vincent's shoulder. "Right?"

Vincent's eyes were to the floor. He nodded his agreement.

CHAPTER 11

The following Sunday, Vincent arrived at the Cardone's tidy row home promptly at two o'clock. The Professor introduced him to Matilda, explaining that Vincent was hired to assist at the funeral home. Matilda accepted her husband's explanation without question and welcomed Vincent into their home with the typical graciousness displayed by all Italian wives. Over the years, she had met many men with whom her husband had business dealings, and to her, Vincent was just another face. She observed, however, that Vincent was younger than the others, odd looking, socially awkward, and unsure of himself.

A young boy stood between Matilda and the Professor. The Professor said, "Vincent, this is my son Robert." With his brown eyes and thin face, the boy resembled his mother.

"Robert, say hello to Vincent."

"I don't want to," Robert said, and he hid behind the folds of his mother's dress. "He's scary!"

Matilda scolded the boy. "Robert, that's not nice. Now, say you're sorry."

"That's okay, Mrs. Cardone. There ain't no reason for him to apologize. How old are you, Robert?"

Robert peeked out from behind his mother's dress but did not answer. Vincent tried to sway him while the Professor and Matilda looked on with curiosity.

"Let's see, hmm. If I'm eighteen, how old are you? Wait. Let me guess." Vincent pretended to do math calculations in his head. "Don't tell me. I bet you're, I would say, sixteen."

"Noo," the boy cooed. "I'm five." He stepped half out from behind his mother.

"Five, like in fifteen? Well, I was close. I thought you were sixteen."

"No, I'm five—five years old," Robert stated. "Not fifteen."

"Really? Five? I think you're teasing me. You look much older. Wow. You're big for five. You're gonna grow up to be bigger than me, that's for sure."

"Yeah," the boy responded. He looked Vincent over from head to toe and asked, "How come you're so little?"

Vincent looked at Matilda, "Because I didn't eat my spinach or drink my milk when I was five years old. If I'd done that, I'd be tall like your father."

Matilda was embarrassed at her son's frank questioning. "Vincent, I'm sorry."

"He's right. I am small for my age. But I bet I can beat him at arm wrestling. You want to try me?"

Robert said, "You can't beat me. I'll beat you!"

"Okay, let's see what you can do—right here, right on the floor."

Robert dropped to the floor. Vincent did the same and propped himself up on his right elbow to do battle with the boy. Vincent let Robert force his arm back and forth, first allowing the boy to show his strength and then pretending to garner his own strength against him. Vincent ultimately lost the battle, but won over Robert in the process—and both Matilda and the Professor as well.

Robert had found a new friend in Vincent. "Let's play cards," he said, and Vincent followed him into the living room. Matilda smiled at her husband then disappeared into the kitchen. Ten minutes later she reappeared, wearing an apron over her house dress and carrying a large plate of antipasto to satisfy everyone's hunger until supper was ready.

Matilda saw substance in Vincent. She was able to look beyond his small stature and dark visage, and was impressed by his thoughtfulness and courtesies, and especially at how he seemed to enjoy playing with Robert. She wanted to ask her husband who Vincent was and what he really did at the funeral home, but she knew Danny would not allow her questions.

Robert asked his mother, "Can Vincent come back next Sunday, Momma?"

Matilda looked at her husband for approval.

The Professor said, "Vincent, we want you to come back next Sunday. Okay?"

"Yeah, I'd like that, Mr. Cardone." Vincent wished he was able to have such pleasant afternoons at his own home. His father was always cold and impersonal, unlike the Professor and Matilda, who made him feel welcome. And, he really enjoyed playing with Robert. He had always dreamed of one day having his own son and being part of an affectionate and loving family, far apart from the harsh rules of discipline his father enacted.

Vincent returned to the Cardones the following Sunday and was invited back for many Sunday afternoons after that. Macaroni with the Cardone family became a regular and pleasant event for Vincent.

CHAPTER 12

In its heyday, Atlantic City, New Jersey, touted itself as the world's playground. The resort town was known for sun, fun, and entertainment galore. The city featured the Miss America pageant, the Steel Pier—which was home to concerts, exhibits, and dance bands—and the first boardwalk in the country. Shops, eateries, and games of all sorts lined the city's boardwalk while dozens of speakeasies remained hidden behind closed doors where illegal liquor flowed freely during the prohibition era.

* * *

For three years, Vincent and Frankie worked nights in the tomb as money-counters while continuing to work for their fathers during the daytime. When they reached the age of twenty-one, the Professor deemed Vincent and Frankie worthy to become full-time associates. They had proven their loyalty and drive. He assigned them to collections, and was not disappointed—they were harsh and eager enforcers.

By the time the boys turned twenty-four in 1936, the Professor touted them to the family leadership, asserting they were worthy of being initiated into the crime family as soldiers.

But they lacked one important qualification.

* * *

The night of August 17 was hot and sultry in South Philly. The dark paved streets and red brick buildings radiated heat from a brutally hot summer day. Vincent and Frankie were sitting on the Vendetti front porch when they spotted Nunzio and Angelo walking toward them. Nunzio was dressed in a light blue seersucker suit while Angelo clutched his suit jacket over his shoulder.

"Ain't you hot with that suit on, Nunzio?" Frankie asked.

Nunzio answered, "We got a couple of honeys waiting for us."

"Oh, that explains it."

"Whose car is that?" Angelo asked. He was eying a black 1936 Ford Standard Tudor Sedan parked along the curb. "Nice."

"It's Vincent's," Frankie said.

"Are you kidding me?" Angelo let out a long, low whistle and got in behind the steering wheel to examine the dashboard.

Nunzio was getting impatient. "Come on, Angelo, we've got to get going."

"Yeah, one minute."

Vincent asked Angelo, "Like it?"

"Beautiful. I don't know where you got the money for it, but yeah, it's beautiful. How does it drive?"

"I don't know. I only got it today."

Frankie said, "He don't know how to drive it, and he won't let me teach him. That's true ain't it, Vincent? You're afraid to drive it."

"I ain't afraid. I just have to get used to it."

Angelo laughed. "Can you see over the steering wheel?"

Vincent disregarded his comment.

"Where'd you get the money to buy this beauty? You ain't been dipping in the till, have you?"

Vincent glanced at Frankie before answering. "I wouldn't take money from the Professor. I've been saving ever since we started working for you guys. I always wanted to get myself a car."

Frankie badgered his friend. "Tell him the truth, Vincent, you're afraid to drive it, ain't you?"

"Are you?" Angelo asked.

Vincent lowered his head. "Yeah, okay, a little. I just need to take it out and get used to it. Frankie wants to teach me, but I've been with him when he drives his father's car. He scares the crap outta me. I don't want to end up in an accident and mess up my car by doin' something wrong."

Angelo said, "I could teach you in ten minutes. Right now, if you want."

Nunzio reminded his cousin about their date. "We ain't got time to screw around. The girls are waiting for us."

"Ah, screw the girls," Angelo said with a wave of his hand.

"That's what we're trying to do. Come on. Let's get going. They're gonna be pissed."

"What are you worried about? They ain't gonna go without us."

"Angelo, it's Friday night, we got two hot broads waiting for us, and you want to give driving lessons. What's wrong with you? Teach him some other time." Nunzio was practically whining. "You don't come with me now, I'm going without you."

Vincent said, "Listen, I don't want to make a problem outta this. Where are you going, anyway? Maybe we can drive there with you."

"We're gonna pick up the girls and head to Atlantic City," Nunzio answered. "They asked us to go with them."

"Jesus, that's nice. You guys do all right for yourselves, don't you?"

Angelo nodded. "We only met them two days ago. The father of one of them has a place there."

"No kidding, a house in AC?"

"You should see these broads. They are beautiful, and hot to trot, but—" Nunzio looked at his cousin before finishing his sentence, "that don't matter because my cousin would rather teach you how to drive a car than be with them."

"How are you getting to AC? You takin' the bus?" Vincent asked.

"The one girl has her father's car."

"I got an idea," Vincent said. "We ain't got nothing to do around here. How about we go down with you, and—"

Nunzio twisted his face into a look of disbelief. "Are you crazy too? Is everybody here stupid crazy? No, I don't want you to go with us. We don't need chaperones."

"I don't mean we chaperone," Vincent explained. "We take two cars. Me, Frankie, Angelo, and his girl go in my car, so Angelo can show me how to drive it. You and your girl go in her car, and we follow you there—that's all."

Frankie lent his support to Vincent's plan, "That's a good idea. We ain't got nothin' else going on tonight. So, we drive down there, drop you and the girls off, tool around on the boardwalk for a while, and drive back by ourselves."

Angelo said, "I like that idea. In the time it takes to get there, I'll teach you how to drive this beauty." He put his meaty arm around Vincent's shoulder.

Nunzio was finally convinced. "Yeah, all right. Let's just get going."

They all piled into Vincent's car—Angelo at the wheel, Vincent in the front seat next to him, Nunzio and Frankie in the back seat. They drove four blocks and entered a lot next to Manucci's Diner, where their dates, Mona and Nina, sat waiting in their car. When they saw Nunzio and Angelo in the Ford, they got out of their car.

Mona's perfume filled the air. Her bleach-blonde hair lay in tight waves and framed her heavily made-up face. The tight baby blue dress she wore showed off her every curve. In a voice hoarse from too many cigarettes, she asked, "Where have you guys been? You're late." She looked at Vincent and Frankie. "And who the hell are they?" Mona was agitated. She folded her arms across her ample chest and tapped her right toe on the pavement.

Angelo grimaced, expecting Nunzio would embarrass him. But Nunzio answered, "We don't have to explain why we're late." Then he explained anyway. "We're late because we ran into these two guys. They're friends of ours. They're gonna drive down to the shore with us. Besides, it's not like we're an hour late, you know."

Mona's friend Nina, a buxom brunette with darting eyes and a tart tongue, dropped her cigarette and ground it out with the sole of her high heel. "You're late enough. And, no. Your little friends ain't going with us," she said. "There's no room for them in the house. If you guys want to go to the shore with them, go right ahead. But we ain't going with you. Make up your damn minds what you want to do." She turned to Mona and said, "Maybe we should go without them."

Angelo envisioned their weekend plans fast falling apart. "Hey, girls, first off, it was my fault for being late." He put his arm around Vincent's shoulder. "I'm sorry. I'm trying to teach my friend here how to drive his new car. He never drove a car before. So, I thought, they drive down the shore with us, I teach him what to do, and they turn around and come back. They ain't gonna stay with us."

"That's true," Vincent said. "We ain't staying."

An apology and a reasonable explanation were all the girls needed. "Why didn't you say that to begin with?" Nina said. "Let's stop all the bullshitting and get going."

The two cars traveled across the newly built Delaware River Bridge and arrived at the shore in three hours. Mona's parent's house was located two blocks from the popular Atlantic City boardwalk. Angelo stood out front and admired the two-story house with its wide front porch and white columns. "Wow. Very nice," he said.

"Shh. Be quiet," Mona said. "We don't want to bother the neighbors." She flicked on the lights and Nina pulled down the shades.

Nunzio looked around and said, "Your father owns this place?"

Mona said, "He does."

"He's got some do-re-mi, don't he?"

Angelo admired the intricate carvings of birds located throughout the house and the shore paintings of fish, boats, and crashing waves that decorated every wall. "What's your father do for a living?"

"He's an undertaker. He used to own Galante's Funeral Home, but now he just works there."

"No kidding." Nunzio caught Angelo's eye. "We did some business with him once."

"You did? That's a coincidence, ain't it?"

Vincent asked, "Can we get a glass of water? Then we're out of here."

"Sure. In the kitchen. Follow us. Hey, Nunzio, Angelo, make yourselves comfortable. Have a seat on the couch. Relax. Take off your jackets."

Nunzio nudged Angelo with his elbow and whispered, "Gonna have some fun tonight." He removed his jacket, rolled up the sleeves of his shirt, loosened his tie, and sat on one end of the plastic-covered couch.

When Mona returned to the living room, she sat on Nunzio's lap and ran her fingers through his hair. "Comfortable?"

"I am now," he said.

A few seconds later Nina came out of the kitchen. She reached for Angelo's hand and guided him to the other end of the couch. She nudged him down and sat on his lap. Like her girlfriend, she wasted no time in stroking his thick, black hair and nibbling on his neck.

Vincent and Frankie walked out from the kitchen, "Okay, we're gonna go," Vincent said. "Maybe we'll go to the boardwalk for a while before we head back. It's been nice knowing you girls. Thanks for the driving lesson, Angelo."

"Yeah, you're welcome," Angelo said. He had other things on his mind. "Go do whatever you want."

"Goodbye, boys." The girls waved without looking up.

Vincent opened the front door, but didn't leave. He and Frankie turned to watch the girls, as they were all over Nunzio and Angelo.

Frankie nodded to Vincent. They tiptoed to the couch—Vincent behind Angelo and Nina, Frankie behind Mona and Nunzio. A floorboard creaked and the girls looked up. Nunzio and Angelo's eyes were closed. Nunzio was fondling Mona's breast while Angelo had one hand halfway up Nina's thigh.

Nina shouted, "Now!" She pushed herself off Angelo's lap and dropped to the floor. Mona slid off Nunzio and landed on the floor alongside Mona.

"What the hell are you doing?" Nunzio shouted.

Pop! Pop! Silencers muffled the shots from Vincent and Frankie's revolvers. Two shots each. The cousins' heads jerked forward and blood rolled down the backs of their necks, streaming from the holes in their heads onto the plastic-covered couch.

Mona and Nina were curled on the floor, their arms covering their faces. With his gun at his side, Vincent walked around to the front of the couch and looked down at them. "You both did good." He tucked the gun away in his belt.

"We owe you."

CHAPTER 13

Before a family considered inducting an associate into the Mafia as a made man, the associate had to either carry out a contract killing as the trigger man or be involved in its planning. Once that obligation was fulfilled, the induction ceremony took place. The initiate drew blood from his trigger finger while crime family members looked on as witnesses to the ritual. A prayer card of a patron saint was burned and cupped in the hand of the initiate who recited a vow to never betray Omertà—the mob's code of silence.

As burn this Saint, so will burn my soul. I enter into this organization alive, and I will have to get out dead.

* * *

When the Professor had learned one week prior to the hit on Nunzio and Angelo that the cousins had been dipping into the till, he sought and received permission from the boss, Salvatore Sabella, to eliminate the cancer from their family.

Cardone had chosen Vincent to carry out the contract killing alone, but Vincent talked the dubious Professor into letting Frankie help fulfill the contract. If Vincent was going to become a made member of the Mafia, he felt his friend should be one too.

He always had Frankie's back.

By killing Nunzio and Angelo, Vincent and Frankie had met the final qualification for entry into the Mafia as soldiers. Soon thereafter, they swore fealty to the family in the ritualistic ceremony of Omertà and, at the age of twenty-four, became made men.

With their vow, Vincent and Frankie now earned the privileges, backing, and protection of the family they honored.

* * *

The next five years saw a rapid turnover of men who controlled the crime family. Salvatore Sabella retired to Florida in 1941, allowing control to pass to the underboss, John Aveno who, in turn, selected the Professor to be his underboss, his second in command.

Vincent and Frankie's rise in the family was linked inexorably to the Professor's ascent. As soldiers working for the Professor, they generated significant revenue for the family by growing the gambling and loansharking organization in their territory and earning a reputation for collecting debts through force and intimidation. Vincent reaped the benefits of the Professor's rise—so much so, that, by the age of twenty-nine, the young protégé had made the progression from soldier to capo.

In 1946, five years after taking over leadership of the family, Aveno was murdered by two unidentified intruders as he and his wife were having dinner in the kitchen of their South Philly home.

The Professor became the new boss and elevated Vincent, then thirty-four, from the rank of capo to underboss. Swayed again by Vincent's pleas on his friend's behalf, the Professor also promoted Frankie to capo, reporting directly to Vincent.

One Sunday afternoon, in the comfort and security of his living room and in a rare show of concern for his own well-being, the Professor made an admission. "Now that I am the boss, I have earned a bull's-eye on my back, Vincent."

"Who wants you dead? Everyone admires and respects you." But Vincent knew the Professor was right. Fear, suspicion, greed, and, above all, ambition, were the way of life in the ruthless world in which they lived.

"Not everyone admires me. I know you respect me, as I respect you. I've been witness to your growth and have been proud of your ascension. You are my protégé. And you are more than just a business associate. You are like a son to me. Someday you will take over the family business. Today, however, some families in New York will believe I arranged to have Aveno killed, and that I did so without consulting with them. They will look for retribution, and want to take from me what is mine and yours. Atlantic City will be big one day. Others want a piece of it, but it is ours, and we must fight to keep it."

Vincent was emotional. "Mr. Cardone, you have my pledge that I will do whatever it takes to protect you and everything we've worked so hard to get. This I promise."

CHAPTER 14

Robert Cardone was in college at Columbia University in New York City, but Vincent continued to spend Sunday afternoons at the Cardone's—the Professor and Vincent sharing a near father-son relationship. The warmth and hospitality the Cardones showed Vincent provided him with a measure of solace from his otherwise violent and solitary life.

But the weekly visits would end.

One Sunday in late October, Vincent and the Professor were discussing family matters in the living room when there was a knock on the front door. The Professor set his pipe down and rose to answer. Vincent heard him greet the visitor with an uncharacteristically loud show of affection. "Matilda! Matilda! Look who's here." Seconds later, he returned to the living room arm-in-arm with Joey "Hammer" Caitano. Matilda looked out from the kitchen. When she saw who had arrived, she rushed to throw her arms around Joey, standing on the tips of her toes to cover his cheeks with kisses.

"Joseph, I want you to meet a friend of mine, Vincent Vendetti. Vincent, meet my favorite nephew, Joseph Caitano. Joseph is my dead sister's son." Vincent recognized Joey immediately. Seventeen years hadn't changed him much. He looked the same as he had in high school, only more mature. Even with the touch of gray in his hair, he was still enviously handsome, especially in his olive drab Army uniform.

Neither man extended his hand. The two former antagonists stared at each other until Joey snarled at Vincent. "What are you doing here, Shorty? I see you ain't got any taller—and you're still ugly."

The Professor thought Joey was kidding. He asked, "You know each other?"

"Shorty and me go way back. We went to high school together and—"

"Call me that again, Joey, and I'll do the same thing I did to you back in school." Vincent took a step toward the bigger man.

Matilda had never seen this side of Vincent before. The shocked way she looked at him tore through his heart. He realized nothing with Matilda would ever be the same.

The Professor stepped forward to clutch Vincent's elbow and pull him away. "You sit down." He directed Vincent to an easy chair. "And you, Joey, sit over there." He pointed to the plastic-covered couch then nodded to Matilda to leave. Matilda lowered her eyes but paused to look at Vincent before stepping back into the kitchen. From behind the door she eavesdropped on the conversation.

The Professor stood in the middle of the room, much like a referee in a boxing match, and spoke calmly but firmly to both men. "Not in my house, understand?" he said, peering over his glasses. "In my house, in front of my wife, you act like gentlemen." The two men continued to glare at each other. "What's the problem here?"

"Uncle Danny, we had a problem back in high school. We had a fight and the nuns threw Shorty here, er, Vincent, out of school for starting it."

Vincent said, "I didn't start it—but I ended it, didn't I?"

The Professor said to his nephew, "Go on."

"That was it. I ain't seen him since then."

The Professor looked at one then the other. "All that time and you two still have a grudge. Forget about it now, okay? That's it. No more. Understand? I want you to shake hands," he ordered. And when neither man made any effort to comply, he said it again. "I said shake hands or I'll throw you both out." Vincent and Joey rose and walked to the center of the room. They extended their hands, allowing their palms to barely touch—more of a brush than a handshake—but the gesture satisfied the Professor.

"Good. Now let's have some wine and talk." He called out, "Matilda! Vino."

On cue, Matilda emerged from the kitchen with a bottle of Chianti and three large water glasses. She set them on the coffee table, then turned to Joey and smiled. "It's so good to see you, Joseph. It's been so long. I want to hear all about what you've been doing, and where you've been. You stay and have ravioli with us, okay? I got plenty."

The Professor answered for him. "Yes. He'll stay."

"No, thanks. I gotta go. You got company. Some other time."

"Vincent is not company," the Professor interjected. "He's family—like you. I insist. You stay."

Joey was stunned. *Family? Vincent was family? What the hell was that all about?*

"Okay. I'll stay." Then he turned on the charm. "Aunt Matilda, I would tell my soldier buddies about your ravioli— the best in all of Philly, I would tell them. But, you know what? Some of those farm boys didn't even know what ravioli were. I'd tell them, "Then you don't know what heaven is until you've tasted my Aunt Matilda's ravioli.""

Matilda blushed at the compliment. She sat alongside Joey on the couch and held his hand in both of hers. Vincent remembered with envy how Joey enchanted the nuns in school, as he now charmed Matilda.

Joey's curiosity about Vincent was piqued. "What have you been doing since high school? How do you know my uncle?"

The Professor answered before Vincent had a chance to respond. "Vincent works for me. At the funeral parlor."

Joey knew Galante's was the front for his uncle's activities in the Mob. With a knowing smile, he said, "Oh, yeah. My mother told me you bought Galante's funeral home. How's business?"

"Not bad. Up and down. People are going to die, you know. Some weeks more than others. But it pays the bills." With Matilda in the room, the Professor changed the subject. "How many more years will you stay in the service?"

"I'm done now, Uncle Danny. Hell, I'm almost thirty-five years old. It's time for me to do something else. I'm looking to get a *civilian* job." Joey failed to explain that he had been forced out of the service when his commanding officer found him in bed with his wife on an Army base in the Philippines. He then asked Vincent, "You ever serve in the War?"

Vincent looked down and away from Joey. "No. The draft board didn't want me." He did not want to discuss that he was rejected because he did not meet the minimum five-foot, four-inch height requirement.

Joey figured as much and would not drop the subject. "Why not? You got flat feet or something?"

"Yeah, that's what it was."

Vincent glanced at the Professor, who sensed his discomfort and turned the discussion back to his nephew. "What year did you join the army, Joseph?"

"1929."

"So, Pearl Harbor happened in 1941, right? And bang, you're in the middle of it. You were with the troops that invaded Italy, weren't you?"

"That's right."

"Ironic, no? Invading the country of our heritage to get rid of that fascist Mussolini. Then they sent you to the Pacific. Thank God you survived all you went through. We're very proud of you, Joseph."

Matilda stroked Joey's arm and smiled. "You're a hero. And thank God you came back safe."

"Yeah, I'm happy to be back."

The Professor nodded to Matilda to return to the kitchen so the men could talk in private. "What kind of job are you looking for?"

"I don't have anything in mind. I hoped you would put in a good word for me someplace. I don't care what it is. I only ask that it pays good and it don't require any experience."

Vincent snickered.

"What the hell are you laughing at?"

The Professor's piercing stare was all Vincent needed to quickly apologize. "Nothing. I just thought of something funny that happened today."

"You know, Joseph, Vincent can always use some good people. Maybe you can work for him."

Joey shook his head. "Not a chance in the world. With all due respect, it wouldn't work out, Uncle Danny. We never got along too good."

The Professor disregarded his nephew's objections. "Vincent, you think you have a good job for Joseph?"

"Mr. Cardone..." Vincent still addressed the Professor with respect, even after all this time, and was never asked to do otherwise. "You know I'd do anything in the world for you, but, like Joey said, I don't think we'd get on too well. He wouldn't take orders from me. Ask him."

"You're damn right about that."

His uncle was irritated. "Joseph, you want a job, yes or no?"

"Not if I have to work for Shorty. No way will I do that."

The Professor bristled. "Listen to me, Joseph. I'm going to say this once. Just one time. You never call my friend that name again. Understand? Not to him, not in my house, not in front of me. No place."

Joey looked sideways at Vincent then nodded. "Yeah, okay. I understand."

"Vincent," said the Professor, "let me ask you again. Can you find a good job for my *nephew*?"

Vincent nodded then looked directly at Joey. "I'll find something for him, yeah. I'll work something out. We'll make a go of it. But, remember, Joey, I don't do this for you. I do it for your uncle. I owe it to him."

Joey took a deep breath and held it for a moment. He shook his head at the ignominy of working for Vincent—but he needed a job.

The Professor moved Joey's decision along. "I'd like to see you work together, Joseph. I believe you can learn from Vincent. He's a good man." Then, wearying of the discussion, he ended with a simple, "Yes or no?"

"Okay. All right. I'll give it a try. It's worth a shot."

"Good. We will meet tomorrow morning at Galante's to discuss it. That's enough talk. Let's drink to your return, Joseph—and to your new job, to family, and to the future."

"And to Aunt Matilda's ravioli."

The Professor made a toast. "Joseph and Vincent, what's done is in the past. Let's forget the past and live for today and tomorrow. *"Cent' anni!* For one hundred years I wish us health, wealth, and happiness." They all clinked glasses.

CHAPTER 15

"Frankie, guess who's gonna be working for us?"

"I don't know, Vincent. Who?"

"I ain't telling you until you take a guess." Vincent sounded more like a juvenile than a Mafia mobster.

"I don't have a clue."

"Come on. Guess."

"Okay, Joe DiMaggio."

"Nope. Guess again."

"Come on. I don't know."

Vincent grinned wide. "Does the name Joey Caitano ring a bell, like in Hammer?"

Frankie recoiled. "You've got to be kidding me."

"How's that for somethin' unbelievable? Joey Caitano!"

"No way! Hammer? You have *got* to be kidding me," he repeated, and shook his head. "Hammer?"

"I ain't shittin' you. He just got out of the Army and he needs a job."

"Well, tough shit. Let him get his own job. He ain't workin' for us."

"Yeah, he is. Turns out he's the Professor's nephew. We ain't got a choice. The boss wants me to hire him."

"I don't like that, Vincent. It's not right. How're we supposed to work with that sonofabitch after all he did to us growing up?"

"Frankie, think about this. He's gonna work for us. *For us!* Don't you get it? Think of the possibilities."

Frankie let the notion sink in, then broke into a grin wider than Vincent's.

* * *

Joey and the Professor were sitting on a couch in the Professor's office at Galante's when Vincent and Frankie arrived to discuss Joey's work assignment.

"Dummy! Is that you? My old buddy, you skinny shit. You look the same. How the hell you been?"

Frankie flipped his head toward Joey. "My name is Frankie, not dummy. Get it?"

Joey said, "Yeah, sure. The last time I saw you, Frankie, you were giving the principal at Saint Theresa's the Italian salute. Uncle Danny, you should've seen him. He was great. We were busting his balls and one of the nuns dragged us all into the principal's office. She's giving us a lot of shit when all of a sudden Frankie gets up and tells her to go screw herself. He grabbed his balls and swore at her. 'Va fongool,' he said. He walked right out of school and the nun went crazy. She followed him home and threw him out of school."

"That's because you guys ganged up on me and that old fart blamed me."

"You should have seen this guy, Uncle. We laughed for days. He was like a hero at the school."

The Professor smiled at the story. Frankie noticed, and said, "I was a hero, huh?"

"I'm serious. Kids talked about what you did for weeks."

"No kidding. After I got kicked out of school, the kids talked about it?"

Seventeen years of pent-up anger toward his boyhood nemesis seemed to dissolve in a minute when Frankie extended his hand in welcome.

The Professor assigned Joey to collections, reporting to Frankie—a step up from the normal assignment of money counter in the claustrophobic tomb. He justified the plum assignment. "Because of what you boys have done since you took over the gambling operation, we have twice the number of betting parlors of five years ago." Although the Professor rationalized that Joey would help speed up the process, his assignment did not sit well with Vincent or Frankie.

CHAPTER 16

Philadelphia's historic Italian Market had its beginnings in the late 1800s when Italian immigrants settled into the South Philadelphia neighborhood in the area around 9th Street. The market, a collection of outdoor vendors selling fish, fruit, and vegetables, was a mainstay of social and business activity for Italians and others who bordered the market.

* * *

Within six months Joey got bored with his collection routine. He was easily diverted by women and idle conversation, and dropped off the betting parlor receipts later and later each day. Joey's late deposits did not sit well with the tomb counters, who were forced to stay and wait for him. The routine had always been for collectors to arrive with their receipts as early as they could, which let counters finish their accounting and check out in a reasonable amount of time. No one wanted to be in the underground room longer than necessary.

Frankie met with Joey to explain how his lateness impacted the tomb counters. But Joey shrugged him off. "Yeah, yeah. Whatever you say. I wouldn't want my uncle to think I'm screwing off. You do know the Professor's my uncle, right?"

"Yeah, I got it."

* * *

Joey finished his collections at five-thirty and was walking through the Italian Market on his way to Galante's. A heavily made-up brunette intercepted him. "Hey, Joey Caitano. You remember me?"

Joey twisted his face as he looked for recognition of the woman. "Pansie? Is that you? Jesus, I haven't seen you in a thousand years." His bear hug lifted her two feet off the pavement.

In return, Pansie gave Joey an open mouth kiss, brief and with intent. Frankie's sister had a reputation in the Italian community of being a *puttana*—a slut. She first had sex with Joey when he was in his early teens, even though she was five years older than he was. Joey thought he was in love with her, but she taught him otherwise. "You don't love me. You'll see. When you're with the next girl, you'll be in love with her too. You're gonna be just like me, Joey. I love to make love."

Joey stood back and took in Pansie from head to toe. "You look great."

She brushed off the compliment. "What have you been up to? I thought you were in the Army."

"Yeah, I was. Not anymore. Are you married or anything?" He took her left hand to examine it for a wedding band.

"Nah, I ain't married. I ain't gonna marry anybody but you, Joey," she teased. Her laugh was throaty and cigarette-strained. "Where are you heading to?"

"I got to take some stuff back to my work."

"What *stuff*?"

"Just some stuff." He lifted a leather case to show her. The case was filled with the day's gambling receipts. "I got to turn this in."

She rubbed against him. "Why don't you come up to my place first? It's around the corner. I can open up a bottle of wine and we can catch up on old times."

"Jesus, that would be nice. But I can't. I got to get back."

Pansie pouted, curling her lips in a sulk. "You sure, Joey?"

"Don't start with me. You know I ain't got no will power."

She looked at him with her large brown eyes and purred. "It's up to you. I mean, maybe, just maybe, if you're a very good boy, we can talk about old times, if you know what I mean."

"I can't, Pansie. I've got to go."

"I live right down the street. So what if you're an hour late taking your stuff back? Who's gonna care?" She licked her tongue against her full red lips.

Joey rolled his eyes skyward, trying to fight off the temptation, but memories flooded over him. He shook his head and put his arm around her waist. "Pansie, you are so bad. I never could say no to you."

* * *

Joey loved Pansie's tight ass and firm breasts. He held his breath and shut his eyes when she played with him, trying to control his urges. She lay on top of him to mirror his body with her own, rubbing her breasts against his chest and kissing the nape of his neck. She nibbled at his ears, his chest, and his stomach. He groaned with pleasure. She kissed him hard and rolled onto her back to allow him to straddle and fondle her. His breathing seemed to stop altogether. "I'm ready, Pansie."

"Not now. I'll tell you when, Joey."

She pulled him down to her and kissed him for a long minute, then whispered. "Did you miss me all those years?"

"Yeah, I missed you."

"Good. That's good."

He struggled to hold off. "You're killing me."

"Not yet, Joey." She dug into his back with her long fingernails, exerting pain to allow him to fight through his passion."

"Okay. Now, Joey!"

CHAPTER 17

Six o'clock turned to seven. The tomb supervisor sent one of the counters to notify Frankie that Joey had not shown up with his receipts. Frankie sent the counters home and called Vincent who, in turn, called the Professor to tell him that Joey had gone missing. The Professor said, "Call me when he comes in. I want to talk to him."

By eight o'clock Joey had not yet shown up. Vincent called the Professor again to express concern. Something was wrong. The Professor wondered if some outsider knew Joey's routine and had held him up for his briefcase full of gambling receipts. Or was it a New York family making a statement over Atlantic City by taking out the nephew of the boss? "I want you and Frankie to meet me at Galante's at nine. Bring a half dozen of your men. Have them check all the parlors to track where Joey was last."

The organized search of the betting parlors turned up no leads and was expanded to include hospitals and even the morgue.

Night became morning. Tired, stubble-faced men sat on the padded benches in the hallway outside the Professor's office offering theories among themselves about what might have happened to the boss's nephew.

Frankie dared to ask the Professor, "Would he have done something stupid like hold back on the money he's been collecting and just take off with it?"

The Professor stared at Frankie. "Why would you say that about my nephew? He's not stupid. Joseph knows if he did that—" The Professor finished the thought by slicing his forefinger across his throat. The gesture was as much a threat about what would happen to Joey as it was a reminder to Frankie that he would not tolerate anyone who had sticky fingers.

* * *

Daybreak arrived to the sounds of the milkman placing empty milk bottles in his metal bottle carrier and setting filled bottles inside wooden boxes next to the front doors of the row houses up and down the street. Joey looked at the clock and saw the time was half past five. He propped himself up on his elbows and looked at Pansie, who was still naked and fast asleep. The room was in disarray, with clothes and towels strewn about, two empty wine bottles on the bureau, and an ashtray full of spent cigarettes. He spied his briefcase near the front door. *Shit. The collection money. I forgot about that.*

The counters would not be back at Galante's until late-afternoon. Joey decided what he would do. *I'll tell Pansie's asshole brother I tried to drop off the money last night but the counters must have left early, so I had no choice but to wait until this morning.* He got dressed and was about to leave when Pansie awoke. She got out of bed and stood naked in front of him.

She was used to men leaving her in the early morning hours, but asked Joey, "Where are you going?"

"I gotta get out of here, Pansie. I'm in deep shit as it is. Everybody'll be wondering where the hell I've been."

"Who's everybody?"

"How about your brother for one?"

"My brother? What do you have to do with him?"

Joey did not want to go into details. "Nothing. We've got a... uh... a business relationship."

87

"Doing what? I thought you hated each other."

"Yeah, I'm not happy about it, but I needed a job when I got out of the Army, and my uncle... my uncle forced me... Aw, never mind."

"Your uncle did what?"

"Pansie, drop it, okay?"

"Yeah, sure. But, Joey, you cannot tell Frankie you've been with me. He don't think much of me as it is. I don't know what he'd do to you if he knew we've been together."

"I ain't telling your brother nothing. If he finds out I've been shacking up with his sister, he'd have my balls ripped off."

"Wait a minute. I have an idea. I've got something for you." She reached into the drawer of her nightstand and pulled out a small pocket revolver. She fingered the pistol gently, then waved it at him.

Joey pushed her aim away. "What are you doing with a derringer? Geez, don't point it at me."

"I ain't gonna shoot you, you jerk. I want you to have it. In case Frankie finds out about us and sends someone to hurt you."

Joey took the gun from her. The derringer fit perfectly in the palm of his hand. "This is a little sucker, ain't it?" He aimed at the wall, his finger off the hair trigger.

"I've had it for years—for protection you know."

Joey slipped the gun into his pocket. "Thanks, Pansie. That's real nice of you." He pulled her toward him, held her butt, and kissed her hard on the lips. "Last night was like old times."

"Yeah, it was." She rubbed her naked body against him. "You sure you have to go?"

* * *

An hour later, Joey stepped out of Pansie's apartment and paused to look up and down the street. He headed north on 9th Street through the open-air market to Galante's. The market was already buzzing with activity. Food stand owners hustled to set up their outdoor stalls and fires were started in fifty-gallon barrels to burn the boxes and trash produced each morning. The cacophony of sounds was amplified by vendors haggling over the wholesale prices of produce and trucks honking as they squeezed through narrow, cart-lined streets to deliver product to shops along the way.

Joey was halfway through the market when a sedan pulled alongside him and stopped. "Hey, Hammer, get in."

Joey peered through the driver's side window and recognized Ralph and Benny, two of Frankie's men. "What the hell you guys doin' here this early?"

"Your uncle wants to see you." Benny disregarded the horn blaring from a truck behind him.

"I've got to go to the tomb. I'll see him later."

"Nah. Better hop in. He wants to see you now."

"What the hell for?" But Joey knew the answer to his question before he even asked it. "Because I was late last night?"

"Can't say. It's better if you get in the car."

Joey climbed into the back seat. "What's going on, guys? Is there a problem with my uncle? Tell me what the hell is going on."

Neither mobster answered.

The drive to Galante's parking lot took no more than two minutes. "Let's go." Ralph led the way into Galante's while

Benny walked behind the two through a gauntlet of grim-faced men waiting in the hallway. Benny knocked on the door to the Professor's office. "Here he is, Professor."

The Professor was seated behind his desk. Vincent and Frankie flanked him on either side. "Thank you, Benny. Close the door and wait outside."

Joey was surprised to see Vincent and Frankie. He noticed the coffee table was littered with coffee cups and two ashtrays overflowed with cigarette butts. The air was thick with cigarette and pipe smoke.

"What's going on, Uncle Danny? Why's everybody's here?"

The Professor said nothing.

Joey looked at Vincent then at Frankie. "What the hell's going on? What's the matter? Benny and Ralph wouldn't tell me nothing."

The Professor glared at his nephew. "Where have you been, Joseph?"

"What do you mean? I ain't been no place."

"What do you mean *no place*? You had to be *some*where. Why didn't you drop off your collections last night?"

Joey cast a quick glance at Frankie before he answered. "I had some things to do."

"You had some things to do? Like what?" Frankie asked.

"The truth is, I was with a girl. That's all." Joey did his best to sound matter of fact. "Just a girl I met. I don't even remember her name. You know how those things go. We had a drink, then one thing led to another and I spent the night."

Frankie said, "See all those men outside? Do you know we had every one of them lookin' for you last night? All because we thought maybe Anastasia's boys nabbed you, or maybe the cops pinched you. We didn't know. We were ready to go to war because of you."

"What's the big deal? I was with a woman. It's not like I'm in the Army."

Frankie snarled at the bigger man. "Yeah? Well, you're right. It ain't the Army. But you know what? Your uncle expects the same things that the Army expects of you. Like, be on time—not twelve hours late. We thought you were maybe dead or something. But I see you ain't dead, so maybe you're right—it wasn't such a big deal. Maybe we shouldn't have worried about you."

"That's what I'm sayin'. It's no big deal."

But Frankie did not let the matter drop. "So, you didn't turn in the money last night because you were with a girl, huh? But you say you don't know the girl's name. Is that right? I find that kinda fishy, to tell you the truth."

Vincent was quiet the whole time, waiting to see how the problem would play out. No one was happy with Joey. He did whatever he wanted, always behind the shield of his family ties to the Professor.

Joey said, "Shit. That ain't the first time I spent a night with a girl and don't remember her name." He turned to the Professor. "I'm sorry, Uncle. I know I ain't no saint. But I didn't mean no trouble."

Frankie lit a cigarette. "You know, Joey, for a couple of months, Vincent and me, we been figuring out that money's been missing from the parlors. We didn't want to think it was you. But now..." Joey stiffened at the accusation. "Let me ask you. Are you the guy who's been takin' money so you could give your girlfriends a good time—those girlfriends who ain't got no names?"

The Professor was somber. He loved his nephew, but it was a given—the penalty for stealing from the mob was not pardonable, regardless of family ties.

"No, I ain't been taking any money. What do you think, I'm crazy?" Perspiration appeared on Joey's forehead.

The Professor challenged his nephew. "You would not steal money from the family, would you, Joseph? If you needed money, you would have come to me, right?"

"I would never take money from you! I don't know what Frankie's talking about. I got yesterday's collection right here." He pointed to the briefcase at his feet.

Vincent spoke for the first time. "Put it on the table." He moved the ashtray and coffee cups to make room.

Joey looked to his uncle and shrugged, but did what he was told. "See for yourself."

Vincent popped the two latches and opened the briefcase. He looked at Joey, shook his head, and lifted the case for the Professor to examine. Vincent squinted at Joey. "It's empty! You sonofabitch. You stole the money."

"Let me see." Joey reached for the case. "What the hell! I don't know what happened to it. I didn't take the money. It had to be the girl."

Frankie put out his cigarette and fronted Joey. "You fuckin' thief!" He sunk his fist into Joey's stomach. The big man doubled over and fell to the floor. He lay curled in a ball, gasping for air.

Vincent tossed the case to the floor. A lone quarter bounced out and rolled around in circles until it stopped a few inches from Joey's face. Vincent picked up the coin and hurled it hard at Joey, catching him in the shoulder.

The Professor had seen enough. "You two, get out," he ordered, and removed a revolver from the shoulder harness tucked under his jacket. The Professor would have to deal with his nephew—no matter it was his own blood—his dead sister's only son. He had no choice. Vincent and Frankie knew there was no other option. They turned to leave the office. Frankie touched the Professor on the shoulder to show respect and said, "I'm sorry." The Professor nodded in return.

Vincent hugged his mentor and kissed him hard on the cheek. He started to say something, but decided against it. A moment later, he closed the door behind him.

The Professor and Joey were alone. Joey rose from the floor, a pitiful figure, begging for mercy and proclaiming his innocence. "Honest to God, Uncle Danny. You can't do that. I didn't take the money. It had to be the girl took it." He pointed to a door at the back of the office. "Let me run out the back door. No one will know you let me go."

The Professor was weary. He pinched the corners of his eyes with his left hand. "Joseph, you betrayed my trust. You make me look bad with my own men. You stole money from the family. I can't let you go. Capisce?"

"Uncle, I didn't do nothin'. It had to be the girl."

"Who was the girl? You know her name, don't you? Why didn't you just say who it was?"

"I couldn't say in front of Frankie."

"He's not here now, so tell me."

"It was Pansie, Frankie's sister."

"Why didn't you say her name? You know what I think? I think it's because you really have been taking money. You've been trouble from the beginning. You have not shown the discipline I expected of you. Because I favored you, you took advantage of me. Frankie has been worried that you've been stealing from me, but I hoped he was wrong. Now I know it's true. You're a thief. You stole from me. You affected the respect my men have for me."

"What do you want me to do? I'm not lying."

"I never thought I would have to kill my own flesh and blood."

"Please don't do that."

"Say a prayer to God with me, Joseph, and may your mother, my dear sister, forgive me for what I'm about to do." The Professor reached out to hug his nephew. "I am heartily sorry for having offended thee and I detest all my sins..."

A shot was fired, but Vincent and Frankie did not hear it. The sound was muffled by the two bodies huddled in a hug inside the Professor's office.

Joey looked at the door hoping no one heard the shot then guided the Professor's limp body gently to the floor. He quickly locked the office door then slid the coffee table in front of it. The back door of the office offered his only escape. He was out and down the steps to the coffin room in a matter of seconds, and exited through an emergency door into a back alley. From there, he disappeared without a trace.

Vincent and Frankie lingered outside the Professor's office. Two minutes passed. When the Professor did not appear, Vincent knocked on the door. It was locked. He knocked again and shouted, "Mr. Cardone!" Still no answer. Vincent and Frankie looked at each other, and Vincent nodded to Frankie to bust the door open. Frankie braced himself and forced the door open with his shoulder, splintering the door jamb. The coffee table was shoved aside from the force of the impact. On the floor lay the Professor—

bleeding from a mortal wound. He had been shot in the heart with the derringer Pansie had given Joey.

* * *

Later that day, Vincent went to Pansie's apartment.

"You want to come in?" she asked.

"No," Vincent said. "I just wanted to thank you for what you did."

"Yeah, sure. Okay to keep the money?"

"Yeah. It's all yours."

"So how did it go?"

"The Professor's dead."

"And Joey?"

"He's gone. I got guys lookin' for him, but we ain't found him yet."

CHAPTER 18

After the Professor's murder, Vincent became the boss of the Philadelphia crime family. He made Frankie his underboss. Both men were thirty-four years old, unusually young to be elevated to such high status in the Mafia.

Vincent and Frankie had money, power, and respect—everything they dreamed about as teenagers. Apart from their own close relationship, however, the two were friendless and unmarried, and they continued to live with their parents in the same row homes in which they were raised.

The Sunday meal routine Vincent had enjoyed for years ended abruptly with the Professor's death. Vincent, however, recalled the times spent with the Cardones and their son Robert. He missed the family atmosphere and longed for a wife and children of his own. He wanted to marry a nice girl who would bear children for him to carry on the Vendetti name. Some girls—gold diggers and women of whorish reputation—threw themselves at Vincent because of his power and wealth, but Vincent longed for more. He wanted to meet an honest, down-to-earth girl with whom he could have a meaningful relationship.

* * *

Vincent's parents had not returned to their birth village of San Bartolomeo since first arriving in the United States in 1912. They spoke often about returning to visit old friends and distant relatives, but were fearful to travel away from Philadelphia on their own.

Maria was determined her bachelor son should go to Italy with them. One night, Vincent arrived home late, long after Dominic had gone to bed. As Italian mothers are prone to do, Maria asked if he had eaten.

"No. I'm starving."

She placed a loaf of thick, crusty bread and a small plate of olive oil in front of Vincent, then turned on the gas stove to fry peppers and a steak. Vincent tore off a chunk of bread and dipped it in the oil.

"Papa and me, we go to Italy."

"Good. When are you going?"

"When you take us."

"I ain't goin' to Italy."

"Why? Maybe you meet girl and get married."

"Are you crazy? No! I'm not goin' to Italy to get married. You and Papa have a great time."

"We no go if you no go with us. Thirty-six years we been here. We come in 1912. You thirty-six years old and still you no marry. No children."

Vincent said nothing.

"I have friend in San Bartolomeo—Caterina Palmero. She have a daughter—Concetta. She a smart girl. Went to school in San Bartolomeo. The nuns, they good teachers. Before I marry your father, I go to school with the nuns. The nuns—"

Vincent was impatient with his mother's endless dialogue and cut her off. "Yeah, I know about the nuns. What about Concetta?"

"Concetta?"

"Yeah. You were telling me about Concetta, your friend's daughter."

"Oh, she nice girl. Work for Caterina and Pasquale at their restaurant. She work hard, and she strong." Maria flexed her arms in a show of physical strength.

"Why are you telling me about her?"

"Caterina and me, we thought, maybe... you know, you both single and you not get younger."

"You're trying to fix me up with her, aren't you?"

"What do you mean *fix*? I told you maybe you meet nice girl in Italy. What I know about fixing up?"

"What does she look like?"

"She go to church every day. She no husband. She quiet girl. No talk too much."

"Momma, what does she look like?"

Maria avoided looking directly at Vincent. She pretended to be absorbed in her cooking and mumbled just loud enough for Vincent to hear, "She nice girl. Twenty-nine."

"Did you say twenty-nine? Why isn't she married?"

"What do I know? Why you no married?"

Vincent was rankled by his mother's evasiveness. "I asked you what she looks like," he repeated. He was tired, hungry, and only wanted to eat and go to bed.

"She nice. Long black hair. Nice smile. She tall and tin."

"You mean thin?"

"Yes. I know you like tin girls. She tin. And she tall." Maria's voice trailed off.

"How thin and how tall? Taller than me?"

"I don't know how tall. I no put ruler against her." She feigned irritation. "She tall. So what? What's wrong with tall girls? Maybe you like her. You such a big shot, you can't meet her?"

"I didn't say I wouldn't meet her. I only wanted to know what she looks like."

Maria lied. "I don't have picture." The truth was, Caterina had sent her a photo of Concetta, but she did not want to show Vincent. "I sent a picture of you and she thinks you handsome." Another lie.

"She said I was handsome? What is she, blind too?"

"No, she not blind. Her mother says she has good eyes."

Vincent absentmindedly tore off another piece of bread and dipped it in the olive oil. His mother's equivocation led him to conclude that Concetta might be okay looking but probably was no beauty. He reasoned that if he accompanied his parents to Italy, he would meet the girl and see for himself. *I ain't exactly Prince Charming, so who am I to talk about looks? I don't have to love the girl, so why not meet her? What's the harm? So she's taller than me. Most girls are. If I marry a tall girl, our children will be tall, and they won't have to put up with the shit I did growing up.*

"So, Vincenzo, you go. Okay? Nice vacation, no?"

He hesitated a moment longer before deciding. "Yeah, okay. I'll go with you and Papa. And I'll meet Concetta. She better not be a dog."

Maria did not understand. "What do you mean *dog*? She a girl, not a dog. I don't want you to meet a dog."

"I know she's not a dog. I meant... Oh, never mind."

CHAPTER 19

With its origins in antiquity, the popular Italian holiday of Ferragosto is celebrated along with the feast of the Assumption of the Blessed Virgin Mary. The August 15 holiday is observed by processions carrying statues of Mary through the streets. Towns also celebrate the holiday with music and dancing in the piazzas as well as nighttime displays of fireworks.

* * *

Maria planned her family's arrival in San Bartolomeo to coincide with the Italian holiday of Ferragosto. Celebrations that included music, dancing, and good spirits would be fun for Vincent to witness and set a positive tone for his introduction to his bride-to-be. Of course, she kept these intentions secret from her son.

Vincent hired a driver to transport them the one hundred and forty-five miles from the Rome airport southeast to the Vendetti family birthplace. Vincent was surprised at the beauty of the village, which sat atop a hill and overlooked a verdant valley where small parcels of vineyards and olive groves were cut geometrically into the land. He expected to see a poor, backward town, and instead saw a village with beautiful stone houses and cobbled streets that led to a tree-lined piazza surrounded by shops and restaurants. Window boxes overflowed with geraniums that added sensational splashes of red, pink, and white throughout the village.

With Vincent in tow, Dominic and Maria worked their way through a throng of people on the piazza to the restaurant owned by Caterina and Pasquale Palmero. Maria had not seen Caterina in thirty-six years, yet the longtime friends recognized each other immediately. They shrieked and smothered each other with kisses and hugs. Caterina took Maria's hand and escorted the Vendettis to a large table outside the restaurant where a dozen relatives and old friends greeted them with more hugs and kisses.

Vincent's reputation and Mafia notoriety were well known to the Palmeros and others in San Bartolomeo, and his visit from America was highly anticipated. Pasquale admittedly admired and respected him. Everyone had seen photos of Vincent and knew he was short and odd-looking, so his looks and stature came as a surprise to no one. Regardless of what he looked like, however, Caterina and Maria had arranged for Vincent to marry Concetta, and by God, this marriage was going to happen.

Concetta stepped out of the restaurant and stood by her mother. She had a pretty face and long, black hair, but Vincent was shocked to see she was rail-thin and six feet tall. She towered over most men in the piazza.

No wonder she ain't married.

Vincent and Concetta looked at each other for the first time—both unsuspecting about what had been planned. Pasquale lifted a glass of wine to toast Vincent. With an arm-waving flourish, Concetta's father announced to everyone seated at the table, "My wife and our dear friends who we have not seen in thirty-six years, Dominic and Maria Vendetti, have informed me that their son, Vincenzo Vendetti, a man of much importance in America, has come to San Bartolomeo to ask for the hand in marriage of our only child, our daughter, Concetta."

Concetta and Vincent were stunned. Neither knew of the scheme Maria and Caterina had plotted to arrange their marriage. Vincent looked at Dominic first, then Maria, but neither returned his gaze.

Pasquale continued his toast, this time directed at Vincent. "We are delighted that the esteemed Signore Vendetti has honored us with his intentions. Dear sir, my wife and I ask that you treat our daughter with respect, and we hope you both live in health and happiness, and—" he paused for effect, "that you will have a dozen children so that the blood of the Vendettis and Palmeros will survive for generations to come." Another pause. "And, Signore Vendetti, may the best day of your past be the worst day of your future."

The diners stood and clinked their glasses. "*Salute*" and "*cin cin*" echoed through the group, and everyone smiled and laughed at the happy news. Soon they all looked to Vincent for a response.

Concetta's cheeks turned a bright red. She was dumbfounded by her father's announcement.

Maria whispered to Vincent, "Say something."

"No," he muttered out of the side of his mouth.

"Give a toast."

"I can't speak Italian."

"Talk American."

"What the hell are you doin' to me?" he said behind a fake smile. "I'm supposed to marry this girl I never even met before?"

Maria nodded and looked away.

Vincent was at a complete loss. He did not want to offend the Palmeros, but he wanted an opportunity to talk with

Concetta to find out what she was like. Did she know about their arranged marriage? How did she feel about immigrating to the United States? What did she think of him? He had so many questions.

The crowd had fallen silent as they waited for Vincent to speak. He scanned their faces, and his eyes landed on Concetta. She shifted from leg to leg, and was clearly as uncomfortable as he was. *Maybe I should go ahead and marry her. She's young and strong and innocent, and she just might give me a dozen children like Pasquale said she would.* Vincent had to say something. He took a deep breath and cleared his throat. Concetta's eyes opened wide when Vincent raised his glass.

He spoke in English interspersed with halting Italian. "Mr. and Mrs. Palmero—and also my mother and father—thank you for arranging to have Concetta... uh... marry me. I know I am not worthy of her... uh..., but my mother says I need to give her some grandchildren. So, I came from America to meet Concetta, and if things work out, then fine. Like I said, looking at her, I don't think I'm worthy of her. If she don't want to marry me, I understand." He knew people did not comprehend what he was saying, and was eager to end his toast. "And if it's okay with my mother and Caterina, then it's okay with me too. I leave it up to Concetta. Thanks, everybody, for trying to make this work. Salute!"

Several of the people present had a basic understanding of English. They were confused by Vincent's words and shook their heads as they explained to the others what he had said.

* * *

From the second floor of a house overlooking the piazza, a man watched Vincent through partially drawn curtains.

CHAPTER 20

Vincent and Concetta married on September 12, 1948, and sailed to the United States to begin their married life. Five years later, after multiple miscarriages, Concetta gave birth to a seven-pound boy. The parents proudly named their son Vincenzo Antonio Vendetti, Junior.

Vincent was ecstatic. He was forty-one years old and had the first of what he hoped would be many children. But his joy was short-lived. Physicians, including the chief cardiologist at Saint Elizabeth Hospital, examined the infant and discovered he suffered from a ventricular septal defect— a hole in his heart.

The cardiologist explained, "The hole is in the wall that separates the heart's lower chambers and allows blood to pass from the left to the right side of the heart. I have to tell you, Mr. Vendetti, that this ailment is fatal. In my estimation, your son has less than a week to live. I'm very sorry, but there's nothing I can do about it."

"What the hell kind of doctor are you? Fix him, you idiot!" Vincent screamed. "So just put a plug in the hole."

The doctor was unfazed by Vincent's shouts. "Yell at me all you want, but I can't help him. I don't know if anyone can. Any doctor I know who's tried to operate on an infant with that condition ultimately lost the child. Understand this, Mr. Vendetti—*immense* skill is necessary to operate on his tiny heart. A surgeon would not be able to see what he was doing because blood would be pumping and coursing through the hole in the heart. No medical professional will take on that risk."

Vincent was incredulous. "So what are you gonna do? Let him die without doin' nothin'?"

"All I can suggest to you is that I'm aware of a father-son team of doctors, Thomas and Matthew Cortland, who've done research at a hospital in upstate Pennsylvania."

"What kind of research?"

"They've been working on an experimental surgical procedure involving a heart-lung machine."

"What the hell does that do?"

"The machine replaces the function of the heart—temporarily. From what I've read in medical journals, the machine would allow your son's heart to be virtually dry, which would enable surgeons to see what they were doing as they repaired the hole."

"Can they help my son?"

"I can't answer that. You'll have to talk to them. I know they've had some success with the machine with laboratory animals, but to my knowledge, they've never used it to operate on a human patient. And the experimental surgeries on animals have had a less than twenty percent success rate."

"Animals? My son's not an animal."

"Of course your son is not an animal, Mr. Vendetti. But medical researchers oftentimes conduct their initial research and testing on animals before they can move onto humans. So, even though the Cortlands have had limited success, that does not mean they're ready to operate on your son. You'll have to find that out for yourself."

* * *

Concetta insisted that their son be baptized immediately, as required by Catholic canon law when an infant is in danger of death. Vincent asked Frankie to be the boy's godfather and explained the urgency to have his son baptized.

"What do you mean, a hole in his heart?" Frankie asked.

"That's all I know," Vincent said. "We're gonna go see a couple of doctors in upstate Pennsylvania. Maybe they can fix the hole." Tears welled. "They've got to, Frankie. I don't know what I would do if Junior died."

Frankie accepted the role of godfather as an honor.

Part II

CHAPTER 21

The heart–lung machine, known in the medical field as the cardiopulmonary bypass pump, assumes the functions of the heart and lungs when a patient's heart is stopped during open heart surgery. Blood is diverted away from the heart at the same time it is oxygenated, and then returned to normal circulation through the arteries. At the conclusion of the operation, the use of the heart-lung machine is gradually halted as the patient's heart resumes normal function.

* * *

Doctor Thomas "Senior" Cortland, age sixty-four, and his son, Doctor Matthew Cortland, age thirty-eight, were pediatric cardiologists at Eaglesmount Regional Hospital, located in Eaglesmount, Pennsylvania. The small town sat at the foot of Pigeon Mountain, in the northeast corner of Pennsylvania.

Both Senior and Matt were strong, athletic, and lean. Senior was six foot one and wore his brown hair closely cropped. His one concession to age was the touch of gray at his temples. Matt was two inches taller than his father, and had inherited his mother's blonde hair and blue eyes. His wide shoulders and square jaw, however, were typical of the Cortland clan.

Matt had followed in Senior's footsteps. He earned his medical degree, specializing in pediatric cardiology, and joined his father's practice at Eaglesmount Hospital. The Cortlands were brilliant surgeons and researchers. Their most important and widely known work involved the development of an innovative mechanical device that would facilitate the surgery necessary to repair congenital heart defects. If successful, their simply termed *Heart-Lung Machine* would mean hope for thousands of people with congenital heart abnormalities. After achieving limited surgical success on dogs, the Cortlands' research drew excitement from their medical colleagues. The machine's hypothetical use on humans was hailed as a potential milestone achievement.

* * *

Senior's wife died of a cerebral aneurysm when Matt was fifteen years old. To fight through their grief, Senior and Matt spent many weekends over the following three years building a twenty-by-twenty-foot log cabin two-thirds of the way up Pigeon Mountain in a clearing alongside Pigeon Creek. Sunlight found its way through the thick branches of tall pines that circled the cabin, dancing over the site each day with the wind as its choreographer. Soft, luscious, green moss carpeted the ground from the cabin to the creek.

The creek, fed by eons of mountain snow, rushed down the mountain, shaping a series of breathtaking gorges and picturesque waterfalls. Small ponds had formed beneath the falls, and were home to spotted brown trout that feasted on buffets of bugs and snails.

Because of the hazardous trek up a narrow, rocky trail with cliff-hugging switchbacks, very rarely did anyone, other than Senior and Matt visit the cabin. The final leg required them to cross over the raging Pigeon Creek by way of a shaky rope bridge.

The cabin had few conveniences. A blackened iron frying pan and two pots hung from nails on one wall. Metal cups and plates were stacked on a shelf alongside cans of beans and corn. Lidded canisters held staples of flour and sugar. They washed their cooking utensils in the creek and slept in sleeping bags on wooden cots they had built. A fireplace made from river rock provided heat for the cabin.

Now, with Matt having married, the Cortlands visited the cabin only occasionally when the two men needed to take time out from the rigors of their medical practice and recoup in the beauty and tranquility of Pigeon Mountain.

* * *

Saturday morning at dawn, father and son drove in Senior's 1951 Chevy pickup to the base of Pigeon Mountain where they parked and strapped on backpacks containing the supplies they would need for the weekend.

However, instead of a relaxing getaway of fishing and quiet chats, Senior and Matt were on edge the entire time. On Monday, they were scheduled to operate on a human being for the first time using their experimental heart-lung machine. Their patient would be the infant Vincenzo Antonio Vendetti, Junior.

In spite of Senior's repeated forewarnings to the boy's father that he and Matt were not yet ready to perform such groundbreaking surgery on a human, that they needed more time, more research on lab animals, Vincent Vendetti had given them no choice.

Senior and Matt did not discuss the impending surgery or the use of the experimental cardiopulmonary bypass pump the entire weekend. As they sat on a log in front of a stone-rimmed campfire heating beans and frying trout they had caught that morning, Matt decided to break the ice. "Dad, I can't stop thinking about tomorrow's surgery."

"We've done everything we can to make this work, Matt, but the odds are not in our favor. There's a huge chance the boy is going to die on the table. Then what happens?"

"What do you mean?"

"I mean, what's the father going to do if his son dies?"

"We can't worry going into this about how he's going to react, can we? I don't want to sound hard-hearted, but Mafia chief or not, we told him the machine is experimental. That we've never used it before."

"At this point, we can't do much more than pray the machine works for us. But, just for the minute, let's say it doesn't. And let's say the surgery isn't successful. Then what?"

Matt shrugged, not because he wasn't concerned, but because he did not know what the next step would be. "Then we're back to the drawing board. That's it."

"Matt, Vendetti's not going to shake our hands and say thanks for trying."

"No, probably not. But what else can he do? I understand he's a bad guy—the Mafia and all that—but he knows the odds are against his son surviving."

"I told him, but he didn't want to hear it. The man simply did not give me any choice. When I think about it, if I were in his shoes, I would probably make the same demands."

"Like any father."

"The boy's got three or four days to live—at best—with or without the surgery, right? So we give it a shot. We're his last chance."

"Dad, what's the worst that can happen? The kid dies. I'd be truly sorry if that happened, but what's the father going to do—put a contract out on us?"

Senior stared at the fire while Matt paced. "Vendetti is a brutal, vengeful killer, Matt. That's his reputation, though it's hard to believe when you see him. He's about this tall." Senior raised his hand to demonstrate Vendetti's short stature, then dropped his hand and let out a heavy sigh.

"What is it?"

"Listen, I haven't been totally honest with you about him."

"About Vendetti? What do you mean? What's going on, Dad?"

Senior had kept some of the details of his initial meeting with Vendetti to himself. Right or wrong, he did not want Matt to worry about what could happen if the surgery was not successful. "At first I thought Vendetti was only a man who was desperate to save his son. His doctor in Philadelphia had told him we were his only hope. And because his son was going to die, he... *demanded*... we operate on him. He wouldn't let up, regardless of every logical reason I gave for *not* doing the surgery. I reiterated that the surgery was too risky and that we would not operate."

"And?"

Senior mimicked Vincent's voice. "He said, 'I don't like it when people say no to me. You will operate on my son, and you will make him better, or else.' Or else what, I said?"

Matt was surprised. "You didn't tell me he threatened you."

Senior hesitated. "Here's what happened. Vendetti picked up the photo I have of you and Kate on my desk and he said,

115

'That's your son and his wife, huh? She's a beautiful girl, blonde, freckle-faced.' Matt, he knew everything about Kate—about all of us, you, me, Mom, even how Mom died. He told me he'd been waiting all his life to have a son, and now that he had one, it wouldn't be fair for him to die. He said, 'God forbid that your son and his wife have an accident or something.'"

"You mean he threatened to hurt Kate and me? Or kill us?"

"He didn't say that, but that's what I read into his words. I wasn't going to take any chances. At the time, I didn't know he was in the Mafia. I didn't know anything about him. But I caved. I said he could have his son transported to Eaglesmount and that we would operate, but only on the condition he understood the risks. He said he did, so that's what we're going to do."

"Dammit, Dad. You should have told me this. How the hell can we operate with that threat hanging over our heads?"

Senior took a deep breath. "I understand how you feel, but we can, and will, operate."

"We need to talk to the police."

"I did. I telephoned the police station right after Vendetti left our office and spoke with a Detective Kelly. That's how I found out Vendetti's a Mafia chieftain. The detective told me all about his reputation and asked if Vendetti had threatened me. I told him not in so many words, but the inference was clear."

"What did he say to that?"

"That I could file a complaint against the guy, but he wasn't recommending I do that."

"Are you kidding me? The police are telling you not to file a complaint against a man who implied he would hurt or kill us?"

"Unbelievable, right? The way Kelly put it was, if I filed a complaint, that could make Vendetti even more of a threat. So I didn't. Son, we're between a rock and a hard place, and there's nothing we can do."

"I wish you had told me all this before."

"If I had, what would you have done?"

"I don't know. Maybe beat the crap out of the guy."

"That's exactly what I was worried about. What good would that have done?"

"I don't know, Dad. You're right. It probably would have made matters worse."

"Enough. Let's do what we have to do."

Senior tried to flip the trout, but the fish was seared to the bottom of the frying pan, burned, crumbled, and unappetizing. "Shoot. Look what I've done to our dinner."

"That's all right. I'm not hungry anymore. Besides, we need to get going. We'll be out of daylight by the time we get down."

They shuttered the cabin and made their descent as the sun dropped behind Pigeon Mountain and darkness arrived like a curtain drawn to shield the light of day.

Senior drove his pickup back into town. He and Matt made empty talk, trying unsuccessfully to break the tension they felt. Both knew this would be a restless night with little sleep. In the driveway at Matt's house, Senior offered words of assurance. "Everything will be okay, Son. We've worked too hard and too long for our pump to fail. One other thing."

"What's that?"

"Don't mention anything about Vendetti to Kate. No need for her to worry."

"I won't, Dad." Matt noticed his house was dark. "Besides I don't think she's home. She must be out with the girls."

CHAPTER 22

A total cloud cover had cloaked the full moon and turned the night pitch dark, even though it was barely eight o'clock. Matt held the railing as he climbed the three steps to his front porch that stretched across the front and both sides of his house. He tried to turn the doorknob to enter his house, but the door was locked. *That's weird. Why did Kate lock the door?* One of the advantages of living in Eaglesmount was the sense of security the neighbors enjoyed in their close-knit community. Like everyone else, he and Kate rarely locked their front door.

Matt knocked, but there was no answer. He peered into the door's side window and saw light in the kitchen at the back of the house. He turned to walk along the porch to enter through the kitchen when he heard the front door latch click open.

"Kate, honey, hi. Were you sleeping?"

Kate did not answer, but the door pulled open a few inches.

"Sorry we're late."

Matt pushed the door open, stepped inside the dark foyer, and flipped on the light. Kate had been crying. "Are you okay? What's the matter?" As he reached to embrace his wife, the door slammed shut behind him. He snapped his head around and felt a rush of fear. A giant of a man—six and a half feet tall, two hundred and sixty pounds—was pointing a revolver at him. He wore rubber gloves and a blue bandana covered his face from his nose down to his neck. His crumpled brown suit looked two sizes too small for his large frame.

The man waved his gun toward the couch in the living room. "Get over there so I can see you both. Sit down and keep quiet." His voice was that of a boxer whose nose had been flattened too many times in the ring. He drew the curtains to all the windows, then turned on a lamp on an end table where a phone rested. He paced back and forth, saying nothing, waving his revolver aimlessly.

Matt held his wife's hand and whispered, "What's going on? Did he hurt you?"

"No. I'm okay. He didn't do anything to me. He's been waiting for you."

The giant said, "If you say one more word, I'll shoot you both."

Matt looked at Kate and put his finger to his lips for them not to speak. Thirty seconds later, the phone rang. Kate flinched at the piercing sound and squeezed Matt's arm. She reached to answer the phone.

"Don't touch it," the behemoth said, and checked his watch. The phone had rung once. Another minute passed and the phone rang again. "Okay. Now answer," the man commanded. "And if you play games again, I'll blow your husband away. Understand?" He leveled his revolver at Matt.

Kate nodded, then picked up the receiver. "Hello," she said, and listened for two seconds before handing the receiver to the man. "If your name is Johnny, the call is for you."

The man mimicked Kate in a falsetto voice. "If your name is Johnny, the call is for you. My name is *Gianni*, not Johnny, you dumb broad." He snatched the phone from her.

"Yeah, this is Gianni... Yeah, they're both here... Nah, no trouble. What do you want me to do now? Okay. Yeah, okay," he said and hung up. He looked around, then walked to the foyer where he opened the door to a small coat closet.

"Stand up," he said with another wave of his revolver. "Come over here and get in the closet."

"What do you want from us?" Matt asked. "You want money? I don't have any in the house, but I can get you some."

"Didn't I tell you not to talk? Now shut up. Both of you, get in there."

The giant turned his head away briefly, as if looking for something. Matt saw his opportunity and threw his weight behind a punch that clipped Big Boy's chin. Big Boy stumbled backward and raised his revolver to shoot, but Matt hit him again, and dug his shoulder into the man's huge chest.

Big Boy muttered guttural sounds and tried to throw his attacker off with his free hand. Kate joined in and yanked and scratched the man's massive forearm to keep the aim of his revolver away from Matt. But she was no match for Gianni's power. He flung her to the floor with a flick of his wrist.

Matt glanced down to see if Kate had been hurt, and in that instant, Big Boy put an arm lock around the doctor's neck with such force that Matt blacked out in seconds. The giant held Matt's limp body for a moment, then released his stranglehold and let the unconscious Matt drop to the floor. Big Boy was out of breath. He stood over Matt and snorted, "I oughta kill you," and kicked him in the thigh.

Kate tried to stand, but Gianni grabbed her by the elbow and dragged her into the closet. He returned to the unconscious Matt and threw him into the closet beside Kate, then jammed the door shut by wedging a chair under the doorknob.

"Stay there or I'll kill you both right now." Big Boy hit the door hard with the side of his clenched fist. "I should kill you anyway."

CHAPTER 23

Senior backed his pickup out of Matt's driveway and drove the three blocks to his own house. He was lost in thought, concerned about the consequences if the Vendetti boy did not survive the operation the following morning. At that moment, however, Senior knew there was nothing else he could do, and he planned to follow the same routine he did every other work day. He would rise at five thirty, make a pot of coffee, read the morning newspaper while eating a bowl of cereal, and drive to the hospital to arrive by seven. With Matt, his team of surgical assistants, nurses, and anesthesiologist in place, the surgery for the Vendetti boy would begin at seven thirty.

Senior entered his house and flipped on the foyer light. Without warning, a bony arm clamped around his throat from behind with such force that he was unable to cry out. Senior pulled on the man's arm to get him to release his grip, but the man bent him backward to further incapacitate him. The man shoved him against the foyer wall and said, "Doctor, if you fight me, you're a dead man." He jammed a revolver against Senior's spine. "Get down on the floor, on your stomach. And don't say a word."

The man, who was in his late twenties, was built like a long-distance runner—thin and about six feet tall. He used a lamp wire to hogtie the doctor, then blindfolded him and dragged him into the middle of the living room. He pulled down the window shades, then removed his hat and suit jacket, loosened his tie, and sank into Senior's recliner. "Doctor Cortland," the man said, "I cannot tell you what this is about, but I can say others are involved. I am going to say this once, so listen carefully. I do not intend to harm you." He

123

laid his revolver on an end table and yawned. "You will be fine if you remain quiet. I am certain you are an excellent conversationalist, but I do not want to hear from you again this evening. Is that understood?"

Senior did not respond, but lifted his chin off the floor and attempted to glimpse his assailant from the opening at the bottom of his blindfold.

The man leaned forward. "Doctor, I ask you again. Do you understand?"

"I'm not sure what I'm supposed to understand. That you don't want me to ask why you've invaded my house or why you're holding me hostage? Is that what I'm supposed to understand?"

"Sarcasm does not become you. I am a man of my word. I do not intend to harm you."

"I guess I'm going to have to believe you. It doesn't look like I have much of a choice, do I?"

"You do not." The man spoke quietly.

The phone on the end table rang once and stopped. The man studied his watch. Another minute passed and the phone rang again. This time he picked up, listened, and nodded in agreement to the caller's commands. "Fine. No problem. I will wait for your instructions."

"I know you are not comfortable in that position, but I suggest you do not struggle against the ties and that you try to get some sleep. Tomorrow will present us with some interesting challenges." The man stood and turned off the foyer light. "Good night, doctor." Certain that Senior would not be able to free himself, the man spent the night in the chair and allowed sleep to overcome him.

Senior twisted and turned, trying to extricate his hands from the wire tie, but with each wriggle, the cord tightened further around his wrist and threatened to cut off his circulation. After only a few minutes, he was exhausted. He spent the rest of the long, sleepless night with his face buried in the carpet and his body contorted in an awkward position.

CHAPTER 24

Matt and Kate met in Philadelphia when Matt was serving his residency at the Hospital of the University of Pennsylvania. Kate had been a student at the university at the time. He was taken by her girl-next-door appearance—her bright smile, and pretty, freckled face. And as he grew to learn, she was indomitable and strong-willed toward anything she set her mind to do.

Kate and Matt were squeezed together on the floor in the dark and claustrophobic closet, underneath the coats that hung there. Kate cradled Matt's head awkwardly on her lap and wiped away the sweat that trickled from his face. Slowly, he regained consciousness.

"How are you, honey?" she whispered, her face inches from his.

"I'm okay," he mumbled. "Where are we?"

"In the foyer coat closet."

"Damn. I asked for a room with a view."

Kate had been drawn to Matt in part because of his humor—his ability to shrug off problems with logic, a joke, or a turn of phrase.

He twisted about and tried to open the door, but it wouldn't budge.

"Matt, I can't breathe. I feel like I'm going to suffocate in here."

He realized from the sound of her rapid, shallow breathing that she was fighting the onset of claustrophobia. He reached up and pulled the coats off the hangers, then bunched them underneath to sit on. "There. Now we have more headroom. Try to sit still and breathe normally. We're going to be okay. Take slow, deep breaths. Okay?"

"I will," Kate replied. She closed her eyes and, with a little effort, slid against a side wall and stretched her legs out as far as the cramped space would allow. Matt stretched his legs in the opposite direction. They both breathed hard from their efforts.

"What do you want from us?" Matt shouted.

Gianni paced back and forth between the living room and the closet, trying to calm down after his struggle with the two. "Shut up in there," he yelled, and banged the door hard. "If you two don't shut up… That's the last time I'm gonna tell you."

Matt and Kate quieted.

Gianni put his ear to the door. Satisfied they had stopped talking, he plopped on the couch near the phone, and in time nodded off.

Inside the closet, they remained quiet until they no longer heard Gianni pacing. Matt tapped each wall with his knuckles in the vague hope he would find a spot to break through. No luck. The plaster walls were thick. He decided to check the ceiling construction as well. He arched his back against the wall and inched his way up, but the coat rod kept him from standing.

"We can't get through and we can't break the door down," Matt whispered, and slid back down to the floor. "We've got to find a way to have him open the door. If he does, I could rush him and we'd take our chances again."

"No. He's too strong. How about I tell him I have to go to the bathroom? Maybe he'd let me out for a minute."

"Then what?" Matt asked.

"I'll try to find something sharp in the bathroom— scissors maybe, or anything we could use for a weapon or whatever. I don't know what. Maybe something will come to me."

Matt gave his wife's plan some thought, then said, "No, I don't want you to take that chance. I'll see if he'll let me out."

"What are you going to tell him? He's not going to open for you. I stand a better chance. Trust me. I promise I won't do anything crazy."

In the darkness of the closet, Matt shook his head and pondered their choices. He concluded they didn't have any, and said, "Okay. Go ahead and try. But no screwing around. Don't even think about trying to fight him on your own. He looks like he'd use that gun on you in a second."

"Don't worry. I won't."

"See if you can find something sharp and bring it back to the closet."

"I will."

Matt pounded on the door. "Hey, Gianni! My wife's got to go to the bathroom."

There was no response at first. Matt shouted again. "Gianni! Open the door! My wife's got to go to the bathroom."

Gianni woke and looked toward the closet. "Shut the hell up."

"Come on. Let her out. She's not going to hurt you."

"I ain't letting her out, so shut the hell up."

"Let me try," Kate whispered. "Gianni, I've really got to go to the bathroom. Please let me out. Just for a minute." Again, no response. She waited a few seconds. "Come on. I need to go. I'm not kidding. I'm not going to do anything. Please, Gianni."

The giant sat up and pondered what to do. He scratched the puffy outer ridge of his ear for a half-minute, then spoke.

"Here's the deal. I'll blow you away if you give me any shit. Understand?"

"We understand," Matt replied.

"I ain't talking to you, asshole."

"Can I come out too? I need to stretch my legs."

"If you try to come outta there, I'll shoot the both of you."

"Okay. Only me," Kate pledged.

Gianni removed the chair that braced the door shut and stepped back with his revolver drawn.

Kate opened the door and crawled out on her hands and knees, groaning from muscles that were cramped and bruised. The fresh air washed over her and cooled her down. "Gianni, the closet is so hot. Can't you let my husband out for a while? Tie him up if you want."

"No! You have to go to the bathroom or not?"

"Can I come out to stretch for a second?" Matt asked. "I'm telling you, it's hot as hell in here."

"One last time, you try to come outta there and you're dead. Understand?" With that warning, he wedged the chair back against the door with one hand, while keeping his revolver leveled at Kate with the other.

She lifted herself off the floor and wobbled into the powder room. When she started to close the door, Gianni stuck his foot out to prevent the door from closing all the way. "Leave the door open."

"You're kidding me. No way. I'm not going to go to the bathroom in front of you."

"Keep the lights off. I ain't gonna look."

"Gianni, it's my time of the month, if you know what I mean. You're a big boy. You understand, don't you?" Kate was lying, but Gianni would never know. "I need light and privacy.

I'm not going anywhere when you still have my husband in that closet. Give me five minutes, okay? Five minutes. Otherwise, I'm going to bleed through my clothes." She hoped her lie would get to him.

She was right. Big Boy felt himself turn red. "Jesus, would you shut up? Make it quick," he snapped. "And listen. If you even think about climbing out the window in there, I will put one bullet between your husband's eyes before your feet hit the ground. Got me?"

"Yes." Earlier, she had debated going through the window but believed Gianni really would kill Matt. Instead, she rummaged through the medicine cabinet and vanity for anything that would serve as a weapon. She found a can of Drano crystals under the sink. An idea struck her. She poured the caustic contents into the metal wastebasket. Then she wrenched the rubber head off a toilet plunger and set the wooden handle nearby.

Big Boy heard her moving about and bellowed, "What the hell are you doing in there?"

"I'm almost done," she answered, and flushed the toilet for effect.

"You got one more minute then I'm coming in."

"I'll be right out."

Acting quickly, she poured water into the wastebasket then watched it react instantly with the Drano to create a hissing cauldron of lye. She covered her nose and mouth with a wet towel to avoid inhaling the toxic fumes.

"Okay, Gianni. I'm ready," she announced, trying to sound calm. "I'm coming out." She clicked off the light and held the metal basket behind her. She stepped into the hallway and, when she got close enough to Gianni, heaved the bucket of lye at his face. She caught him flush on the left side and caused him instantaneous burning and pain.

The giant bellowed, dropped his gun, and yanked off his bandana mask. He tossed Kate aside and rushed into the darkened bathroom to throw handfuls of water on his burns.

Just as quickly, Kate ran to the closet and pulled the chair away from the door. "Matt, hurry! Hurry!" she shouted, and raced back to the bathroom. With Big Boy bent over the sink, Kate used the wooden plunger handle to pummel him across his back. He tried to ward her off with one hand while flushing the searing lye off his face with the other.

Matt crawled from the closet amid the confusion and screams, not knowing what had happened. "Get the gun!" Kate yelled. "Get the gun! It's on the floor!"

He spotted the revolver. "I got it. Get away from him!" he yelled. Matt was afraid to fire for fear he would hit Kate, but he knelt and aimed the revolver at Gianni. "Get your hands up, Gianni! Kate! Move away!" he shouted again.

Big Boy would not give in so easily. In one swift move, he snatched Kate by her elbows, lifted her up, and threw her on top of Matt. He slapped at the light switch to turn on the bathroom light and slammed the door shut behind him. He looked in the mirror and saw the side of his face had turned scarlet red. "I'll get even with you, *bitch*," he shouted through the door. He then opened the window and clumsily climbed through, tumbling to the ground and vanishing into the night.

CHAPTER 25

In Pennsylvania and other states, remote communities have often found they are able to improve police services by establishing one regional police department to cover two or more neighboring communities rather than employ separate police departments for each. By combining small, sometimes part-time, police forces, municipalities enjoy the benefits of a larger, cooperatively funded department with well-trained, specialized units and professional, full-time police and administrative personnel.

* * *

Two black and white police cars raced to Matt and Kate's house—their sirens piercing the quiet Eaglesmount night and flashing red lights reflecting off houses along the way. From one home to the next, lights in the dark neighborhood flicked on and people peeked out of windows to see what was going on.

Detective Nick Kelly arrived in his unmarked black sedan five minutes later. Kelly was one of two full-time detectives in the regional, multijurisdictional police force of twelve cops. Both detectives were responsible for investigating crimes committed in the borough of Eaglesmount as well as in the four surrounding townships, an area of approximately one hundred and fifty square miles.

Matt and Kate were seated at the kitchen table giving a statement to a cop when Kelly walked in. Kelly identified himself and extended his hand to shake Matt's, but Matt did not extend his in return. "Sorry. My hand is swollen from the fight with the guy who attacked us."

Kelly was concerned about their condition. "You both look pretty banged up. Shouldn't you go to the hospital to have yourselves checked out?"

Matt answered, "We're okay. But we'd be in worse shape if it weren't for Kate."

"Tell me what happened, Mrs. Cortland," Kelly said. He put department-store spectacles on the tip of his nose to take some notes and tilted his head down to gaze over them to address Kate. At fifty-five, Kelly was fit, but his age showed in the thinning gray-brown hair he wore in a wide comb-over. He stood five feet eight, and the reddish complexion on his round face gave him a sunburned appearance. In a voice that was a few decibels too loud, he asked Kate, "I understand your husband wasn't here when the man invaded your home."

"That's right," Kate said. "I was in the kitchen when I heard the front door open. I thought Matt had returned from his weekend away at the cabin."

Kelly interrupted, "Cabin?"

Matt explained, "My father and I have a cabin up on Pigeon Mountain. We spent the weekend there."

"Okay. Mrs. Cortland, please, go on."

"I went to greet Matt, but instead saw this huge guy. He was holding a gun and wearing a bandana to hide his face. I tried to run out the back door, but he caught me and dragged me to the foyer. He told me to sit on the floor and that if I tried to warn Matt when he got home, he would shoot us both."

"How long did you wait for your husband?"

"At least an hour. Then we heard dad's pickup truck pull up. Gianni—that was the guy's name—heard Matt walk up the steps to the front porch, and he whispered to me to open the door. He held me by the back of my collar. I remember feeling his gun against my back. I was scared to death, but instead of opening the door, I locked it. I didn't know what else to do. I guess I should have screamed or something, but I didn't. I thought if I did, Gianni would shoot us. Instead, I thought if I locked the door, Matt might figure something was wrong because we never lock the door."

Kelly asked Matt to explain what happened next. "I did think it was strange that the door was locked, but I thought maybe Kate was out with her girlfriends. I was going to go around back to come in through the kitchen when I heard the front door lock open. I stepped inside the foyer and saw Kate was upset. I asked her what was wrong, but before she could answer, that man, Gianni, slammed the door shut behind me. He flashed a gun and ordered Kate and me to sit down." Matt then described the sequence of events that led to Kate flinging the acid solution at Big Boy and the assailant's subsequent escape through the bathroom window.

"Mrs. Cortland, throwing that Drano concoction at your abductor was foolish on your part."

Matt disagreed. "Maybe it was, Detective, but it was also brave. I'll put it this way. If it wasn't for her, we'd still be in that closet—or worse."

Kelly smiled and said, "Then perhaps I should apologize for my comment, and say nicely done, ma'am."

"Thanks."

Kelly noticed a revolver lying in the middle of the table. He pointed to it, and asked, "Whose gun is that?"

"It's Gianni's. He dropped it after I threw that stuff on his face."

"We'll take the revolver and try to track its owner. Did this man—Gianni—give you any idea, any idea at all, what he wanted?"

"No. He never said," Matt answered.

"You think you can identify him from mug shots?"

Kate nodded. "Yes. One thing's for sure, he's huge. His nose was flattened and his ears were swollen and deformed, like cauliflower. He looked like a boxer."

"What about you, Doctor Cortland? You think you could identify him?"

"Kate's right. He might have been a boxer at one time. I'd say he was about forty-five years old and so large he could probably still do some damage in a boxing ring. Yes, I'm pretty sure I could identify the guy."

"Then we'll have you down to the station tomorrow to look through mug shots."

Matt asked, "Detective Kelly, here's a thought. My father and I are supposed to operate in the morning on Vincent Vendetti's son. Do you know who Vendetti is?"

"Yes. Your father called me a few days ago to ask about him. He said Vendetti threatened to harm you and your wife if you didn't operate on his son."

Kate recoiled. "What? Who is this? Who are you talking about?"

"Kate, listen. You already knew we were going to operate on an infant using the heart-lung machine. What I didn't tell you is that this child is the son of the head of the Mafia in Philadelphia."

"Are you kidding me?"

"I'll explain later, honey. Dad told me about the threat this weekend. Anyway, Detective, is it possible Gianni could have something to do with Vendetti?"

Kelly thought about the possibility then shook his head. "I guess anything's possible, but why would Vendetti arrange to have someone invade your house? That doesn't make any sense. I don't think there's a connection. Vendetti wants you and your father to operate on his son, so what would be the point?"

"Yeah, I guess you're right."

"I can't explain what happened here tonight. Maybe it was supposed to be a kidnapping for ransom. I don't know right now. But for sure, it's most likely a coincidence about the Vendetti kid."

Matt said, "Then that means he might try again."

"I don't think so. Even though in this business you never say never, my guess is it's played itself out. I think you foiled the bad guy's plans, whoever the bad guy is. I don't think you're going to have to worry about him again."

Matt wasn't so sure. "I hope you're right."

"We're going to dust the house for fingerprints and see if we can find any other clues to this guy's identity. We'll be out of here in a bit. Call me tomorrow to arrange a time to come down to the station to look at mug shots. In the meantime, we'll keep a black and white out front to keep an eye on your house."

"We would appreciate that." Matt observed the detective to be competent and thorough, and his manner purposeful and reassuring. Kelly and his cops left well after midnight. On his way out, the detective assigned Officer Mike Kuberski to guard the house.

* * *

The phone rang once at Senior's house, waking the intruder who was guarding Senior. A minute passed and the phone rang again. This time, the man picked up the receiver and listened in silence before asking. "Where is he now?" His voice was low, calm, even flat. "Okay... When?" He hung up and spoke to Senior. "It seems your son and his wife have created a problem for us." The man spoke with perfect diction, pronouncing every word with precision. He also spoke so quietly Senior found it difficult to hear everything he was saying.

"My son and his wife? What do you mean? Where are they?"

"Calm down, Doctor. They are fine."

"Tell me what's going on."

"In due time."

Senior stammered, "You sonofabitch." He struggled against the wire that secured him, trying to pull his hands through the knots, rolling back and forth, straining until he was out of breath.

"Are you through?"

Senior ended his struggle then started to issue a warning. "If anything happens to them... If you harm them, I'll..."

Quiet Man interrupted Senior before he finished his threat. "You will what?"

Senior knew he was powerless to do anything. He changed his tone and pleaded with his captor, "Listen, I'm not a wealthy man, but if you want money, I'll get you some."

"We do not want your money, Doctor Cortland, and we are not going to harm any of you. I realize you may not believe me, but I am a man of my word. Follow my orders. I would rather not have to ask you again."

CHAPTER 26

The alarm clock awakened Matt at five. He silenced the buzzing, relieved the noise had not awakened Kate. His battle with Big Boy had left him bruised, so he took a long shower, hoping to quiet his aching muscles. Afterward, he iced his swollen hands again, but quickly realized he would not be able to assist Senior with the delicate Vendetti operation. He asked the operator to ring his father's house.

* * *

The phone rang multiple times. "I need to answer that," Senior said. He had spent the night on the floor with his knees bent and ankles tied behind his back unable to extricate himself from the wire ties.

Quiet Man read the time on his wristwatch and asked, "Who would be calling you at this hour, Doctor Cortland?"

"The hospital," Senior lied.

Quiet Man asked. "Why would the hospital call you at five thirty in the morning?"

"My son and I are supposed to operate on an infant with a heart condition this morning. The hospital calls me every morning when I'm scheduled for surgery to make sure I'm awake. If I'm not there soon, they'll send security to check on me."

"Is that right? Are you lying to me, Doctor?"

"No, I'm not. Why not let me go? I won't say anything about this."

"I will not be able to do that. We will go ahead and let your hospital security staff visit you, but we will not be here long enough to welcome them."

Quiet Man went to the kitchen to make a pot of coffee. The phone rang again—this time only once. It was the prearranged call Quiet Man had been expecting. He didn't pick up, but waited for the phone to ring again sixty seconds later. When it did, he picked up the receiver. "Yes... Okay. I understand." He hung up, removed a knife from his jacket pocket, and unfolded a serrated blade.

"You will be pleased to know your discomfort will be over soon." Quiet Man cut the cord at Senior's ankles, allowing the doctor to unfold his knees. Senior groaned with relief as circulation curled back into his long legs. "Get up, Doctor."

Senior tried to stand, but was unable to do so without support. He was on his knees, his legs still half asleep. "I can't."

Quiet Man grabbed the wire tie at Senior's wrists and lifted him to his feet. Senior's legs buckled once, but he was able to remain upright.

"Doctor Cortland, please continue to follow my instructions. I will explain our plan of action. Listen to me, please. We will be leaving soon and walk out to a car that will be awaiting us in your driveway. You will remain blindfolded. I caution you not to attempt to remove the blindfold. Trust me when I tell you it will be in your best interest to retain it. We will be taking you to another location. Do you understand?"

Senior nodded once.

Thirty minutes later, as dawn was breaking, a dark blue sedan pulled into the driveway behind Senior's truck. Quiet Man heard the car and looked out the living room window. "Our ride is here, Doctor," he announced. "Shall we go?" He maneuvered his blindfolded hostage out of the house and to the waiting car. "Be careful getting in." He placed his hand on Senior's head and helped him ease into the back seat.

From inside the car, Big Boy grabbed Senior by the back of his neck and shoved him to the floor.

"Take it easy with him," Quiet Man said, and climbed in the back seat. In the dim overhead light inside the car, Quiet Man saw the left side of Big Boy's face was blistered and smeared with petroleum jelly. "What happened to your face?"

"That other doctor's wife—that bitch—threw some stuff in my face and burned the shit outta me. That's how the two of them got away. I don't know what the hell she did, but I don't know how my eyes ain't blind."

"You are indeed a true linguist, Gianni" Quiet Man said.

"Screw you, Bobby—you and all your fancy words."

Senior listened to the exchange, and made a mental note that the name of the man who had held him hostage overnight was Bobby and the man who had struck him was Gianni.

Big Boy reached down and slapped the top of Senior's head. "That's for what your son's wife did to me, but that ain't nothing compared to what I'm gonna do to get even with the both of them."

Senior was horrified. "What? What did you do to my son and daughter-in-law? Where are they?"

Quiet Man said, "Doctor, I must remind you to remain completely quiet. We will not be answering any of your questions." He then addressed Big Boy. "Gianni, don't hit him anymore."

"Go screw yourself. I'll do what I want when I want, and you ain't stopping me, Bobby. You got that?"

Till then, a man in the front passenger seat wearing a felt hat had been quiet. But he had had enough. He turned to look at both men in the back and said, "Shut up, both of you! You sound like a couple of old ladies."

Big Boy whined, "The sonofabitch is always on my case."

"I told you to be quiet. Capisce? You too, Bobby," Felt Hat repeated with authority. "Now let's get going."

Senior now knew there were four men involved in his abduction—Bobby, Gianni, a driver, and the man in the passenger seat who sounded like the leader of the gang.

The occupants of the car fell silent while Driver made turn after sharp turn to thwart anyone who might have been trying to trail them. He kept a wary eye on the rearview mirror. At one point, he warned, "There's a white Olds 88 coming up on us. Hold on." He made a fast U-turn, to see what the driver of the car would do. A second later, he said, "False alarm" when the woman who was driving the Olds drove on by. No one said a word about Driver's sharp maneuver. They knew he was doing his job.

The car soon reached cruising speed. Senior reasoned they had to be on Route 11, a north-south roadway from Eaglesmount. Soon after that, Gianni's snoring was the only sound in the car. Some thirty minutes later, his snoring ended abruptly when the car pulled onto what felt to Senior like a potholed dirt roadway. The vehicle drove slowly and came to a stop a quarter of a mile later.

"Get him in the house and tie him up," Felt Hat ordered.

Senior heard the sound of water lapping against a shoreline and deduced they were on one of the many lakes in northern Pennsylvania—but he had no idea which.

Big Boy held onto Senior's collar and dragged him from the car. He shoved him ahead with such force that the doctor stumbled and fell hard onto his stomach, scraping his chin and knocking the wind out of him.

Quiet Man darted over to help Senior get up. He glared at Big Boy and, uncharacteristically, raised his voice, "What is wrong with you? Do you get pleasure hurting people for no reason at all?"

"Yeah, that's right. I like hurting people, Bobby," he answered, and took several menacing steps closer to him. "You keep talking to me like that, and I'm gonna hurt you too."

Bobby and Gianni were opposites in every way. Quiet Man loathed violence without purpose. Big Boy had no such compunction and believed Bobby was soft and weak and not to be trusted.

As Big Boy approached him, Quiet Man slid his hand inside his jacket. Felt Hat reacted quickly and grabbed Quiet Man's forearm before he removed his revolver. "Bobby! What's the matter with you? Are you crazy?"

Big Boy spat out, "He's sweet on that doctor. That's what the matter is."

"Enough, both of you. Shut up! You understand me? Gianni, take him down to the cellar and tie him up—and do not take his blindfold off."

Quiet Man interjected, "Let me take him down. Gianni never learned how to make a knot."

Felt Hat was annoyed. "Okay, okay. If it's gonna make you happy." The two antagonists were wearing him down.

While Big Boy huffed at Felt Hat's decision, Quiet Man grasped Senior's elbow and guided him to the back of a two-story wood-framed farmhouse with peeling paint and dangling gutters. They stepped through a screen door into a large kitchen with simple white cabinets and a pale green linoleum floor. A table and four metal chairs with red plastic seats sat in the center of the room. "Doctor Cortland, I am going to take you to the cellar," said Quiet Man, and he steered Senior through the kitchen and down a dozen steps to a dark, musty cellar.

Senior felt a metal chair nudged against the back of his legs. "Please sit." Senior did what he was told and Quiet Man tied him to the chair. "I apologize for the actions of my associate."

Senior was confused about this man who showed he could be both harsh, almost cruel, and gentle, protective. "I promise I'll do what you say, Bobby, but in the car, Gianni said something about my son and daughter-in-law. Can you tell me if they're okay?"

Quiet Man bristled at Senior addressing him by his first name. Nevertheless, he answered. "Your son and daughter-in-law are fine. Now, I will entertain no further questions. Understand?"

Senior nodded. He was learning how far he might go with his assailant.

Quiet Man climbed the stairs to the kitchen, leaving the cellar door ajar. A minute later, Senior heard a loud debate break out. He recognized Bobby and Gianni's angry voices, but struggled to make out the gist of the argument. His concern grew when he heard Quiet Man say, "What do you mean they can identify you? You let them see your face?"

"I had to take my bandanna off when she threw that stuff at me. It burned the shit outta my face. I had to wash it off."

"You were supposed to blindfold them."

Big Boy looked at Felt Hat and shrugged. "I forgot."

After a few seconds of silence, Senior heard Felt Hat say, "We have to find a way to get the other Cortland and his wife too."

Quiet Man closed the cellar door so Senior could not hear them discuss Vendetti's kid.

Gianni said, "Let's just whack 'em. We got the one downstairs. Let him operate on Vendetti's kid."

Quiet Man argued, "I'm in this because you said we would let the doctors operate on the kid and then we would let them go. No one would get hurt—not the doctors and not the wife."

"It's a new ballgame now," Felt Hat said. "They can identify Gianni."

"Then let's just whack Gianni," Bobby said.

Felt Hat looked at Quiet Man, uncertain if he was serious.

"You think that's funny?" Gianni retorted. "How about I whack you right now?" Big Boy reached for his shoulder revolver.

Felt Hat fumed. "If you two don't stop all this shit, I promise I will personally shoot the both of you."

They knew he meant it.

Driver said, "Hey, boss, why don't we get the hell outta here before the cops find out where we are."

"No. We need to get Cortland and his wife, and we need to do it quick before they have a chance to look at mug shots. If they identify Gianni, the feds will be able to track him to us."

Quiet Man shook his head and stared at Big Boy with a sour look on his face.

Big Boy bellowed, "What are you looking at? I told you I didn't have any choice. I'm lucky she didn't blind me."

"Right. No doubt they now have the feds involved because of you."

"As God is my witness, Bobby, I'm gonna hurt you some day."

"Try, and it will be the last day of your life."

The heated discussion in the kitchen continued until Felt Hat ended it by shouting at Bobby and Gianni. "Enough! Shut up so I can make a phone call." They quieted. Senior heard Felt Hat talking on the phone, but was unable to make out what he was saying.

A minute later Senior heard the creak of the kitchen door as the men left the house. He counted three car doors being slammed shut outside. The next sound was the car speeding down the driveway.

Overhead, heavy footsteps walked toward the cellar door.

CHAPTER 27

When Senior did not answer his phone, Matt tried to contact him at the hospital, but head nurse Gladys Risner told Matt his father had not yet arrived.

"When he gets there, tell him I hurt my hand last night. Let him know it's nothing serious, and I'll be able to help operate the bypass pump for the Vendetti infant procedure this morning, but I won't be able to assist on the actual surgery." Matt did not want to go into specifics and would explain the events of the previous night to his father later at the hospital. "I'll try reaching him again at home, but if you see him, tell him I'm on my way."

He rang Senior's home phone, and again there was no answer. Matt was curious, but not overly concerned. Before leaving for the hospital, he decided to update Kate on the situation. Upstairs, he stroked her arm to wake her. "I've tried to phone Dad to tell him about last night, but I can't reach him. He might be on his way to the hospital. I'll let the cop out front know I'm leaving. This afternoon we'll check in with Detective Kelly to look at mug shots."

She smiled and said, "Love you." Exhausted from the events of the night before, she fell back into a deep sleep.

Matt backed his car out of the driveway, pulled up alongside the patrol car parked at the curb in front of his house, and reached across the passenger seat to roll down the window. Officer Michael Kuberski, a former Marine, stepped out of his squad car and spoke to Matt through the open passenger window. "Good morning, Doctor Cortland. Everything okay?"

"I've got to get to the hospital, Officer. My wife is still sleeping. Keep a close eye on the house, okay?"

"She'll be fine. I'll be right here." Matt was pleased to note that the cop was powerfully built and could probably hold his own in a fight with Gianni.

The drive to Eaglesmount Regional Hospital was short—an eight minute ride up Main Street and past the high school. Matt parked in one of the spaces reserved for doctors and took the elevator to the third floor to check on the Vendetti infant. Nothing had changed since Friday.

Gladys told him, "Your father hasn't been in yet. The baby's parents have been here all night, but they went to the coffee shop for some breakfast."

A hospital-wide page for the elder Cortland went unanswered, so Matt used the phone at the nurse's station to call Senior at home one more time. No answer. *What's going on?* he wondered. He was becoming concerned. "I'm going to my father's house," he told nurse Gladys. "I'll be back as soon as I can." He took the steps down to the ground level. When he rounded the corner, he saw a short man walking toward him accompanied by a much taller woman wearing a black dress and black lace mantilla. Matt recognized the Mafia chief from Senior's description. The man had to be Vincent Vendetti and the woman, his wife.

Matt looked away when they passed in the hallway, but Vincent recognized him from the photo in Senior's office. "Hey, you," he shouted at Matt who continued to walk toward the exit. "Hey, you. Cortland!" he shouted again and raced to catch up to him.

Dammit. Matt stopped.

"You're Cortland's son, ain't you?"

"Yes. But listen, I can't talk to you now."

"Why the hell not? Why ain't you gettin' ready for the operation?" Vincent's loud voice drew stares from several nurses waiting to use the elevator.

"I'll be back in a couple of minutes, Mr. Vendetti. I'm in a hurry. I'll see you back in your son's room. Wait for me there." Matt turned on his heels and dashed out the door and to his car."

"Sonofabitch!"

* * *

Matt pulled up to his father's house and was relieved, yet irritated, to see Senior's pickup truck in the driveway. He parked behind the truck and ran up the front steps two at a time. His father's tardiness was unusual given that Senior constantly preached punctuality to his staff. Matt would have to give him some friendly jabs. He opened the door and entered the house with a loud, "Hey, Dad. You okay in here?"

There was no response. He continued to shout, "Dad? Where are you?"

Matt recognized the acrid smell of burning coffee and went into the kitchen. He unplugged the coffee pot that Quiet Man had neglected to turn off. *Dad left the coffee pot on? That's not like him. He's always so careful.* "Are you here, Dad?" No answer. He checked the backyard, the basement, and each room of the house. The last place he looked was in the detached garage. Nothing. Senior was nowhere to be found. *Maybe he tried to reach me at home.* Matt called Kate. The phone rang four times before she answered. Her voice was hesitant, sleep-laden. He had awakened her.

"Honey, I'm sorry to wake you, but did Dad call?"

"No." She sat up. "Is something wrong?"

149

"I don't know. I'm at his house now. I know he was here this morning because the coffee pot was still on and his truck is in the driveway, but I can't find him anywhere. I've already been to the hospital, and he's not there either."

"I'm sure there's an explanation, Matt. You might have passed each other on the way. Maybe he walked to the hospital."

"No. I think something's wrong—with what happened to us last night, and now Dad's nowhere to be found. I think they're related. Look, I'm going to drive back to the hospital to see if he's shown up there. If he hasn't, I'm coming right home. Look out the front window and make sure the cop is still there."

Kate went to the window and parted the curtain. She had a clear line of sight to the car and saw that Officer Kuberski was still in his patrol car. "He's still out front."

"Good. Stay put, please. I'll call you from the hospital."

Matt's mind was racing with the concern that had set in. His father's disappearance added to his confusion about the episode with Big Boy.

He decided to follow his father's usual path to the hospital, hoping Kate was right and he had walked there. Along the way, he popped into a cafe where Senior sometimes stopped for a quick breakfast and asked the manager, "Was my father here this morning?"

"No. Not today. Is there a problem?"

Matt didn't answer. *Yes, there's a problem. Something is seriously wrong.* He left the restaurant and raced back to the hospital.

* * *

Vendetti paced his son's hospital room, growing more and more agitated. His watch read seven thirty, the time the operation was to begin, but his son was still in his crib with an oxygen line into his tiny nostrils. "What the hell is going on? Why ain't they here?"

Concetta didn't know and couldn't answer. She was seated next to her son's crib, bent at the waist, her hands covering her face to mask her wracking sobs. Vincent stopped ranting, reached out to her, patted her shoulder to try to calm her, and then stormed out to the nurses' station.

Gladys looked up from her paperwork. She could be stern with patients and their families when she had to be. "Yes, sir? May I help you?"

In a voice too loud for a hospital, Vincent said, "My son is still in his room. Why ain't Cortland here?"

She glared at Vincent and corrected him, "You mean *Doctor* Cortland."

"Yeah, okay. *Doctor* Cortland."

Though she knew both doctors were to operate, she asked, "Which Doctor Cortland are you referring to?"

"What do you mean which one? Both of them. That's which one. If they don't show up in the next ten minutes, I'm gonna tear this fuckin' place apart. You got what I'm saying?"

Over the years, Gladys had seen her share of hot-tempered and unreasonable patients and family members. She was inured to their tirades. Vincent's volcanic temper did not impress her. She scolded him in a clipped manner that recalled long-ago memories of his Catholic school nuns. "Keep your voice down, Mr. Vendetti. I don't appreciate you cursing at me. Kindly go back to your son's room and maintain some decorum in this hospital. I will page the doctors."

Vincent shook his forefinger at her and said, "Don't push me, lady!" He returned to his son's room and a minute later heard Gladys's page.

"Doctor Thomas Cortland, Doctor Matthew Cortland, dial extension 454. Doctor Thomas Cortland, Doctor Matthew Cortland, dial extension 454."

Matt had arrived back at the hospital and also heard the page. He stepped into the Admission's Office to call Gladys. "Is my father here yet?"

"No, we haven't heard a word from him. It's not like your father to be late and Mr. Vendetti's throwing a fit. He wants to know where you both are. He's cursing a blue streak. What do you want me to tell him, Doctor?"

Matt said, "Stall him. Don't tell him we talked. I have no idea where my father is. I'll call you when I know something more."

CHAPTER 28

Kate hung up the phone and got dressed but, unable to clear the cobwebs of sleep from her head, she lay back down on her bed, struggling to keep her eyes open. Moments later, she heard footsteps on the stairs and smiled thinking Matt was already back home. She sat up.

When the door swung open, it was Big Boy, not Matt, who barreled into the room.

Kate screamed and tried to jump off the bed, but he was on her in an instant, holding her down with his elbow across her chest.

"Where's your husband?" Big Boy was mere inches from Kate's face. His lye burns were weeping and his offensive breath reeked of cigarettes. She struggled and writhed to get free, but he grabbed her face and forced her to look at him.

She screamed again, hoping to get Officer Kuberski's attention. "You're hurting me. Get off! Help!"

"That cop ain't gonna help you. Where's your husband?"

"Out back with the police."

"Don't give me that crap. I know he ain't here. Now where the hell is he? I ain't gonna ask again. I'll snap your neck in two."

"All right, all right. I don't know where he is. He's looking for his father."

"See my face? You're gonna pay for what you did." Big Boy flipped Kate over like a ragdoll, straddled her, and dug a knee into her back.

"Get off me. Get off me!"

Quiet Man and Driver were downstairs searching for Matt. When they heard Kate's screams, they ran up the stairs and into Kate's bedroom in time to witness Big Boy rolling her in a blanket.

Quiet Man yanked on Big Boy's jacket to stop him. "What the hell are you doing?"

Big Boy snapped back, "What does it look like?"

Quiet Man tried to calm him. "Hold on a minute, Gianni. Let's find out what she has to say." He pulled the blanket away from Kate's head and in his quiet manner asked her, "Mrs. Cortland, your husband is not in the house. Please tell me where he is."

"I don't know."

Quiet Man took her at her word. "Gianni, we will worry about her husband later. Take Mrs. Cortland to the car, but do not wrap the blanket around her head. She will suffocate."

Big Boy sneered, "You're not the boss of me, Bobby. I'll do what I want. The boss is the only guy who can tell me what to do and when to do it. And since he ain't here, I'm making myself the boss." He cradled his right arm around the small of Kate's back and lifted her over his massive shoulder, then carried her to the sedan and shoved her onto the floor. Quiet Man followed and quickly got into the back seat alongside Big Boy.

Big Boy lifted his sleeve against his weeping burns. "You bitch. You almost blinded me," he said, and ground his shoe into Kate's back.

She shrieked in pain from under the heavy blanket.

Quiet Man said, "Ease up on her, Gianni."

"Why? You goin' sweet on her too?"

Quiet Man tried to reason with Gianni. "We need her to execute our plan."

"What plan? She knows what we all look like now. She's no use to us. Why don't I throw her outta the car?"

"No. We need to know what she can tell us about her husband. Besides, you are not authorized to make that kind of decision."

"The hell I ain't."

"Let's have her sit up. We will be back to the house in a little while, and then we can decide what to do with her."

"No. She's fine where she is."

"Gianni, I know she harmed you, but you would have done the same thing if your roles were reversed. Mrs. Cortland, Gianni will allow you to sit between us if you do not cause any problems. Will you comply?"

"Yes," she murmured.

Surprisingly, Big Boy lifted his foot off Kate's back. "She does one thing, she goes back."

"Fine, Gianni," Quiet Man agreed. He helped Kate onto the seat and unfurled the blanket from around her.

Big Boy looked her up and down and said, "She's got nice titties, don't she, Bobby?" He reached over with his left hand to clutch her breast.

Quiet Man snatched Gianni's wrist and, with astonishing strength, pulled it away. He warned him, "If you touch her again, I will cut your hand off." He tucked the blanket back under Kate's chin.

"You want her for yourself, don't you."

Quiet Man did not respond. Nothing else was said until they arrived at the farmhouse. From the kitchen, Felt Hat heard the car approach. He stepped outside, allowing the screen door to snap shut behind him.

Big Boy pulled Kate out of the car. "Let's go, sweetie-pie."

Felt Hat shouted when he saw only the girl, but not Matt. "Where the hell's her husband?"

Driver answered, "He wasn't at the house. She said he went looking for his father."

"Sonofabitch! Do I need to do everything myself, for Chrissake? Get her down to the cellar."

Quiet Man said, "I'll take her." He removed the blanket from around Kate and guided her toward the farmhouse. Big Boy leaned against the car and let out a long-layered whistle. "She's got a nice ass too, huh, Bobby?"

Big Boy intended the comment to rattle Quiet Man, but it pierced Kate, too.

Quiet Man wheeled around to face Big Boy, who smirked and turned away. Inside the kitchen, Quiet Man apologized for Big Boy's behavior. "I am very sorry for the manner in which Gianni has treated you. Sometimes he is difficult to control—much like a wild animal."

Kate wasn't going to show any weakness, even though fear threatened to overwhelm her. "Your name is Bobby, isn't it? I don't understand what you want from my husband and me. Maybe if you told me, I could help you."

"No. It is not anything you need to know. And don't be frightened by Gianni. I will do my best to protect you from him." At that moment, the three other gang members walked in.

Felt Hat said, "Why ain't she down in the cellar?"

"I told you the sonofabitch was sweet on her."

Felt Hat said, "Get her down there now."

Bobby latched onto Kate's elbow and guided her down the narrow steps. She squinted through the dim light and was shocked to see Senior tied and blindfolded. "Dad! Oh, my God, Dad. Are you okay?"

"Kate?"

She tried to pull away from Quiet Man's grasp, but he was too strong. "Please do not do that," he said, and tied her in a chair next to Senior.

For the first time, she cried. "Dad, I don't know what's going on. They won't explain a thing."

"Don't cry, Kate. We'll be okay, honey. Have they hurt you?"

"No, but only because of Bobby."

Quiet Man didn't acknowledge her.

"Kate, where's Matt?"

"He's been out looking for you all morning."

"Is he okay?"

"Yes. But he's worried to death about you and doesn't know they took me. They're trying to get him too."

CHAPTER 29

Kate and Senior listened as the four men above them spoke. They craned their necks toward the kitchen, but were unable to make out what the men were saying. The conversation suddenly turned loud and angry. Someone slammed the table hard, rattling cups and saucers. A chair was shoved back and sent crashing to the floor. Footsteps shuffled about and voices sounded threatening. After another minute, Felt Hat put an end to the disagreement. "Shut the hell up—all of you. Now!"

Everyone quieted, but one of the men continued to stomp heavily back and forth. Kate said, "That's probably Gianni. It sounds like he's arguing with that guy, Bobby. I think they're arguing about what to do with us."

Senior said, "That's not good. We've got to find a way to get out of here."

The cellar door opened. Kate and Senior sat completely still. Someone listened for a brief moment then slammed the door shut. The heavy footsteps started anew.

Kate looked around the cellar to see if there was a way to escape. She described to Senior in detail what she saw. On the far wall of the cellar, she observed daylight filtering in through a window that was secured with three iron bars across the interior frame. The only other light came from two low-wattage bulbs, one hanging from a bare wire over the stairs and another in the center of the cellar. She also saw a worktable with tools strewn haphazardly on top, a wooden winepress, and just behind those, an empty fifty-gallon oak wine barrel. A set of three long, deep shelves filled with dusty bottles of homemade wine and Mason jars holding tomato sauce and preserved fruit lined another wall.

Senior asked, "Do you know where we are?"

"We're on a farm next to a lake. When they drove me here, all I could see for miles around were fields of corn. Lord knows what happened to the owners. We may never find out unless we find a way to escape. And that won't happen if Gianni has his way. He would just as soon kill us for what I did to him last night."

"What happened?"

"Oh, Dad. It was so frightening." Kate recounted the encounter with Gianni that ended when she threw Drano at him. "I couldn't think of any other way to get away from him." Senior listened and grew more concerned about what Big Boy might do to Kate in revenge.

In the kitchen, Felt Hat was exasperated with Big Boy and Quiet Man.

Big Boy pleaded loud enough for the hostages to hear, "Let me kill the bitch. Look what she did to me."

"You can't," Quiet Man said. "We may need her."

"For what?"

They continued to argue, storming about the kitchen, threatening each other. Felt Hat had had enough. The bickering needed to end so they could get on with their plan, but he felt he had to throw Big Boy a bone. Over Quiet Man's objections, Felt Hat made his decision. "Okay. Go ahead, do it, Gianni. But get it over with quick. Take her outside, away from the house. Dig a hole and bury her out back next to where you buried the owners."

Big Boy grinned in appreciation. "Thanks," he said and walked down to the cellar.

Felt Hat looked at Quiet Man, shrugged, and shook his head. "He likes the killing part. I gotta let him do it. We really don't need her."

In the cellar, Big Boy stood in front of Kate. In a fake, high-pitched voice he taunted her, "You're gonna die today. Kiss your sweet ass goodbye today!"

Senior twisted against his ropes and shouted to the giant. "Are you Gianni?"

"You got it."

"So, *Gianni*, you like hurting girls, is that it?" Senior tried to draw Big Boy's attention away from Kate. "Take this rope off me and we'll see how tough you are."

"Don't tempt me." He ducked to avoid the low-hanging light bulb, shuffled behind Senior, and slapped him hard across the back of his head. Senior fell onto the concrete floor, tied to his chair.

Kate screamed at the hulk. "Why did you do that, you sorry excuse for a man? He's defenseless. Why do you want to hurt people so much?"

Gianni answered, "I just like it. Like I'm gonna like hurting you, bitch. Do you know you almost burned my eyes out?"

"My father-in-law had nothing to do with what happened last night. Pick him up," she demanded. "You are not going to leave him like that. Pick him up, I said."

"Screw you. You know what, sweet pea? The boss said it was okay for me to whack you. Say goodbye to the old man, because you ain't gonna see him again." Gianni cackled with delight. He untied Kate and pushed her up the steps to the kitchen. She was terrified.

"Gianni, you sure you don't need help?" Quiet Man said. "I mean, she might hurt you again. After all, she's a big strong girl."

Driver laughed.

"What are you laughing at?" Gianni said. "Get me the shovel before I whack you too. You're gonna help me bury her."

Big Boy opened the screen door to exit the house. Kate's only thought was to escape any way she could. She pulled away from Big Boy and dashed across the yard, but Driver caught up to her before she got twenty yards. He held her arm in a hammer-lock and led her back into the kitchen.

Big Boy said, "Nice try, sweet pea."

Felt Hat ordered, "Get it over with quick, before I change my mind."

Quiet Man argued one last time to Felt Hat. "We can always kill the girl, so why do it now? I have an idea. She will help us get to her husband. We do not have much time left to pull off this scheme. Remember, he can identify Gianni. It is imperative we find him."

Big Boy said, "I'm telling you, Bobby's getting soft. We don't need her. We'll find Cortland without her."

"How do you propose we do that?" Quiet Man asked.

"Just go find him, that's how."

"I asked you *how* do we find him?"

"How the hell do I know? Just go out and do it, that's all."

Driver chuckled. "Good plan, Gianni. Sometimes I think you took too many punches to your head. Bobby said he had an idea, so let's hear what he has to say."

Gianni took a step toward Driver, but Felt Hat interjected before Gianni could act. "What are you saying, Bobby?"

"We give her husband the option of exchanging himself for her. He will agree. Any man who has a modicum of honor would sacrifice himself for his wife."

"I wouldn't," Big Boy said.

Driver said, "He said a man *with honor*. That leaves you out."

"That's true. I ain't got none." Big Boy chortled and the other men laughed. And like that, the tension was diffused.

"Take her back downstairs. Let's hear Bobby's plan. If, after that, we still can't find her husband, you got my permission to whack her."

Big Boy held Kate's arm behind her and half dragged her down the cellar steps. Senior was still lying on the floor. "Get him up," she ordered.

"Screw you, sweet pea." He pushed her down to the chair and tied her tighter than before. "How does that feel, bitch?"

"You're such a big man, aren't you Gianni? Hurting me and hitting Doctor Cortland when he's tied up. I'm so impressed."

Big Boy knelt down to Kate's eye level, his face inches from hers. His acid breath made her flinch. "Look close at my face, sweetheart. Take a real close look, because I'm the guy who's gonna blow your brains out." He held the barrel of his gun against her temple. She felt the cold of the revolver and held her breath. "They don't want me to kill you, but I'm gonna do it anyway." He cocked the revolver, then pulled the trigger. The sound of the shot filled the cellar. "Oops. I missed." He had fired at the empty wine barrel.

Quiet Man raced down the stairs, followed by the others. "What happened?"

"Nothing. My finger slipped."

"And why is the doctor on the floor?"

"He tripped," Big Boy laughed.

Quiet Man sat Senior upright. "Are you okay, Doctor?"

"Yes, but do me a favor. Put that animal in a cage someplace."

CHAPTER 30

Unable to find Senior at the hospital, Matt drove home to check on Kate. When he pulled into his driveway he waved to Officer Kuberski who was still parked at the curb. Kuberski didn't wave back. Matt wasn't certain the cop had seen him, so he walked to the cruiser to ask if everything was all right.

Kuberski was leaning forward, his chin against his chest as though he were asleep. When Matt leaned down to talk to him through the open driver side window, he recoiled. Blood was oozing from a gunshot wound to the officer's left temple. Matt reached through the window to search for a pulse, but there was none.

Matt looked over the roof of the black and white and noticed the front door to his house was open. *Oh, my God. Kate!* He bolted across the lawn and up the porch steps. Inside, he climbed the stairs to the bedroom two at a time, calling out to Kate and praying he would find her stretched out in bed still asleep. Instead, he saw rumpled bed sheets and pillows tossed about, signs there had been a struggle. "Kate, where are you?" he shouted.

He ran through the house, calling out in each room, "Kate! Kate!" Matt had never known such dread. In his desperation, he thought she might have been hiding from whoever killed the cop. "Kate, you can come out now. It's me."

In the kitchen, he grabbed the phone and blurted out to the phone operator, "This is Doctor Matthew Cortland. This is an emergency. Connect me with Detective Nick Kelly at the police station. Hurry!"

A minute later, Kelly was on the line.

Matt was in a panic. "Detective Kelly, this is Doctor Matthew Cortland. They killed the cop out front of our house and now my wife's missing, and... Yes, my wife is missing," he repeated. "I think that guy from last night took her... You know, the guy from last night.... Had to be him. Of course I'm sure the cop is dead... I said he's dead. For Christ's sake, I'm a doctor. He's dead." Matt struggled to compose himself. "And my father's disappeared too. I don't know what's going on."

Kelly tried to calm him. "Doctor Cortland, slow down. Stay put. I'll be right there. Don't let anyone in but me. And don't touch anything."

Within five minutes, a police car with a single flashing red beacon swung across the road to block traffic from both directions. The cop drew his revolver and stood by Kuberski's patrol car in shock at the sight of his dead fellow officer. Detective Kelly arrived seconds later and screeched to a stop in front of Kuberski's car. Two other cop cars and an ambulance followed.

Kelly leaned into the car to examine the body and shook his head. Kuberski's revolver was still holstered and a cup of coffee from a thermos rested on the seat beside him. He had been ambushed.

Matt rushed out to talk to Kelly, but the detective put his hand on the doctor's shoulder and turned him around. "The Medical Examiner will be here in a few minutes. Let's go inside to talk." He ordered one of the cops to rope off the crime scene.

They went into the house, followed by another cop. "Last night you and your wife were held hostage," said Kelly. "This morning you think your wife was kidnapped. And now you say your father is missing. Let's try to find out what the hell's going on here. First, what makes you think your wife has been taken? Could she be out grocery shopping or at a neighbor's house?"

"Detective, it's seven thirty in the morning. There's a dead cop outside my house and you think my wife is out shopping. She's missing. Period. I talked to her half an hour ago. I asked her to check to see if your cop was still out front, and she said he was. I told her I was coming home. And when I got here I saw Officer Kuberski had been killed and my front door was wide open. I panicked and ran into the house to look for Kate."

"Did you have any concern about her safety when you left her this morning? Where did you go?"

"To look for my father. And, no, I didn't have any concern at first. Everything was fine here. She was still in bed. Your officer was out front. I felt she was safe. Detective, I don't understand. Why is all this happening? No one has contacted me to pay a ransom or anything."

Kelly removed his glasses and looked at Matt. "Last night, after that man invaded your house, I thought, yeah, maybe it was an attempt at kidnapping for ransom. But now I don't think so. If it was about a ransom, they would have kidnapped *one* of you, not try to take you, your wife, and your father. Who would be left to pay the ransom?"

"What other reason would there be?"

"Let me ask you something. Have you had any problems with the staff at the hospital, maybe someone you fired?"

"No."

"What about your father? Did he have any problems? Do you know if he's borrowed money from someone and hasn't been able to pay it back?"

"No. He's frugal. He's never had a need for a lot of money."

"Does he gamble?"

"No, no, and no—to all of the above. My father got along with everyone. I don't know a single person who ever had a bad thing to say about him. I know you've heard that before, but that's the truth."

Kelly probed deeper. "What about you and your wife? You two have any kind of problem?"

"What do you mean?"

"Marital problems. I mean, everyone's got some kind of problem in a marriage. Hell, I've been divorced for ten years now. I had my share of problems. Everybody does."

Matt shook his head. "Not us."

"What about financial problems? You're a doctor. You make a lot of money, don't you? Does she spend it all? You know what I mean? My wife spent all I earned and more."

Matt was angered by the insinuation. "No, we don't have any financial problems. What are you implying? You think I had something to do with this?"

"Don't be pissed. I'm just asking."

"If I had anything to do with this, Detective, how do you explain Gianni's invasion of our home last night?"

Kelly disregarded Matt's question. "You said the front door was open when you got home—and that was after you saw Officer Kuberski had been killed."

"Yes. It was open."

"Which means there was no forced entry of any kind. Why would that be? You suppose your wife might have let the perpetrator in because she knew the person?"

"There was no forced entry because we don't lock our doors."

Kelly looked confused. "Let me see if I get this straight. You mean to tell me that after last night, after you were both supposedly attacked by a thug, held hostage in a closet, beaten and bloodied, the next day you leave your wife alone in the house with the doors unlocked?"

Matt said, "I never thought I had to lock the door. I don't remember the last time we did. Besides, your cop was outside."

CHAPTER 31

Chief of Police Gary McCay arrived on scene and approached the Medical Examiner, who was standing alongside Kuberski's patrol car making notes on a clipboard. The ME explained that the extent of rigor mortis and lividity indicated Kuberski had been shot within the hour.

Detective Kelly exited the house to talk with the chief. "Kuberski was a good man, Chief. Someone needs to tell his wife. Do you want me to do it or will you?"

"I'll do it, Nick. From what I could see inside the patrol car, I'd say he never saw it coming. Any witnesses?"

"No, sir. Not yet. I'm going to have the neighborhood canvassed to see if anyone heard or saw anything suspicious."

"Brief me on the Cortlands?"

"We think Doctor Cortland's wife, Kate Cortland, was taken from her bedroom after Kuberski was shot. Doctor Matthew Cortland said he was out looking for his father at the time. When he returned, she was gone. He called me right away. From the looks of things in their bedroom, there was a struggle, so we're assuming she was taken by force. Thus far, we don't know what's happened to Senior Cortland either. I had a couple of cops check his house on Maple Street. They found his truck parked in the driveway, but the doctor wasn't home and there was no sign of a struggle. Matthew Cortland said he and his father were supposed to be at the hospital early, but Senior never showed up."

"Can we assume he's a kidnap victim too?"

"He could be."

"Is Matthew Cortland a suspect in the disappearances?"

"I don't know. It's all still sketchy to me."

"I'd like to meet him," said Chief McCay.

"He's inside."

On their way into the house, the chief asked Kelly, "How have you been, Nick?"

"I'm okay. Another six months."

"Still planning to head to Florida?"

"Yeah. Time for me to retire in the sun—do a little fishing, maybe take up golf. Who knows."

"We'll miss you, that's for sure."

Kelly stole a glance at McCay, uncertain of his boss's sincerity. The two men were the same age and both had been on the police force for thirty years. Together they climbed the ranks from rookie cops to well-respected detectives. When their chief retired, both Kelly and McCay were candidates to replace him. McCay got the nod. That had been ten years earlier. Ever since, Kelly harbored a grudge against him, feeling McCay had gotten the promotion because he was better at playing politics within the department. To his credit, McCay recognized Kelly's silent animosity toward him and took every opportunity to laud him for his work. In truth, he was not unhappy that Kelly would soon be retiring.

"Doctor Cortland, this is Chief of Police Gary McCay." The men shook hands.

"Rest assured, Doctor, we will do everything possible to find your wife. I understand your father might also be a kidnapping victim. I know you've already described to Detective Kelly what has happened, but would you explain it again to me?"

Matt explained about the home invasion, his search for his father, his discovery that Kuberski had been shot, and the realization that his wife was missing, and perhaps kidnapped.

The chief said, "I understand Detective Kelly had Officer Kuberski keep guard out front, but it appears he was ambushed. When was the last time you saw the officer alive?"

"This morning, at about five thirty, quarter to six. I talked with him for half a minute, then went to the hospital. My father wasn't answering his phone at home so I figured he was at the hospital preparing for surgery on Vincent Vendetti's son."

The chief raised an eyebrow. "Vincent Vendetti. The Philadelphia mob boss?"

"Yes." Matt explained how it came to pass that the mobster was in Eaglesmount.

The chief said, "Vendetti's a murderous thug. The FBI has been working to take him down. Could he be involved in Officer Kuberski's death or the disappearance of your wife and father?"

Kelly answered, "Doctor Cortland and I have talked about that possibility. We don't see a connection. In fact, the opposite. Vendetti needs the Cortlands to operate on his son. There wouldn't be any reason for him to pull these acts and delay the surgery."

Chief McCay asked Matt, "When did you last see your father?"

"Yesterday evening. We spent the weekend at our cabin up on Pigeon. He dropped me off last night, and I assume he went home from here. When I went to his house this morning to look for him, the coffee pot was still on, so I know he made it home last night."

"Has there been a ransom demand for your wife or father, or both?"

"No."

Kelly said, "I'm not convinced this is a kidnapping. I don't know what it is—maybe a grudge or act of revenge—but I don't think it's a kidnapping."

"I'm going to contact the FBI to have them determine what's going on."

"With all due respect, Chief, it might be premature to bring them in. We don't know for sure if we have a kidnapping or if it's something else."

McCay was well familiar with the fact that when the FBI is called into a local investigation, the agents and the local cops often face a struggle of wills, and questions of jurisdiction come into play. Local cops seldom want the Bureau involved.

The chief didn't want to debate Kelly in front of the doctor. "Nick, walk with me, please." McCay knew Kelly was not going to agree with his decision. "Here's my take of this. We've got a renowned physician and his daughter-in-law missing. It won't be long before reporters try to make this into another Charles Lindbergh kidnapping story. I believe it would be in our best interest to have the FBI involved. You may disagree, Nick, but until we know for sure that this is a kidnapping, you will still have jurisdiction."

CHAPTER 32

Vendetti was mad as hell. The Cortlands were not at the hospital to operate on his son. *Where the hell are they?* He demanded answers from Gladys. "Did you hear from them?"

"No, I did not, but I am quite confident they're on their way."

"They were supposed to be here first thing this morning."

"They've gotten delayed somehow. But you shouldn't worry. They are very reliable and, I might add, excellent surgeons. Perhaps you and Mrs. Vendetti might want to enjoy another cup of coffee while you wait."

Vincent stood on the tips of his toes and leaned over the desk as far as he could. "I don't want any stinkin' coffee. I want the doctors to operate on my son. That's it. Catch my drift? No coffee. No nothin'. Just the fuckin' doctors."

Gladys rolled her chair back away from him. "Curse all you like, Mr. Vendetti. It will not do you any good with me."

Vincent narrowed his eyes. "Give me the Cortlands' home phone numbers."

"I will not. I'm not allowed to give out phone numbers to anyone."

Vendetti got louder each time the nurse refused his demands. "Yes, you will."

"Sir, keep your voice down. You are disturbing the patients."

Vincent pounded his fist on the top of the nurses' station desk and shouted. "Give me their phone numbers or I will disturb the whole fuckin' hospital."

Gladys was not intimidated. She reached under her desk for the local Eaglesmount phone directory and shoved it in front of him. "Get them yourself. I will not give them to you."

Vincent snatched the book, turned to the page where the Cortlands were listed and ripped it out of the directory. "Gimme the phone."

Gladys realized it was no use resisting. She placed the phone in front of him. He had the operator connect him to Senior's home first, but there was no answer. He slammed the phone down hard. Next, he tried Matt's number.

When the phone rang at Matt's house, Matt and Detective Kelly stiffened. "Don't answer it yet, Doctor Cortland. I want to listen. Do you have an extension?"

"In the kitchen."

"I'll give you a sign when to pick up."

Matt took a long breath then exhaled equally long, trying to get his voice under control. Kelly gave him a thumbs-up sign to pick up the receiver.

"Hello?"

"Cortland?"

"Yes."

"This is Vincent Vendetti. Why ain't you at the hospital?"

"Vendetti?"

The voice got harsher and louder. "Yeah, this is Vincent Vendetti, and I want to know where your father's at?"

"I don't know where my father is. But I've got to get off the phone. I can't talk to you now. I'll have someone call you later." Matt hung up.

"The sonofabitch hung up on me," Vendetti swore to Gladys. "No one hangs up on me. You understand? No one."

Vincent stuffed the page of the phone book into his pocket and stormed back to his son's room. He raged to his wife in broken Italian that he was going to the doctor's house, and directed her to stay put at the hospital until he returned.

Concetta nodded. She had seen her husband act like this so many times in the past five years—angry and loud. She knew not to question his actions for fear he would storm at her too.

Vincent leaned over the crib and kissed his son on the forehead. He whispered to him, "Everything will be okay. Don't give up. You hear me?"

Vincent drove to Senior's house and entered without knocking. *I'll drag him to the hospital if I have to.* "Cortland, where the hell are you?"

He rumbled through the house shouting time and again, "Cortland! Where the hell are you?"

Finally, when he realized Senior was not there he called Matt using Senior's house phone.

"Cortland, where's your father? Do not hang up on me again. I want to know when you and your father are operating on my son? I'm in his house and I can't find him. Where's he at?"

"What the hell are you doing inside his house? Listen to me, Vendetti. I don't know where my father is. He's disappeared, okay? I know you're worried about your son, but right now, I can't help you. So get the hell out of my father's house. Go back to the hospital. I'll get hold of you later." He hung up again.

Vendetti slammed the phone down. "That's the second time the sonofabitch hung up on me," he shouted to an empty room. "I'm gonna kill him."

Vincent got in his car and raced to Matt's house. He was surprised to see a large circle of neighbors gathered on the sidewalk in front of the house. *What the hell is going on?* He worked his way to the cop who was keeping onlookers from encroaching on the crime scene. The flashing lights on the police cars and ambulance were at odds with the quiet neighborhood where manicured lawns and well-kept homes sat on a street lined with rows of maple trees.

Vincent asked the cop, "What's going on?"

The cop studied Vincent before he answered. "One of our officers was killed. Over there," he said, nodding to Kuberski's patrol car where the ME was still examining the body.

"Who killed him?"

"We don't know." The officer asked Vincent, "Do I know you? I haven't seen you around here before."

Vincent did not answer. "Can you tell me if both the Cortlands are in there?"

"They're not. Just the younger doctor. Why do you want to know?"

"I need to talk to him. He's supposed to operate on my son this morning."

The policeman studied Vincent, stretching his memory for recognition. This strange-looking little man was familiar, but the officer couldn't quite place him.

"Who killed the cop?"

The officer did not answer, but a neighbor standing next to Vincent said, "From what I heard, the cop was guarding the house."

"Why?"

"Last night, some guy assaulted the couple that lives here, Doctor Cortland and his wife, but they fought him off. The cop was stationed in front of the house to guard against the guy coming back."

Vincent said, "So what happened? The guy came back and killed the cop?"

"They don't know for sure, but they think that's what happened. What they *do* know is that someone took the doctor's wife this morning. Kidnapped her."

"But the doctor's okay?"

"As far as I understand."

By the most optimistic measures, Vincent's son had no more than forty-eight hours to live—seventy-two hours at the outside. Although the experimental heart-lung machine could help save his boy's life, Vincent understood the surgery had a far greater chance of failure than of success. But surgery was his only hope.

Vincent asked the cop, "Where's the other doctor?"

"What other doctor?"

"This guy's father."

"Don't know."

"Listen. I need to talk to the doctor who lives here. Tell him if his wife was kidnapped, I'll pay the ransom for her."

That got the cop's attention, "What did you say?"

"You heard me. Tell Cortland I'll pay the ransom."

The big-waisted cop looked down at the man dressed in an ill-fitting suit. "Forget about it, pal."

"Didn't you hear what I said? What the hell are you waiting for? Go on. Tell him I can help. Go tell him I'll pay the ransom. All I want to do is talk to him."

The cop was irritated by this little man. He took a step toward Vincent. "I said no."

"Do you know who I am?"

The cop did not respond.

"I'm Vincent Vendetti."

The cop flinched when he recognized the name. "Vendetti? You're Vincent Vendetti?" He studied him a few seconds longer. "Wait here." He left his station to talk to Detective Kelly and Matt, and emerged a minute later.

"The doctor said he can't see you now. He knows you're worried about your son and will talk to you when he knows something more about his wife."

Vincent seethed. He started to duck under the crime scene rope, but the cop grabbed him by the crook of his elbow. "Doctor Cortland said he can't see you now. So, drop it, pal. They got other things on their minds in there."

"Take your hands off me."

The cop let Vincent go but watched to make sure he didn't try to get under the rope somewhere else.

Vincent walked back to his car. *I'll kill the sonofabitch if my son dies.* He got into his car, made a fast U-turn, bounced his car over the far curb, and sped back to the hospital.

CHAPTER 33

Congress passed the Lindbergh Act, named after the celebrated aviator Charles A. Lindbergh, whose baby was kidnapped and killed in 1932. The Act provided that if a victim is not released within twenty-four hours after being abducted, a court may presume that the victim was transported across state lines, which then makes the kidnapping a federal crime. At that point, the Federal Bureau of Investigation has jurisdiction to investigate the crime.

* * *

At Chief McCay's request, the Scranton, Pennsylvania, FBI Bureau Chief sent Special Agent Alan Dryer and his partner Agent Mark Harris to lend assistance to the Eaglesmount police force.

The two agents, dressed in dark suits and white shirts, arrived before noon. They showed their credentials to the cop standing guard on the porch, entered the living room, and introduced themselves to Matt, who was standing at the bay window looking out at the activity surrounding Officer Kuberski.

Dryer spoke to Matt in a terse, assertive manner. "Doctor Cortland, our understanding is your wife has been kidnapped. Is that your understanding too?" The special agent was a fit fifty-five-year-old with cropped gray hair and narrow eyes that held a perpetual squint.

"Yes. There's no doubt my wife was taken forcibly from our bedroom. The bed covers were in disarray. And you know about the cop who was killed out front. So, yeah, there's no question my wife was kidnapped."

Agent Harris asked, "Doctor, which one is Detective Kelly?" In contrast to his veteran partner, Harris, a recent graduate of the FBI Academy in Quantico, had a more personable air about him—not as officious as Dryer.

Matt pointed to Kelly, who was talking to one of the cops.

The agents continued questioning Matt. "What about your father?" Agent Harris asked.

Matt explained, "I haven't been able to find him. He's not at the hospital and he wasn't at his house, but his truck is still parked in his drive." Matt shook his head.

"Has he ever disappeared like this before?"

"No, never. He's as reliable a man as you'll ever know."

When Kelly finished talking to his cop, the two FBI agents displayed their credential to him.

Dryer explained the FBI's role. "As you know, Detective, since the motive of kidnapping hasn't been definitively established, all the bureau can do is provide support. The final decision on any investigative action is yours to make."

Kelly responded disingenuously, "I will appreciate your advice in helping us apprehend the individual who killed my cop and may have taken Mrs. Cortland."

"You mean *individuals* who may have taken Mrs. Cortland," Dryer corrected. "Appears there is more than one."

Kelly had an immediate dislike for Dryer. "Yes, of course, *individuals*. We know at least two were involved in the home invasion last night—one was a man by the name of Gianni. He had an accomplice who gave him instructions by phone. So yes, *plural*. We're assuming it's the same people from last night."

The phone rang, quieting everyone. Dryer stood alongside Matt who allowed him to lean in close to the phone to eavesdrop on the conversation while Kelly hastened to the kitchen to listen on the extension.

A disguised voice spoke, "Doctor Cortland, we assume the police are there. We have your wife."

"Do you have my father too?"

"Yes, we have your father also. Both are fine—for now."

"What do you want from me?"

"You."

"What do you mean?"

"We will exchange your wife for you."

"What about my father?"

"That is another matter which I prefer not to discuss at this juncture."

"Let me talk to my wife."

The caller responded in a colorless voice, "Not now, Doctor Cortland. Please understand what I am saying. This is not subject to negotiation. I will call you back in precisely one minute for your decision. If you do not agree to an exchange, your wife will die within the hour and your father will follow. I will not be able to alter that progression of events. You have one minute to decide on your course of action."

Matt spoke quickly, "Listen to me. I will pay you a ransom instead. How much do you want? If you hurt my wife—" He was too late. The caller had hung up.

Matt turned to Dryer, "You heard, didn't you? They want to exchange Kate for me."

Dryer spoke bereft of any outward sign of emotion, "You will not be doing that."

"Yes, I'm going to—of course, I will."

Dryer had witnessed much in his thirty-one years with the Bureau and was inured to emotional influences when he worked his cases. "Doctor Cortland, listen to me. You cannot do that without a guarantee that your wife will be released. You'll both be killed. There's no reason to believe they'll make the exchange."

Agent Harris concurred with his partner's assessment. "Doctor, Special Agent Dryer is right."

"I don't care if he is."

"Do you have any idea why anyone would want to harm any of you? Are you and your father having a dispute with a patient, or a patient's family perhaps, or anyone—"

Matt broke off the conversation. "No. Even if we were, it doesn't make any difference. I'm going to do what they want."

Dryer cautioned, "Listen, we understand you feel it's your obligation—your duty to your wife—but without knowing the kidnappers will comply, you're making matters worse. They'll end up with your father, your wife, *and you*."

Matt reminded everyone, "The kidnapper said he would be calling back in one minute. I'm going to do what they ask of me, and—" The phone rang. "I don't want anyone listening on the extension. Understand, Detective Kelly?"

Kelly didn't respond.

"Understand, Detective?" Matt insisted.

Kelly nodded reluctantly.

Matt answered the phone. The voice on the other end was straightforward. "I am going to say this once. If you tell anyone where you are going, if anyone follows you, or if you attempt to do something foolhardy, your wife and father will die. You must do precisely as we say. Is that clear?"

"Yes."

"Very well. Drive to Dunellen and Willow Streets—alone. Do you know where that is?"

"Yes."

"Park your car there. Open the trunk and return the key to the ignition. Do not close the trunk. Wait alongside your car until we give you further instructions. Again, I remind you that if someone follows you or the police elect to have you wired, your wife and father die. If you do what we ask, your wife will be released. Do you understand?"

"I do, but, what about my father? When will you let him go?"

"In twenty-four hours. That's enough questions. You have five minutes to get to your destination."

Click.

Matt looked at his watch.

Kelly asked, "What do they want you to do? Did he ask you to meet them somewhere?"

Matt did not respond, but Dryer surmised what the kidnapper had directed him to do. "They want you to meet them somewhere. Listen, you can't do that without backup. If you go and they don't honor their pledge, we have no leverage."

"I know you're right. It might not be wise to go, but I have no choice. They say they want me, not my wife, so I've got to take the chance they'll keep their word and release her. I wouldn't be able to live with myself if something happened to her."

"Doctor, let me go in your place," Agent Harris said. "We look a little alike. I could pass for you." Harris stood over six feet tall with a lanky athlete's build and a blond crew cut. He was right. He did resemble Matt.

Matt studied the agent briefly, looked at his watch, and said, "No. I'm going. All of you, listen. I know you're trying to do your jobs, but I'm going. I take full responsibility for anything that happens. You cannot follow me. It's *my* decision. Do you understand?" He examined the faces in the room and, convinced everyone would abide by his request, ran out of the house to his car.

Unable to back up because of the police cars parked in his driveway, Matt swung his car onto the lawn, ran over the curb, and sped to the intersection of Dunellen and Willow.

CHAPTER 34

Vincent tore into the hospital parking lot, left his car parked haphazardly across two spaces, and bolted up the stairs to the nurse's station outside his son's room. "Is Cortland here yet?"

"No, sir, he is not. If you wish, I will page him again right now."

Gladys's suggestion preempted another outburst from him. "Thanks. I appreciate that," he said. She was surprised by his pleasant response.

Vincent turned and stood at the door to his son's room. He closed his eyes and took a deep breath to compose himself before entering.

Concetta was in a chair she had pushed up against their son's crib. She looked at her husband, searched his face for a sign of hope and, seeing none, returned to her prayers.

Even with an oxygen tube patched into his tiny nostrils, the infant struggled for air. Vincent whispered, "I won't let you die. I promise." Unable to hold back his emotions any longer, he hid his face in his hands and cried.

Concetta reached out to touch him, but drew her hand back when Gladys entered the room. Although Vincent stood with his back to the nurse, his distress was evident to her. Gladys felt compassion for this profane man whose love for his son was clearly genuine and tender. Without hesitation, the nurse put her arm around his shoulder to console him, but her attempt at comfort only made Vincent feel worse. Embarrassed by his show of emotion, he shrugged her off and walked to the window. Viewing Pigeon Mountain with its lush green blanket of pine trees calmed him after a moment.

He regained composure, wiped his tears away with his jacket sleeve, and turned back to face the nurse.

"I don't know what's going on in this town. First, Cortland goes missing. Then I go to see his son and find out a cop was killed in front of the guy's house."

"No! Oh, mercy," said Gladys. She put the palm of her hand to her chest in disbelief. "What was the name of the cop? I know most of them."

"I don't know."

"Tell me what happened."

"The cop was supposed to be protecting the doctor's wife, but he was killed and the doctor's wife was kidnapped."

Gladys was shocked. "Kate Cortland! She was kidnapped?"

"Yes, kidnapped. I don't know what the hell is happening. I came up here to have those two doctors fix my son. That's all. Fix my son before he dies. Is that too much to ask? What do you think? Do you think they can make him better?"

Gladys had been asked hundreds of times by anxious families if their husbands, wives, sons, or daughters were going to survive and recuperate from surgeries, illnesses, or injuries. She knew to hedge—to offer an air of optimism—but also to measure her responses with caution. "Can they fix your son? Mr. Vendetti, there are so many factors involved. The Cortlands are not God. Your son is very ill…"

He raised his voice, "I asked you a simple question. Can they fix my son?"

Gladys stiffened for the inevitable explosion. "Mr. Vendetti, I understand you are angry, but let me suggest to you that if are a religious man as I see your wife is, right now your son needs prayers more than anger. Praying is the best thing you can do for him."

Vincent's calm ended. "Prayers? You want me to pray for a miracle? Here's a miracle for you. If the Cortlands don't operate on my son, it'll be a miracle if I don't blow up this fuckin' hospital."

Gladys looked to Vincent's wife, but Concetta never wavered from her rosary, even when her husband's calm exploded to fury. "I'll keep paging Senior." She turned and left the room.

Vincent walked in and out of his son's room, each time checking with Gladys to see if she had heard from Senior. Each time her response was no. By early afternoon, Vincent's patience was spent. He would have to rely on the younger Doctor Cortland to perform the surgery alone.

He asked Gladys, "Tell me about Cortland's son."

"What do you want to know?"

"Can he do this operation without his father? Is he good enough to operate on my son alone using that machine they invented?"

"Doctor Matthew Cortland is a fine physician—the equal of his father."

That's all Vincent needed to hear. "Then he's got to operate by himself now. He ain't got no choice. My son can't wait no more. I'm gonna call him right now."

Vincent placed a call to Matt's home, but the line was busy. At that very moment, Quiet Man was on the phone giving Matt final instructions about making the exchange for his wife at Duncllen and Willow.

Vincent waited one minute and had the operator call again.

Agent Dryer answered.

"Who's this?" Vincent asked.

"This is Special Agent Alan Dryer of the Federal Bureau of Investigation."

"Let me talk to the doctor."

"He's not here."

"What do you mean he's not there? Where the hell is he?"

"Who is this?"

"My name is Vincent Vendetti."

"Vincent Vendetti? What do you want?"

"I need to talk to him about my son. I gotta talk to him now, do you get me?"

Detective Kelly heard the interchange and whispered to Dryer, "Both Cortlands are supposed to operate on his son."

Dryer nodded and said, "Okay, listen I've just been told about your son. But I repeat, Doctor Cortland is not here."

"He better be there."

"Mr. Vendetti, I said he's not here and am ordering you to stop calling so we can keep this line free." Dryer hung up.

Vincent called a third time. "Don't hang up on me again. You hear me? Don't hang up. You know who I am?"

"Yes, I know who you are. But unless you can tell me something about the whereabouts of Doctor Cortland's wife, I want you off the phone."

"Well, I ain't getting' off the phone. Now let me talk to Cortland."

"I'll say it again. He's not here. He just left."

"Don't tell me you let him go? What's he gonna do? Give himself up for his wife?"

Dryer was surprised, "Yes. How did you know that?"

"I know because I know."

"What does that mean?"

"Go after him. Bring him back before it's too late, you asshole. I know for a fact that his wife is dead. She's dead, and you let him go. Now they'll both be dead. Go after him!" Vendetti shouted. "You gotta stop him before they nab him."

"How do you know his wife is dead?"

Vincent hung up.

CHAPTER 35

Matt waited at Dunellen and Willow. He looked around but saw no one. As instructed, he unlocked and opened the trunk, returned the key to the ignition, and stood waiting alongside his car.

From a short distance away, someone bellowed, "Get in the trunk of the car." The voice was unmistakable—it was Big Boy, who was crouched behind a dense wisteria bush, hidden from view.

Matt pivoted toward the bush. "I know it's you, Gianni. I'm not going anywhere until I know my wife is safe."

Big Boy came out from behind the bush and looked down at Matt, "If we ain't at the next spot in ten minutes, your wife's gonna be dead. I couldn't care less if you get in the trunk or don't get in. If you don't, I can go ahead and kill her for what she did to me. It's up to you. Get in the stinking trunk or don't. I don't care."

Quiet Man observed the encounter from twenty yards behind Big Boy.

Matt knew events would be moving fast, making it impossible for him to study all the options at every turn. The kidnappers had established a series of checkpoints to thwart anyone who might attempt to follow him.

He was about to comply with Big Boy's order to climb into the trunk of his car when the wailing of police sirens startled him. He looked up the street and saw Kelly's unmarked car, Dryer and Harris's black sedan, and a black and white squad car, all steaming in his direction.

Big Boy shouted, "Your wife's gonna pay for this," then lumbered back around the wisteria and through some back yards to a car waiting on Spring Street.

190

"Gianni, wait!" Matt shouted after him. "I told them not to follow me." He ran after the giant, but Big Boy tumbled into the back seat of the gang's sedan. Quiet Man had raced ahead of Big Boy and jumped in the passenger seat.

"Hit it. Quick," Quiet Man ordered.

Driver sped off.

Matt returned to his car which now was encircled by the three cop cars. He shouted, "Didn't I tell you not to follow me? What the hell is wrong with you?"

Agent Dryer said, "Doctor Cortland, we got a phone call about your wife." He put his arm on Matt's shoulder. "I'm sorry to tell you this, but we were informed she is dead."

* * *

Felt Hat pulled a handkerchief from his pocket and used it to wipe his forehead and the inside brim of his hat. All the while, he enfeebled Big Boy with an angry stare.

Big Boy squirmed and glanced at Quiet Man for support. He said, "What was I supposed to do? When the guy's climbing into the trunk, the cops come flying down the road. If we didn't hightail it out of there, they would have nailed my ass."

Bobby said, "I hate to agree with Gianni, but he's right."

Gianni said, "Hey, boss, why don't we just kill Vendetti and get the hell out of here?"

"Get this through your head. We ain't gonna kill Vendetti. I told you that from the beginning. We stay with our plan."

"Why?"

"Because I said so. I don't want you to tax your brain by thinking. I just want you to do what I tell you to do. Got it?"

Gianni lowered his eyes. "Yeah, boss, I got it."

CHAPTER 36

Agent Dryer, Agent Harris, and Detective Kelly huddled in the living room with Matt. They explained what had occurred—why they had followed him and how Vendetti's phone call had left them uncertain if Kate was dead or alive. "That's the reason we went after you. Vendetti called and said your wife was dead. We didn't know if it was true, but we didn't want to take the chance that you were giving yourself up for no reason."

Matt was stunned at the thought that Kate was dead. "Did he tell you how he knew?"

"No."

Kelly caught Matt's eye and motioned him to follow him into the kitchen. "Doctor, listen. I think your wife is still alive."

"You do?"

"Yes. I think Vendetti was lying so you would operate on his son."

"Where's Vendetti now?"

"He's still at the hospital. I'm heading over there to bring him back so we can find out what he knows."

"I'll tell you this much. I'm praying the kidnappers call again. If there's another chance to get my wife released, I'm taking it."

"You'd be taking a hell of a risk, but I'd do the same if I were in your shoes. I'd go in a heartbeat."

* * *

Kelly found Vincent sitting in the third-floor waiting room. Vendetti was bent over, his forearms resting on his knees, and looking like he had lost all hope. Kelly identified himself, presented his badge, and immediately told Vincent he was under arrest.

"What for?"

"For interference in a police investigation."

"You gotta be shittin' me."

"Nah, I'm not," Kelly said in a matter-of-fact manner. "Stand up." He frisked Vincent, confiscated his revolver, and cuffed him.

"I can't believe you dicks were gonna let Cortland walk into a trap. Did you stop him?"

"Yeah. He's back home. Let's go. You wanted to talk to him. Now's your chance."

"Someone's gotta tell my wife I went to talk to the doctor."

Kelly said, "Yeah, we'll tell her." He drove Vincent back to Matt's house and escorted him into the living room. "Here's the famous Vincent Vendetti," Kelly said to Matt and the agents.

Vincent was still in handcuffs. "Hey, asshole, you gonna take these cuffs off me or do I have to get my lawyer to come up here and sue your ass for harassment?"

Kelly removed the cuffs.

Dryer and Harris flashed their FBI badges.

Kelly said, "Tell us what you know about Mrs. Cortland. The truth, Mr. Vendetti, the total truth. And if we don't get it, we have enough to take you down on obstruction charges."

Vincent said, "Ha! Obstruction my ass! Like that charge would stick." He plopped down on the couch.

"What do you know about Mrs. Cortland?"

"I don't know if she's dead or alive. And I don't give a shit. All I care about is my son." He turned to Matt. "I know one thing for sure. If you give yourself up for her, you're dead and so is she. You don't have to be a genius to know that."

Matt moved a desk chair to the couch and sat facing Vincent. "Mr. Vendetti, did you know they also took my father?"

"Oh, no! They didn't." Vincent did not want to believe what Matt had just told him. "Did they tell you that?"

"Yes."

"Why do you think they took my wife?"

Vincent shrugged his shoulders and said, "Why do people kidnap people?" He gestured by rubbing his thumbs against the tips of his fingers. "Money. That's why."

"But they haven't asked for anything."

"They're asking for you, ain't they?"

"What the hell does that mean?" Matt shot back.

"All I know is if you give yourself up, she dies, your father dies, and you die too. Don't ask me how I know—just trust me that I know. So, if you have a death wish, go ahead—give yourself up. But I'll tell you one thing, I know when something is going down that don't make sense. And this don't make sense."

"I have no choice," Matt said. "If the kidnappers give me another opportunity to give myself up, I'm going to take it."

Vincent nodded toward the FBI agents. "Doctor, if you think you can get your wife back by giving yourself up, you're as stupid as them FBI dicks. And let me tell you somethin' else—my son's dying, and you're gonna take care of him. I don't give a shit whether you like it or not. You want to play hero and trade yourself for your wife, that's okay with me. But you do it *after* you operate on my son. Got it?"

Matt had heard enough. He rose from his chair and bent his six-foot frame so his face was inches from the mobster's and said, "I swear to you on all that's holy, that if you ever threaten me or my family again, I will beat the living shit out of you. I don't care who the hell you are."

Vincent smirked and looked away unconcerned. He was used to threats. Matt's words did not faze him.

"Look at me," Matt demanded. "I said look at me." Vincent turned back to face Matt. "See these?" Matt held his hands up for Vincent to see. They were black and blue, his knuckles swollen, and his pinky and ring finger were bandaged together. "Some guy invaded my house last night and held my wife and me hostage. I ended up fighting him, and that's why my hands look the way they do. Do you see them?" he demanded. "Even if I wanted to operate on your son, I wouldn't be able to. I can barely tie my shoelaces, much less tie stitches in the heart of an infant. Yeah, I can help operate our heart-lung machine, but I can't do the actual surgery. My father is the only one who can."

Vincent turned away so Matt wouldn't see he had tears in his eyes. He understood now that Senior was his only hope. After a few seconds, he looked back at Matt and pledged, "I promise you I will do anything I can to help. If whoever took your father wants money, I'll take care of it. I don't care how much."

Just then, the phone rang, making the tension in the room palpable. Matt answered and the same muffled voice as on the previous call spoke to him. "That was a foolish thing you did to have the police shadow you. You betrayed our trust."

Matt was defensive, "I told them not to come, but someone called and said my wife was already dead. That's why they followed me. Where is she? I want to talk to her."

"Your wife is alive and well. I promise you that much. Mercifully, you have one final opportunity to see her and your father." There was silence.

"Hello? Are you still there? Hello?" Matt thought the caller had hung up.

"I am still here. Who told the police your wife was dead?"

"That's not important. Look, all I want to know for certain is that my wife is still alive. I'm not going anywhere unless I get proof she's okay."

"I said she is alive, did I not? So is your father—although how much longer depends on you. I will call you again in half an hour. You will be able to speak with your wife at that time." The caller hung up.

Matt checked his watch. Eleven o'clock. He faced Dryer, and announced, "If there's an opportunity to win my wife's freedom, I'm going to take it. This time, do not try to stop me."

"Listen, Doctor—"

"No, I will not listen. I've made up my mind. I'm going to wait and see what they want me to do. You cannot stop me from doing what I feel is best for my family." Matt looked at each of the three law enforcement agents standing in his living room. "Do you understand that I don't want any interference?"

All three nodded.

Vincent sat with his legs crossed and his head resting against the back of the couch. He stared at the ceiling, angry at Matt's judgment, but he recognized nothing would change his mind.

To get away from the men and activity in the living room, even if only for a few minutes, Matt went upstairs to his bedroom. He sat on the edge of the bed and thought about what might be in store for him after the kidnappers captured him. Somehow he needed to conceal a weapon that he could use if the opportunity arose. A sudden thought struck him.

He hurriedly put on his hiking boots, went back downstairs, and exited the house through the kitchen door. He went to his garage where he rummaged through a fishing tackle box and retrieved a one-inch, one-bladed penknife. He tucked the knife under the tongue of his right boot and tied the laces loosely.

When he walked back into the living room to wait for the next call, Dryer asked him if he would wear a wire so they could listen in on any discussion that might take place.

"No!"

"Will you let us tail you from a safe distance?"

"No!"

Matt scanned the room and shook his head in disbelief. *What a bizarre mix of people—a middle-aged FBI agent, his rookie partner, and a street-smart local detective—all working in alliance with the brutal head of the Mafia who happens to be sitting on my couch.* Outside, the continued police activity at the Kuberski crime scene caught his further attention.

The phone rang. Kelly started for the kitchen, but Matt shouted, "Don't even think about getting on the extension."

The muffled voice on the phone asked, "Why did it take you so long to answer?

"No one else is listening. Trust me. This is between you and me."

"As you must trust me, I must trust what you are saying too. Here is the framework for our demands. In exchange for you, we will release your wife today and your father tomorrow. You will be released when we are through with your services—in a matter of days. We want only you—not your father, nor your wife. We will explain why when we see you."

"What services are you talking about?"

"We would rather not disclose that at this juncture."

"And how will I know you won't kill my father and me afterward?"

"Trust. You must trust me."

"All right. What else?"

"Your wife will call you in a few minutes. When you accept that she is fine, I want you to get into your car and drive to the corner of Main and Mechanic Streets. I assume you know where that is."

"I do."

"You will note a mailbox just off the corner of Mechanic. Taped to the side will be an envelope with further instructions. Follow them precisely. When we are convinced you are not being followed, we will intercept your vehicle and take you to your father. Is that understood?"

"Yes."

"Please explain to the police that if they follow you or wire you, it will result in a final and unpleasant action. Is that point also clear?"

"Yes, it is. I've made it clear to them, but will re-emphasize it."

"Good. I will hang up now. Wait for the call from your wife and do as I have explained. If you do not follow my orders to the letter, as much as I dislike the concept of killing a woman, your wife will die, and your father will die as well."

Click.

Vincent had edged closer to Matt to eavesdrop on the call, but he heard little. When Matt hung up, Vincent asked, "What do the sonsofbitches want you to do? They say anything about your father?"

Matt did not respond. He went to the window and watched as the Medical Examiner removed Officer Kuberski's body from his patrol car. He was not going to answer any questions about the phone calls or let his own intentions be known. He hoped the kidnappers would be true to their word.

Vincent punctuated the unease in the room. "You don't know what the hell you're doin'. You're gonna get your family killed. Listen to these dicks. They know better than you do."

Matt turned to the mobster. "I told you before and I'll say it again. Stay out of this. I know what I'm doing." He sounded more confident than he felt.

"You say you can't operate on my kid because of your hands. How long before you could?"

Matt lifted his hands and flexed his fingers. "I don't know. But they said my father will be released tomorrow."

Vincent sunk back onto the couch. "I don't believe them."

"We have no choice but to believe them."

Ten minutes later, the phone rang. Matt picked up right away. "Kate?"

"Yes, Matt. It's me."

"Where are you?"

Tony Spallone

"They let me go. I don't know where they went or if they're watching me now."

"Tell me where you are."

"They dropped me at a phone booth outside of Binghamton and told me to call you. I'm at an Esso gas station on Hillsdale Avenue."

"Binghamton! Stay put! I'll have Detective Kelly get the local police to you." Matt tilted the phone up and told Kelly, "She's calling from a phone booth at an Esso gas station on Hillsdale Avenue outside of Binghamton. Call the cops up there to get them to pick her up. Right away."

Kelly went to his car to place the call.

"Detective Kelly is calling the police there now. They'll be there in a few minutes to bring you home. Are you okay?"

"Yes, I'm fine. Scared, but fine."

"Keep talking to me. Don't hang up."

"Matt, it was Gianni from last night and three other men."

"Did they hurt you?"

"No, but Gianni said he wanted to kill me because of what I did to him. One of the other men, a guy named Bobby, talked him out of it."

"What about Dad?"

"He's tied up in the cellar of some old farmhouse. That's where they had me tied up too, although I don't know where it is. He's okay, though. They said they'd let him go tomorrow after they finished doing what they're doing, whatever that is." Kate heard sirens heading toward her. "The police are here already, Matt. I'm going to hang up now. I love you."

"Don't hang up!" Matt yelled. "Honey, don't hang up!"

Kate did not hear his shouts. She dropped the phone and ran to the approaching police car waving her arms frantically.

For now, Kate was safe and Matt had to trust the kidnappers would be true to their word and release his father the next day. He had no choice but to believe them.

Matt looked at the men in the room before issuing one final warning. "I'm going to say it again. Don't follow me. They said they would release my wife, and they did. They said they would release my father tomorrow. They want me for some reason or another. I don't know what that reason is, and yes, I know I'm at risk, but I've got to believe they will do what they say. I've got to go. I know you're just doing your jobs, but I'm leaving now. Do not follow me!"

Chief McCay entered Matt's house just as Matt rushed out. "Detective Kelly, what's going on?"

"The kidnappers promised to release Kate Cortland if Doctor Cortland gave himself up in exchange."

"And?"

"She called just now and said the kidnappers released her. I contacted the police in Binghamton to pick her up at a phone booth where they left her. The kidnappers said they would be releasing the senior Doctor Cortland tomorrow."

CHAPTER 37

Matt drove to Main and Mechanic Streets, six blocks from his home. He checked his rearview mirror often to ensure no one was following, then parked and retrieved the envelope taped to the mailbox on Mechanic Street. The instructions read "Drive onto Route 11 northbound."

Matt saw no vehicle waiting for him at the intersecting streets, so he proceeded onto Route 11.

A blue sedan with Driver at the wheel appeared and followed him at a distance of less than fifty yards. After driving for two miles, Driver took advantage of an open stretch of the road to pull up alongside Matt's car. Quiet Man, seated in the passenger seat, gestured for Matt to roll down his window. "Follow us."

Matt glimpsed Quiet Man for the first time as Driver pulled out ahead of him. To lose anyone who might have been following, Driver made two unexpected sharp right turns, first to exit Route 11, then to quickly re-enter the roadway. When it was obvious no one was tailing the sedan, Driver took another right onto a dirt lane that was hidden from Route 11 traffic by a thick strand of pine trees. Driver and Quiet Man waited for Matt to pull up behind them.

Matt drove up, turned off his engine, and waited for the kidnappers' next move. Driver and Quiet Man got out of their car with guns drawn and approached Matt's car with caution. They checked the back seat to make sure no one was hiding there and ordered Matt to get out of his vehicle. Without warning, Driver fired his revolver three times into the trunk of Matt's car. "In case someone is in there," he said without emotion.

Matt said, "No one's in there."

Driver laughed. "If they are, I bet they wish they weren't."

"I promise you no one is in there and no one's going to follow me."

Quiet Man said, "Well, I promise you this, Doctor, if someone does follow, it will not bode well for you or your family." Matt recognized the cadence and articulation in Quiet Man's speech as that of the man who had called him at home.

Driver shoved Matt against his car, lifted his shirt to check for a wire, then frisked him. He told Quiet Man, "No gun. No wire."

Quiet Man opened the trunk of Matt's car. "I am delighted to see no one is in here. Now, would you please climb in, Doctor? We have a short drive remaining. I trust the ride won't be too rocky for you." Matt did as he was told.

Quiet Man slammed the trunk shut and drove Matt's car while Driver followed in the sedan. They got back onto Route 11 and drove for fifteen minutes before pulling off onto the dirt driveway that led to the remote farmhouse.

Quiet Man opened the trunk. "You can exit now, Doctor."

Matt climbed out and looked around to see if he recognized where he was.

Felt Hat came out of the house. "I see you got him. Good job. Get him down in the cellar. Tie him up with his father."

Matt immediately assumed Felt Hat was the leader of the gang and pleaded with him, "Tell me, please, why you're doing this."

Felt Hat responded, "You'll know soon enough. Just do what you're told."

The air cracked with the sound of a siren. A police car with flashers on came speeding up the driveway. The gang members rushed Matt into the house. Felt Hat pulled out his revolver and stood at the kitchen door. He yelled, "You *sonofabitch*. The cops followed you."

Quiet Man grabbed the back of Matt's shirt and ordered him to sit in the corner of the kitchen floor. "You have betrayed my trust. Do not do anything to give me a reason to shoot you."

Matt nodded.

Driver raced to the second floor, parted the curtains from a bedroom window, and trained his gun on the police car as it careened up the drive.

"They followed you, the bastards! They followed you," Felt Hat screamed at Quiet Man. "I oughta shoot him right now."

Matt was as surprised as his captors at the doggedness of the police. They had disregarded his orders not to follow him, but this time he was happy they did not comply.

The black and white spun to a stop alongside the house. Big Boy stepped out of the car wearing a policeman's hat perched at an angle on his massive head. He grinned and waved to the men in the farmhouse.

Felt Hat opened the kitchen door and yelled out, "Gianni, you asshole, you scared the shit out of us."

Big Boy opened the door to the back seat of the cruiser. In his mocking falsetto voice that sounded so absurd coming from such a big man, he said to the passenger, "We're home, sweetie-pie!"

CHAPTER 38

Big Boy yanked Kate from the back seat of the police cruiser and pushed her ahead of him into the farmhouse kitchen.

Matt jumped to his feet, "Kate!" He tried to go to her but Big Boy intervened. He then turned to Quiet Man and swore, "You lied to me, you sonofabitch. You lied! And I was stupid enough to believe you. I trusted you. You dirty sonofabitch."

Big Boy reached around and slapped Matt hard on the back of his head, "Shut the hell up. You gonna let him talk to you like that, Bobby?"

"I did lie to him, so he can say what he wants. I am not proud of it."

Felt Hat stepped in. "Both of you, take them downstairs and tie them up."

"Let me kill 'em now!"

"You're getting on my nerves, Gianni. Do what I say."

Big Boy held Matt by his elbow while Quiet Man followed with Kate.

As Matt descended, his eyes adjusted to the dim light of the cellar. When he saw his father blindfolded and tied to a chair with his head bowed to his chest, Matt thought the worst. He shouted out, "Dad! Dad!"

Senior lifted his head toward Matt's voice. "Matt?"

"Yes."

"I'm back too, Dad," Kate said.

Senior asked, "Are you both okay?"

"Yes, we're good."

Bobby and Gianni tied the hostages to chairs alongside Senior and then headed back up to the kitchen. Halfway up the stairs, Big Boy paused and pointed his cocked forefinger at Kate, then Senior, then Matt, and back again at Kate.

"Eenie, meenie, miney, mo, catch a tiger by the toe." He pulled the trigger of his imaginary gun and blew on the tip of his finger as if blowing smoke from a gun's barrel. "Later, sweetie. You and me," he said, and gave her a crooked grin.

Quiet Man said, "Are you through, Gianni? How about giving it a rest?"

Gianni smirked and brushed past Bobby to get up the stairs.

When he heard the door to the kitchen close, Senior asked, "Does anyone know what's going on?"

"I don't have a clue," Matt answered. "The bastards had me convinced they were going to let Kate go and I fell for it. The FBI agents told me not to believe them—that they weren't going to release her—and obviously they were right."

Senior asked, "The FBI's involved?"

"Yes. When they found out you and Kate were kidnapped, they took over jurisdiction of the case from Detective Kelly. Remember him, Dad?"

"Yes. I talked to him about Vendetti."

"Well, if you can believe it, even Vendetti was offering advice. He agreed with the FBI and warned me not to give myself up. I didn't listen to him either. I thought he was just saying that out of desperation to have his son operated on. But he was right. He said these guys would never be true to their promise to release Kate. I should have known he understood what he was talking about."

Matt explained the events of the past day involving Vendetti, Kelly, and the FBI agents. "I've been so stupid."

Senior told him, "You did what you thought was right. I would have done the same. Don't beat yourself up."

Kate said, "I believed the goons too. They dropped me at a phone booth so I could call Matt to have the police pick me up. But they had no intention of letting me go. Gianni, that ugly gorilla, wants to kill me." Kate tried to remain strong, but the stress had finally gotten to her. She started to cry. "I'm scared to death of him, but I'll be damned if I'll let him know that."

"Kate, I don't know how, but we *are* going to get out of here," Senior said.

"I'm afraid what I did to Gianni has made matters worse for us," Kate said."

"Honey, we'd still be in our coat closet if it weren't for you—maybe even dead by now. Gianni's got a loose nut. You don't know this, but the cop who was on guard outside our house was shot and killed this morning. Gianni's probably the one who shot him."

"Oh, no!"

The kitchen door creaked open. The Cortlands quieted when they saw Big Boy stomping down the steps. He stood in front of Kate with his feet wide apart but didn't say a word. He just dabbed at the weeping burns on his face with a handkerchief then took his revolver from his shoulder holster. "Nice what you did to my face, huh? You'll pay. Trust me. You'll pay." He hunched down to Kate's eye level, and started his nursery rhyme again, "Eenie, meeney, miney, mo..."

Kate stared back at him. She was defiant. "Put the damn gun away before you hurt yourself."

"...catch a tiger by the toe. My mother said to choose this here one."

Felt Hat shouted from the top of the steps, "Gianni, what's taking you so long? What the hell are you doing?"

"Nothing. I'm getting the wine like you asked." With a grin and a nod to Matt, he said, "You're next after her," and slapped Matt on the back of the head.

The giant holstered his gun and walked to the end of the cellar where he pulled two bottles of wine from a shelf. On his way back, he stopped in front of Kate again and didn't say a word—he just stared at her.

"What do you want?" she snapped.

"Bang, bang!" He lifted the bottles toward her and blew the dust from them into her face.

Kate held her breath and exhaled only after Big Boy started to climb the stairs. At the top, he turned to look at her again and grinned, "Bang, bang!"

As night fell, Quiet Man descended to the basement to check on the prisoners and announce that someone would be on guard in the kitchen all night. "I know it will be difficult, but please try to get some sleep. I will check back with you in the morning."

Kate asked, "What's going to happen to us?"

Quiet Man gave an almost imperceptible shake of his head but did not otherwise respond.

Thirty minutes later the Cortlands heard a car drive off. "I heard three doors slam," Kate whispered. "That means there's only one guy upstairs in the house."

CHAPTER 39

Vincent paced between the kitchen and the living room of Matt's house waiting for the Binghamton police to arrive in Eaglesmount with Kate. With normal traffic, it should have taken no more than forty-five minutes. But the wait had stretched to over an hour. From the outset, he had been suspicious about the arrangement Matt had made with the kidnappers. "Where the hell is she? I'm telling you, something's gone wrong."

Detective Kelly looked to Agent Dryer for an answer, but Dryer looked away.

"Call the cops up there to see where the hell she is," Vincent demanded.

Kelly said, "I called them ten minutes ago."

"So call them again. You want me to call them for you?"

The phone rang.

"That's probably them calling back with an update."

The Binghamton police had disturbing news. They had searched the three Esso gas stations along Hillsdale Avenue and Kate was nowhere to be found. But at the Esso farthest south of Binghamton, they found one of their officers shot and killed, and his police cruiser was missing.

Vincent shouted, "They double-crossed us. I told you they would, the no-good sonsofbitches. Now they got all three Cortlands and you're all sittin' here on your asses. I knew they'd double-cross you, but no one would listen to me." He threw his hands in the air. "I'm outta here. You dicks couldn't find a quarter in your pocket. I'll find 'em on my own."

Dryer did not try to stop him and offered a weak challenge in response. "Mr. Vendetti, I'd advise you not to intrude on this investigation. We will charge you with obstruction if you attempt to interfere with our ongoing federal investigation."

"Yeah, yeah. All bullshit. Give me my gun back. I got a right to carry it."

* * *

Concetta remained at her son's bedside hour after hour. She hoped her prayers would penetrate the infant's veil of illness and that God would bestow a miraculous cure.

Vincent entered the room and stood beside his wife. He put his hand on her shoulder to show he understood and felt the same pain she was feeling. With tears rolling down their cheeks, the two looked down at their son. They grieved in silence at what looked like the boy's inevitable death.

Nurse Gladys opened the door and told Vincent a call had come in for him.

Vincent used his coat sleeve to wipe away his tears and followed Gladys to her station.

"Hello? Who is this?"

"This should go without saying, but I assume you want both doctors released to operate on your son. Is that correct?" The voice was disguised.

"Who the hell is this?"

Gladys looked up from her desk and braced for another explosion of cursing.

"I will repeat. Do you want the doctors to operate on your son?"

"Yeah, of course I do."

"We will release them under certain conditions."

"Conditions? Like what?"

"Tonight at midnight you must be at LaGuardia Airport. You will be met there by our associates who will escort you on a flight to Rome tomorrow."

"To Rome? Italy? Are you shittin' me?"

"I repeat. You must be at LaGuardia by midnight. When we know you are on board the airliner to Rome, we will release both doctors so they can operate on your son."

Vincent removed the phone from his ear, held it six inches in front of him, and shouted into it. "You can go screw yourself!" He returned the receiver to his ear. "Did you hear that? That's what I think of your conditions."

"If that is your definitive answer, there is no need to discuss this further. Let your son's death be on your conscience."

Vincent's tone changed. "No! Wait! Okay, wait. Okay. I need some time to think about it. Tell me exactly what you want me to do."

"We will let you know. Remain in the hospital. Expect to hear from us again. If you do not comply with our demands, the consequences will be catastrophic for your son. Do you understand?"

"Yeah."

* * *

Pigeon Mountain encircled Eaglesmount and masked the sun, shortening the light of another day. The hospital room seemed to turn colder. Vincent removed his suit jacket and draped it over Concetta's shoulders. He fidgeted with the radiator then stood at the window, arms crossed, watching traffic below enter and leave the hospital grounds. His head swirled with thoughts. *Why Rome? What's in store for me there? Who are these kidnappers? I know dozens of people who want to do me in, but why in Rome? Why not kill me here and let my son live?*

Vincent realized he was going to have to turn back to the FBI and Detective Kelly for help. He would have to explain the kidnappers' demand without divulging the specifics. And he'd have to find someone to care for Concetta.

He phoned Matt's house. "This is Vincent Vendetti. Who's this?"

"Kelly. What do you want?"

"Let me talk to Dryer."

"You can talk to me. What do you want?"

"I'm at the hospital. They called me."

"Who called you?"

"The kidnappers. They took the Cortlands because of my kid. The sonsofbitches ain't gonna let the doctors go until I give them what they want." Vincent was on the edge of rage. "They're playing games with my son's life. What kind of lowlife would do that to my kid?"

"What do they want from you?"

Vincent regained control of his emotions and said, "Tell Dryer I need his help. Tell him to come to the hospital." He hung up the phone and returned to his son's room.

He was convinced one of the five New York crime families was orchestrating his removal to take over control of the Philadelphia family. He slammed his fist against the window ledge, rattling the pane of glass.

The noise startled Concetta. "*Che cosa?*"

"It's New York. That's what the matter is."

Concetta nodded as though she understood what he was referring to, then turned back to console their whimpering son who had been startled by the sudden noise.

Vincent went to the crib, and softly brushed the dark fuzz of hair on his son's head, trying to calm him. The hard-hearted mobster knew he would give away all he owned and had worked for to have the Cortlands released. His son was all that mattered. He would do what the kidnappers demanded.

Twenty minutes later, Dryer, Harris, and Kelly arrived. Vincent huddled with them in the corridor outside his son's room. He told them of the earlier phone call from the kidnappers but did not provide details. "They told me to leave Eaglesmount. I can't tell you where I'm supposed to go, but I'm gonna do what they want me to do." He explained he had to comply as a precondition to the Cortlands being released. "My son don't have much time. The Cortlands are the only doctors who can do this operation. That's why I came to this hospital in the first place. And the guys who took them know it. They say once I do what they say, they'll let the doctors go. They're using my son to get to me."

"Do you have any idea who it is?" Kelly asked.

"Yeah, I think I know who it is, and I think I know why, but I ain't sayin'. There's nothin' I can do. They got me over a barrel. But I promise you this, if my son don't survive, there will be a war to end all wars."

"A war between so-called *brothers*, eh?" Kelly said. His derision was not lost on Vincent.

Dryer said, "So it's another family? Tell us who's behind this. We can't help you unless you tell us who's responsible for these kidnappings."

"Yeah, right. I saw how you handled things today. You let them take Cortland and his wife too. Now I'm gonna let you handle this? I don't think so. I'll wait for them to call and work it out myself. All I want from you is to make sure that as soon as they let the doctors go, you get them to the hospital quick to operate on my son. You don't have to do nothin' else. That's all I'm asking. Think you can handle that?"

Dryer took a deep breath. He didn't appreciate Vincent's sarcasm and didn't answer.

Vincent asked again, "I want to know if you'll do what I'm asking."

Again Dryer would not answer, but Agent Harris spoke up. "Yeah, we'll take care of it."

Gladys interrupted the gathering. "Mr. Vendetti, there's another phone call for you."

Vincent glanced at the three men and said, "I need to talk privately with these guys."

The same disguised voice asked him, "Have you made your decision?"

"Yeah. Go ahead and let them go. I'll do what you want."

"It is not quite that simple. You see, if we let the doctors go, you may decide to not honor your part of the agreement."

"Why do you want me to go to Rome?"

"The reasons will become clear once you get to LaGuardia."

"No way I'm goin' *any*place unless I know my son is gonna be okay. You can go ahead and kill me now."

"If we wanted to kill you, you would have been dead some time ago. We have had countless opportunities. However, if you present us with no other option, we will not

214

shirk from taking that step. But I must tell you, it is not our intent."

"What about my wife?"

"Your wife will be allowed to remain. She will join you as soon as your son is well enough to travel. All details have been worked out quite meticulously. Arrangements have been made for you to leave now. A hired car will be made available to you as soon as we hang up. You will be driven to LaGuardia so you can board the plane to Rome in the morning. Once in Rome you will be met by one of our associates and given further instructions. I presume the FBI is with you now as we speak. If you discuss the specifics of this plan with them, and they, in turn, notify their counterparts in Italy, the transaction is off. Furthermore, the transaction will also be off if the FBI tries to follow you to LaGuardia. We will know if they follow you. If either event occurs, we will know that you have betrayed our trust, and we will end our communications. On the other hand, if you comply with our wishes, everything will be set in motion after you depart for LaGuardia."

"You mean you'll let the doctors go as soon as I start for LaGuardia?"

"No, but preparations will begin. The Cortlands will be released once you are on board the airliner."

There was a long pause before Vincent spoke. "Okay. I'll do it. Let's get going. What do you want me to do?

"Speak with your wife. Explain what is happening. Do not tell her where you are going. I repeat, do not tell her you are departing for Italy. It is best at this juncture that she not know. You may, however, tell her she will be able to join you after your son is better. Do not go into any other detail with her. Do you understand?"

"Yeah. I get it."

"A car will be dispatched and waiting for you at the main entrance of the hospital. As of now, you have thirty minutes before departing for New York. I will not be calling again. Please remember, your son's life is in the balance."

Vincent thought the man's voice sounded familiar, but he was unable to place it.

* * *

Concetta did not handle the news well. The thought of losing her son was too much for her to bear, and now she was going to be alone. She was scared and homesick and did not understand why her husband would leave her in such a time of need.

CHAPTER 40

"Have you seen the men who are holding us?" Senior asked.

"Yes. We saw Gianni when he was in our house last night, and I guess because we've seen him, the others don't care if we see them too."

"Dad's been blindfolded the whole time," Kate said.

"You have?" Matt asked.

"Yes, from the time I walked into my house from our weekend at Pigeon Mountain to right now, they've had my eyes covered. But I don't understand why they keep me blindfolded and not you."

Kate said, "I think they plan to kill Matt and me, since we can identify them."

"And because I've been blindfolded they aren't going to kill me? Why? That doesn't make sense."

Matt said, "I don't think they were going to kill any of us at first. But when we escaped from Gianni, they realized we'd be able to identify him and that changed their plans. I think you're both right. They'll get rid of us, but then use you for some other purpose. We need to get out of here, now."

"The only way out is upstairs through the kitchen," Kate said.

Matt strained to examine the cellar. "Wait. I see something."

"What?"

"A coal-burning furnace in the far corner to our right. And a small pile of coal against the wall. There has to be an opening in the wall for the deliveryman to shovel the coal into the cellar, right?"

Kate scanned the wall above the pile of coal. "I see it," she said.

The hinged coal chute was three-quarters of the way up the wall.

"How big is the opening?" Senior asked. "Does it look wide enough for us to climb up and out?"

Matt eyeballed the chute. "Maybe. It'll be a tight squeeze, but I think it's wide enough."

Kate agreed. "But we've got to find a way to cut ourselves loose. How are we going to do that?"

Matt said, "I've got a penknife underneath the tongue of my right boot."

"You're kidding me," Senior said in disbelief.

"I thought it might come in handy. Is there any way you can pull it out if I get close enough to you?"

"We'll have to inch close together—and be quiet doing it."

"Not you. Just me. You stay put and let me come around behind you," Matt said. "That way, you can reach down to my boot."

Matt moved inches at a time to minimize the scraping sounds of his chair against the concrete floor. After a couple of minutes he was positioned facing his father's back. "Okay, Dad. I'm behind you. Now stretch your hand down as far as you can. My boot is down a bit from your right hand."

Senior strained against his ties.

"You're close. A little bit more."

Senior felt the boot.

"Great," Matt whispered. "Untie the lace. It's in a loose knot."

Senior loosened the lace.

"Okay. The knife is inside the tongue on the right. Can you feel it? Hold it tight. If it falls to the floor, we're done for."

"I got it." Senior held the knife tight. He held it between his forefinger and thumb at an awkward angle.

"I'm going to move my chair around so we're back to back. Reach for my hands and see if you can cut the rope."

A moment later, Senior said, "Matt, I feel the rope." With surgical dexterity, Senior cut Matt's rope one strand at a time until Matt freed himself with a yank of the last fibers.

Working quickly, Matt cut the rope from Senior's wrists, then from Kate's. Senior removed his blindfold, then squinted until his eyes acclimated to the light from the bare bulbs.

Matt tiptoed to the worktable to search for tools to use as weapons. He kept a hammer for himself, handed another one to Kate, and gave Senior a screwdriver. "Let's take a closer look at the coal chute."

They were examining their possible escape route when footsteps above moved toward the cellar door. The hostages scuttled back to their chairs.

The door creaked open, and a long shadow Kate recognized as belonging to Felt Hat started down the steps. All three Cortlands dropped their chins to their chests, pretending to be asleep. Matt tightened his grip on the hammer he held behind his back, ready to strike at their captor if he came close. But the gang leader descended only three steps and peered down to check on the prisoners. Satisfied nothing was amiss, he went back to the kitchen and latched the door shut.

A few minutes later, the captives heard loud snoring overhead. Senior whispered, "It's going to be hard to climb through that chute without making any noise. It's right underneath the kitchen. Maybe we should try to overpower the guy upstairs before the others come back."

Matt disagreed with his father. "I heard him lock the door behind him. I say we go up the chute. If we can't fit through it, then I agree we have to find a way to overpower the guy. But let's try the chute first."

Kate found a ball of twine on a peg above the workbench. "I have an idea. I'll booby-trap the steps. If he hears us and rushes down the steps, he'll trip on the twine. We can overpower him then."

"Good idea. Do it."

Kate tied twine across the bottom step at ankle height. In the dim light of the cellar, it would not be visible to anyone who rushed down the stairs. Senior gave her a thumbs-up.

Matt moved a chair to the coal chute to stand on and slowly pushed on the metal door. It opened to the outside with a slight creak that, to them, sounded as loud as a passing freight train. They froze, waiting to see if the noise had awakened Felt Hat, but his snoring continued. Matt pushed the chute door again. This time, coal dust that had accumulated on the hatch showered down on his face and into his eyes. The dust blinded him, but he held tight to the door, unwilling to let go for fear it would spring shut. With his eyes closed and tears streaming down his cheeks, he closed the door quietly and stepped down from the chair.

"What do you think? Can we fit through?" Senior whispered.

Matt stood blinking the coal dust away. "Yeah. I think so. It's not going to be easy, but we can do it."

Senior was anxious to get started. "Let's do it then."

"Okay. I'll go first. Once I make it out, you help Kate up, then I'll pull you out."

Matt climbed back on the chair and, with a boost from Senior, squeezed through the narrow opening one shoulder at a time. Once outside, he closed the door to the chute gently and looked around to get the lay of the land. The farmhouse sat on a crown of land that sloped gently toward a large lake. Cornfields covered the rolling land in every direction as far as the eye could see. The moon was full. Its silver beams danced off the lake's surface to light the entire area surrounding the lake.

Matt opened the hatch and whispered, "The coast is clear. Help Kate get out." Just then a vehicle turned into the driveway and approached the farmhouse. Matt dropped his head into the coal chute and warned, "Wait. A car's coming. Stay there." To avoid the headlights silhouetting him against the farmhouse, Matt closed the hatch and scrambled low to the back of the house.

Driver beeped the horn to let Felt Hat know they had returned. "We got good news. Bobby, tell him."

"I spoke to Vendetti. I told him what we expected, and he agreed to fly to Italy. He is on his way to LaGuardia as we speak."

"Good job." Felt Hat was ecstatic that his plan was coming together.

Senior and Kate were up against the concrete block wall of the basement, waiting to get a signal from Matt that all was clear. They heard the gang's animated conversation continue as they entered the kitchen.

Matt maneuvered his way back to the coal chute door and whispered down, "Dad, hurry! Boost her up!"

Matt pulled his slender wife easily through the opening.

Senior was last. He held Matt's hand, but was not able to hoist himself out as easily as Matt had. His knees scraped against the wall and his foot slipped off the chair, causing it to topple backward and clang against the furnace.

Felt Hat asked, "What the hell was that?"

Big Boy yelled, "It's from the cellar." He unlocked the door and bolted down the basement steps, followed by Driver and the others.

Senior made it through the chute just in time.

"Sonsofbitches," they heard Big Boy yell.

Matt whispered, "Run! Run! Run!" The three raced toward the lake.

As Big Boy ran down the cellar steps, he tripped on the twine that Kate had stretched across the steps and took a thunderous fall, crashing to the concrete floor, hard on his shoulder. "Sonsofbitches. I'm gonna kill 'em."

Driver saw the chair alongside the furnace. "They must have climbed through the coal chute."

Quiet Man examined the ropes. "They've been cut through. Somehow, they got hold of a knife."

"We can't let them get away," Felt Hat raged. He was first up the steps and out of the house. The others followed close behind.

The four men raced around the perimeter of the house in search of the escapees. Driver caught a glimpse of them running along the lakefront, the light of the moon spotlighting the three. "There they are," he shouted. "Down near the water."

Felt Hat ordered Driver to drive the sedan around the cornfields and down to the lake from the west. "Gianni, take the police car and drive it down to the lake from the other side. Me and Bobby will come at them from the front. With the lake behind them, they won't have no place to run."

The escapees ran along the edge of the lake, but Senior was falling behind.

"Dad, come on. Hurry!" Matt slowed down to urge his father on and shouted to Kate. "Wait for us up ahead at that tree. We'll rest for just a second."

Kate veered from the lakefront and ran behind the large pad of an uprooted oak tree. Matt and Senior caught up to her a few seconds later. All three stood with their hands on their hips, trying to catch their breath.

"We can't stay here long," Matt said.

"You two go ahead. I'll just slow you down," Senior said.

"No, Dad. We're not leaving you. Let's get into the cornfield. They won't find us there."

Kate was the first to see the headlights as Big Boy and Driver's cars crashed toward them through the cornfields, mowing down rows of corn like so many bowling pins. "Oh, no! Here they come!"

"Okay, forget the cornfield. Let's head back to the lake. Hurry!"

Senior said, "Please, you two go. Try to get up to the road we came in on to flag down a car. I can't go any farther."

"No. Dammit, Dad, you're coming with us."

Before running off again, they heard Felt Hat call out, "We're not going to hurt you. We need you to operate on Vincent Vendetti's son."

Matt turned to his father. "What the hell? Vendetti's son?"

Senior shook his head. "I don't know. That doesn't make any sense."

"Forget it. Let's go." They raced to the shoreline. "Look!" Matt shouted. "There's a boat up ahead." He spied a small aluminum fishing boat lapping off the shore, its oars leaning against the center bench. During an earlier storm, the skiff had broken loose and sailed pilot-less across the lake, its owner's fishing rod still propped up in the stern. "Get in! Quick!"

Matt, Kate, and Senior sloshed through ankle-deep water. Kate climbed in and sat at the bow, Matt on the middle bench. Senior turned the boat so the bow faced the lake, then he tumbled into the stern. The boat rocked precariously until he settled down into it.

Matt rowed as fast as he could. "Hurry, Matt. Hurry!" Kate urged, as she and Senior paddled with their hands to help Matt open up the distance between the boat and the shore.

Big Boy arrived in his cruiser before the weighted-down skiff had a chance to get out beyond the shallows. He jumped from his car, threw off his jacket and shoes, and splashed into knee-high water where he grabbed the stern and spun the boat around so the bow pointed back toward land. He tried to grab Kate to pull her from the boat, but she used the fishing rod to lash out at the giant. Big boy covered his face with his arms to protect himself from her vicious whipping.

Big Boy bellowed, "I'm gonna kill you all," and retreated. When he got back to the shore, he pulled out his .38 revolver and fired a shot at the skiff.

Matt shouted, "Get down! Get down!" but by then the boat was out of range for the small caliber revolver. The bullet skipped off the surface of the lake yards away from the boat.

Big Boy was about to fire again, but Felt Hat shouted to him. "Gianni! Stop shooting. People will hear the shots."

Big Boy said, "Look what they did to me." His shirt was shredded from Kate's lashing.

"You'll live," Felt Hat said. "Let's get back to the house."

CHAPTER 41

Outside the main entrance to the hospital, a skinny, pockmarked-face man with slicked-down red hair and a bulbous blue nose stood beside an unwashed car. A Kool menthol cigarette dangled from his lips. He held up a section of cardboard cut from a corrugated box with the name "Vendetti" written on it.

Vincent stepped out the front door of the hospital and studied the man. "Are you the driver taking me to New York?"

"Are you *Ven... daddy*?" the man replied.

"*Detti*, not *daddy*. Vendetti."

"Yes. I am the driver taking you to New York. I'm Tennessee."

"Tennessee? What the hell kind of name is Tennessee?"

"I was born in the great state of Tennessee."

Vincent smelled alcohol on the man and eyed him with suspicion. "Hey, pal, you been drinking?"

"No, *pal,* I have not," he lied.

"You know where you're takin' me?"

"I'm driving you to LaGuardia Airport in New York. If you please, sir." Tennessee bowed from the waist and made a sweeping gesture with his right arm.

"Do you know how to get there?"

"Of course."

Vincent was hesitant but knew he had to have this character drive him to New York. He looked up to his son's room on the third floor and saw Concetta standing at the window. Vincent had explained to her what was happening. He asked her to call his friend Frankie, the godfather of their son. "Have Frankie drive up here to be with you. I'll call you from the airport."

His marriage to Concetta, like most other arranged marriages, had been one of convenience. He wanted children, and she had been committed to him. There was no love between the two, just a sense of obligation from both. She was his wife and the mother of his son, and he vowed to take care of her. He had hoped for more children, but now, even the life of the son he had was in jeopardy.

Vincent waved to Concetta, but she didn't see him. She was looking at the sky, praying to all the saints in heaven for her son's recovery.

Tennessee was getting impatient. "Mr. *Vendetti*, if we don't get moving, we're not going to get there in time."

Vincent didn't budge. He watched Concetta at the window a while longer as he questioned her ability to handle decisions she might need to make. "I ain't goin' no place 'til I know you can get me to New York without killing me. If you're drunk, I'll drive."

Tennessee was concerned he was going to lose his fare. He pleaded, "I... am... not... drunk. I had a couple of beers, but I am not drunk. I am fully capable of driving you. See?" He extended his hands to show they weren't shaking. "Now get in the car. Please."

Vincent relented and fell into the back seat of the dirty, brown sedan. "Is this a taxi or your own car?"

"It's my car. And I'm licensed to use it as a taxi, thank you very much."

"Don't you ever clean it?" The front floorboard of the cab was littered with empty soda bottles, cigarette packs, and paper bags, and the upholstery on the back seat was stained and torn.

"I cleaned it out a couple of days ago."

"Yeah, right. It looks like you did. It looks like a pig sty."

The car pulled away from the curb and Vincent craned for one last glimpse of Concetta, but she had left the window.

"Oh, yeah. I'm supposed to give you this," Tennessee said, and handed an envelope over his shoulder to Vincent. The words *Give to Vendetti* were written on the front. Vincent tore the envelope open to find a counterfeit passport in his name and a one-way Pan American Airways ticket to Rome via London.

The bastards thought of everything. "Who gave this to you?"

"I don't know. I found it on the front seat of my car."

"What did the guy look like who hired you?"

"I don't know. I never met the guy. He called me at my house and asked if I wanted to make a couple hundred bucks. I said, 'Yeah. Who do I have to kill?' I thought it was a joke. But then he tells me about driving someone to LaGuardia. He said he'd call me when he needed me, but I had to be ready to go with fifteen minutes' notice, anytime, day or night. I figured, why not, and said I would do it. The next day I found two envelopes in my car—one with my money and another for you."

"What else did he say?"

"He promised me another two hundred dollars when I got back from New York, as long as we made it to the airport on time. But, like I said, I talked to him that one time and never saw him. I'm trying to make a buck is all."

"How'd you know to get me at the hospital?"

"A half hour ago, the guy called me again and said to rush over to the hospital and wait for you out front. That's all I know." Tennessee looked at Vincent in his rearview mirror. "Who are you, anyway?"

"Nobody." Vincent looked in despair out the side window. The drive from Eaglesmount through New Jersey, into Flushing, and on to LaGuardia would be three hours. Vincent was exhausted from the day's events and decided to get some sleep, but Tennessee turned on the radio and flipped from station to station.

"Do me a favor, Tennessee, turn that radio down so I can get some sleep."

Tennessee paid no attention to Vincent's request. He thumped the steering wheel, keeping the beat with the music.

Vincent leaned forward. He thought Tennessee might not have heard him. "Hey, pal, would you mind turning that radio down? I'm gonna try to sleep a little."

"No."

"What did you say?" Vincent was still uncertain the driver had heard him. "I asked you to please turn down the radio."

"It's my car, my radio, and you aren't the one who's paying me. So I'll play what I want, as loud as I want. You have a problem with that, Mr. Vandaddy?"

"Yeah, I have a problem with that. I asked you nice to turn the radio down."

Tennessee said, "I'm not going to. Cover your ears if it's too loud."

Vincent yanked his revolver from his shoulder holster, leaned forward on the seat, and jammed the tip of the gun barrel in Tennessee's ear. "Maybe you didn't understand me. I said, turn the fuckin' music down."

Tennessee wanted to nod his okay, but Vincent held the gun so hard against his ear he was afraid to move. He reached for the radio dial and clicked the radio off.

Vincent reholstered his gun. "Now that wasn't hard, was it, Tennessee?"

Tennessee was quiet the rest of the way, and Vincent was able to catch a few minutes of fitful sleep. At exactly eleven o'clock, they pulled up to the main entrance of Pan Am. "We made it with an hour to spare," Tennessee said. He rushed around to the passenger side of the car, opened the door for Vincent to get out, and stood with his hand extended, waiting for a tip. "Sorry for the misunderstanding about the radio."

Vincent looked in disbelief at Tennessee's outstretched hand. "You shittin' me? You want a tip?" He grabbed the driver's hand with his own right hand and bent it backward until Tennessee crumbled to the ground, crying in agony. "You ain't getting nothin' from me—*nothin'*, you wino, get it?"

Inside the concourse, Vincent used a payphone to call Concetta and check on their son. There was no word yet on the Cortlands. Vincent promised to call her again.

CHAPTER 42

Vincent looked out at the tarmac as the flight crew on the Lockheed Constellation prepared for boarding. With his son's life at stake, his rage had turned to acceptance. There was nothing he could do about the kidnappers' plan to have him fly to Italy. He played out the scenario in his mind and considered any number of people who might be involved. *But why this way?* They could have killed him at any time—in Eaglesmount or Philadelphia. It wouldn't have been the first time an attempt was made on his life. In his world, a word of honor was balanced on a thin line of deceit. He agreed to fly to Italy, but would be back in short order if the Cortlands were not released to operate on his son. He would comply with the kidnappers' demand until he knew for sure that all was well with his son.

"This don't make no sense," he said out loud.

A passenger seated next to him said, "I'm sorry, what did you say?"

"Nothin'. Talkin' to myself."

The public address announcement asked passengers to board the airliner. As a line formed, Vincent stood off to the side. He studied everyone who walked by, hoping to spot his escort to Rome.

When all the passengers in line had boarded, Vincent heard a last-call announcement. He stepped up to the ticket agent and presented his boarding pass. The agent studied it and said, "Mr. Vendetti, you have been summoned to meet with a customs agent at the end of Concourse C."

Vincent spat out, "I'm not meeting with anyone. I'm not missin' this plane. You tell the customs guy to come here if he wants to talk to me." Vincent felt a tug on his sleeve.

"Hello, Vincent."

"Pansie. Well, I'll be a sonofabitch. What are you doin' here?" She looked older—crow's feet had developed at the corners of her eyes, and tiny vertical wrinkles above her lip were noticeable underneath her heavy makeup—but her shapely body still drew attention.

"How have you been, Vincent? I haven't seen you in a couple of years."

"Not too good. It's a long story, but I'm supposed to be flyin' to Rome. I can't talk with you right now."

"Yeah, I know. Listen, you've got to follow me. You can't board this plane. You'll take another flight later."

Vincent suddenly realized that *she* was his escort. "Don't tell me. You're the one who's taking me to Rome?"

"It'll all be clear to you in a couple of minutes. Follow me, okay?"

Vincent did not know what to expect, but he followed Pansie through the airport. His eyes darted back and forth as he checked for other people he might know. He was unaware there were three men following them.

When they reached the end of Concourse C, a uniformed customs agent approached and said, "Mr. Vendetti, Miss Impolito, follow me." The agent ushered Vincent and Pansie through a door and into a large, windowless interview room. He signaled for them to sit then turned and left the room. The three men who had been following waited outside.

Vincent was getting angrier by the minute. He scowled at Pansie, "What the hell are we doin' here? What's goin' on? Am I supposed to fly to Rome or not? Let me tell you something, Pansie, if my son ain't bein' operated on, like, right now, I'm gonna make sure you never live to see another day."

"Hello, *Shorty*." A tall man with thick black hair entered the room and greeted him.

Joey "Hammer" Caitano.

He was older-looking, gray at the temples and with a few wrinkles on his brow, but he was still handsome. He wore a double-breasted dark blue suit, a stiff-collared white shirt, and expensive Italian leather shoes. Smoke curled from a cigarette in his right hand.

Vincent was surprised. "Joey Caitano," he said. "I knew someday we'd meet again."

"Yeah, me too. I been looking forward to this day."

"What's it been—ten years? We been lookin' for you a long time. Where you been hiding?" Vincent asked.

"Seven years, to be exact. But who's counting?"

Vincent looked Joey up and down. "Looks like you done okay for yourself since I last seen you."

Joey blew a vaporous stream of cigarette smoke into Vincent's face, "Yeah, I done okay. But, you know, one can always do better."

"The word on the street was you went to Italy after you killed the Professor. But you been here the whole time, huh? Working for who? Tell me—Anastasia? Lucchese?"

Joey did not answer.

Vincent looked around the room, trying to maintain his composure. "What's next?" he asked. "How come we ain't on the plane to Rome?"

"You know somethin', Shorty? We don't trust you. If you told the FBI where you were headed, they'd be on the plane with you. So we decided, let's take a different flight. If the feds are on that other flight, I hope they enjoy Rome. It's a beautiful city."

Vincent said, "I didn't tell the FBI shit."

"I hope not, for your son's sake."

"So, what are we doing?"

"I'll tell you when I'm ready to tell you."

"What makes you think I'm going with you? You know, Hammer, I can plug you right here, right now."

"I don't think so—if you want your kid to live. I got three guys outside the door waiting for my word. If you try anything stupid, you'll be dead in five seconds. I'll have you killed right here. And you know what? I'll get away with it too. We got major connections here in New York, and you ain't got shit. My friends own this airport, if you know what I mean."

Vincent looked at Pansie. "You whore. I can't believe you're doing this."

"Don't talk to her like that."

"Screw you."

"You know, Shorty, I owe you for what you did to the Professor."

"What are you talking about? You killed the Professor, not me."

"Yeah, I killed him. You made sure of that," he said.

"I don't know what you're talking about."

Joey dropped his cigarette to the tile floor and ground it out with the sole of his shoe. "Yeah, you do. You're good. I gotta admit that. Back in Philly, you planned that whole thing, down to me killin' my own uncle. But I'm okay with that now. I moved on. That's what you're gonna be doin'—movin' on."

"Kill the Professor? What? Are you crazy? He was like a father to me."

Joey bent down to Vincent's eye level. "Don't give me that bullshit. I know different." Joey jerked his chin toward Pansie. "She's how I know. She told me everything. I was pissed at her at first, but I could never be mad at Pansie for too long." He smiled at her. "Right, Pansie?"

She nodded and smiled back at him.

Vincent shook his head at her and bit on the knuckle of his right forefinger to show his contempt. His anger boiled over. "You *are* a *puttana*—a slut whore. I thought we were friends. What's Frankie gonna say when he finds out about this?"

Pansie did not answer.

Vincent turned to Joey, his anger brimming. With spittle flying from his mouth, he swore, "You shit-for-brains. You were gonna let my kid die. You kidnapped the doctors to get even with me?"

"Nah, I didn't plan nothin' about your kid. I'm your Italian connection—your *coordinator*—that's all. Yeah, that's it. I'm your coordinator. I like that."

"Who's the ringleader?"

"I ain't tellin' you that."

Vincent wanted to know what Joey had in mind. He gritted his teeth. "Then what's the deal? We wait 'til we get to Rome before you whack me?"

"I ain't gonna kill you, Shorty. I'd *like* to blow your brains out right here, but I ain't supposed to. I'm supposed to take care of you. I don't know why, but that's what I'm supposed to do." Joey rubbed his temple and winced. "Here. Right here. I still get headaches from when you sucker-punched me in high school. Why'd you do that? We were havin' a little fun and you turned around and nailed me when I wasn't lookin'. I ain't never gonna forget that."

"You know what, Hammer? I gotta thank you for that. If it wasn't for me being thrown out of school, I don't know what the hell I would have done. Maybe work for my father the rest of my life. But thanks to you, I met your uncle. So, thank you for that, asshole."

"Yeah? My uncle was a good man, you fuckin' ingrate! "Now it's my turn to nail you. I'm supposed to watch you close from now on, take care of you, make sure you don't get into no trouble. I'm gonna take you back to San Bartolomeo. Ha! You want to know my idea? You like pigs, Shorty? I hope you do, 'cause I'm gonna turn you into a pig farmer—in San Bartolomeo." He nearly spat the words. "That's where you got married to that beanpole wife of yours, and San Bartolomeo is where you're gonna go back to. You look like a pig, so bein' a pig farmer makes sense. You'll go from bein' the boss, the *capo*—the family big shot—to bein' a pig farmer. What do you think about that, Pansie?"

Pansie felt Joey was going too far with his insults. She pursed her lips and shook her head.

Vincent had had enough. He reached for his revolver, but before he was able to remove it from his jacket, Joey said, "I told you already. You try that and you're dead—and worse than that, your kid's dead too. Trust me. I been told one thing—I'm supposed to take care of you. But if you get out of hand, I also been told I can do whatever it takes to straighten things out, including blowin' your brains out."

Vincent removed his hand from the gun.

"So you want to know where I been, Shorty? Remember when you were in San Bartolomeo five years ago? That's where I been all these years. You don't know it, but I almost killed you there. I could have, but now I'm happy I didn't."

"You know, Hammer, Frankie ain't gonna let your asshole buddies in New York get away with this."

"Oh, we'll get away with it all right. Why don't you let me have your gun so you won't be tempted to do nothin' stupid?"

"You ain't gettin' my gun."

"You give me your gun or we call my boss. He ain't gonna be too happy with you. Up to you, Shorty. If you don't do it my way—if you don't do what I say—your son dies. Do I have to keep repeating myself?"

Vincent glared at Joey. "You lowlife sonofabitch. I can't believe you'd do this to my kid."

"Yeah, and I can't believe what you did to the Professor, so we're even."

Vincent had no choice. He pulled back. "I'll tell you what, Hammer. First, I call my wife to see what's happenin' with my son. If the doctors are operating on him, then I give you my gun."

Pansie chimed in, "That's fair, ain't it, Joey?"

Joey nodded his okay. "Fine. You talk to your wife—that's all. You don't say nothin' about what's goin' on here. Nothin'. And you don't talk to nobody else. Got me? Let's go."

Joey, Pansie, and Vincent walked out of the room to a bank of payphones near the escalators that led to the terminal gates. Joey's men followed.

Joey shoved a phone to Vincent. "Here. Go ahead. Make your call." He removed a handful of coins to pay for the call. "Make it snappy."

"I want to talk to my wife in private."

"I'm stayin' right here or you don't make the call."

Vincent placed the call and announced to the operator at the hospital that he wanted to speak to his wife. "How is the baby? *Come sta il bambino?*"

"*Lo stesso,*" she answered.

"No change? Have you seen *il Dottore* Cortland?"

"No. *Non ho visto il dottore.*"

"Has he called? *Ha chiamato?*"

"No."

Joey was getting fidgety. "Get off the phone!"

"*Chiamo in un'ora.* I'll call you back in an hour." Vincent placed the phone in its cradle and remained a moment longer as he tried to control his anger.

"What's your problem?" Joey asked.

"I'll tell you what my problem is," Vincent said. "The Cortlands ain't showed up yet, and I'm about ready to tear your face from your head. If your boys are playin' games with me, they're screwin' with the wrong guy. Where are the doctors?"

"They don't get released until we board the flight to Rome."

"That's not good enough. Find out where they are or this whole deal is off. You understand me, you moron?"

Joey removed a piece of paper that had a phone number scrawled on it from his coat pocket. "Move away from the phone and stand over there. I'm gonna make a call."

"I'm stayin' here."

"Then I don't make a call."

Pansie gave Vincent a weak smile. "Come on, Vincent. Let's move, so he can find out what's going on."

238

Without acknowledging her, Vincent moved out of earshot.

Pansie was frightened. *Why did I ever let myself get talked into this?* If the plan didn't work, she was dead—and Joey, her lover—was too.

The operator attempted to connect Joey to the phone in the gang's Pennsylvania farmhouse, but the men were out searching the lake for their escaped hostages. The operator interrupted several times to inform Joey no one was answering. "Would you like to try again later?"

Joey whispered, "Yes," after which the operator ended the call. Joey, however, continued to talk into the dial tone. He needed to convince Vincent he still was talking to his contact and that all was well with the Cortland plan. He shrugged every few seconds, gestured, and nodded convincingly. Out of the corner of his eye, he saw Vincent walk toward him and muttered a quick, "Yeah. Got it," then hung up.

"What did they say?"

"They said everything was goin' okay and they're waitin' for me to call back to tell them when we're about to board the plane."

"Somethin's wrong. I don't know what, but somethin' don't smell right," Vincent said.

"I'm tellin' you, everything is okay. Now let's get going." Joey nodded to his men to close in on Vincent.

"I ain't goin' nowhere. Tell them to back off or I promise I'll blow your head off right here. I don't know if you're stupid or deaf, but we ain't goin' *no* place until I know my son's okay. And you know what else? You can tell your friends I'm about ready to change my mind and I'm thinkin' about goin' back to Pennsylvania."

Joey pulled his revolver from his holster, shoved it into his coat pocket, and jammed the barrel of the gun against Vincent's back. He bodied him toward a vinyl-covered bench on a far wall across from the ticket agents. His men encircled them. Joey said, "You ain't goin' back to Pennsylvania, Shorty. Let me make this clear. You try to leave, and your son's the one who's gonna pay."

Pansie tried to calm Vincent. "He's right, you know. Don't do anything stupid like that."

Vincent glared at her.

Joey, Pansie, and Vincent sat side by side on the bench, each stealing an occasional glance at their watch. Pansie tried to break the tension. "You talk to Frankie, Vincent? How's he doing?"

An expressionless Vincent turned to her, bit his knuckle again, then looked away without saying a word.

Joey didn't know what to do next. He needed direction from Felt Hat, but he hadn't been able to reach him. Half an hour passed. "Our flight is in an hour. I'm gonna call again. I'll be right back," Joey said. He huddled with his men, ordered them to keep an eye on Vincent, and walked back to the phone to attempt another call to Felt Hat. He returned a few minutes later.

"What did you find out?"

"The Cortlands are back and operating on your son as we speak. Everything's okay."

"Both Cortlands?"

"Yeah, the father and the son. Now let me have your gun."

Vincent fumed. "You ain't getting' my gun because you're a lying asshole. The son can't operate on account of a fight he was in two nights ago. His hands are too banged up to operate. I always knew when you was lying. Even when you lied to the nuns in school, I knew."

A stern-looking airport cop who was patrolling the terminal walked by the three on the bench. When Vincent saw the cop, he stood to approach him. Joey tried to yank Vincent back down, but Vincent shrugged him off. Pansie smiled faintly at the impassive cop. The cop didn't react.

Vincent called out, "Officer."

The cop stopped and looked at the small man. "Yeah?"

With his back to Joey and Pansie, Vincent spoke in a low voice so only the cop heard. "I'm from Philadelphia."

The cop stared down at him. "Yeah? And I'm from New York. What do you want?"

Vincent pretended he was nervous, and rolled his eyes. He spoke in a low voice. "See that man and woman on the bench behind me?"

The cop looked over Vincent's head. "Yeah. What about them?"

"I think they're the ones the police are looking for in Philly. I seen their pictures in the newspapers yesterday."

"Who are they?"

Vincent thought quickly. "I don't know their names, but I think they're the ones who killed a couple of people. I think the guy is in the Mafia or somethin'."

The cop continued to look at Joey and Pansie, who looked away. "Are you sure?"

Playing his lie to the hilt, Vincent said, "Pretty sure. And see those three other guys? They've all been talkin' together."

The cop leaned his head in the direction of the men and put his hand on his service revolver. Realizing they had been identified, the men dispersed.

"The sonofabitch. What the hell is he doin'?" Joey whispered through clenched teeth. "Come on. Let's get outta here." He took hold of Pansie's hand.

"Stop!" the cop ordered. Joey and Pansie pretended not to hear and kept walking. "Stop or I'll shoot!" The cop removed his revolver.

"Keep walkin'," Joey said through the side of his mouth.

But Pansie stopped, frozen in place. Joey tried to pull her along with him, but she wrenched her hand from his.

Joey reached for his gun.

The cop yelled, "Drop it, or you're a dead man."

Joey crouched to put his gun on the floor.

"Get down on the ground! Now! On your stomach. Now!"

The cop kept his gun trained on Joey and ordered Pansie to the floor too. She did as she was ordered.

The cop kicked Joey's gun away and took out his handcuffs.

Passersby in the busy airport gawked at the scene and formed a large circle away from the suspects on the floor. The cop looked around for Vincent and Joey's men, but they had disappeared into the crowd of onlookers.

CHAPTER 43

Matt didn't stop rowing until they reached the middle of the lake. They were out of harm's way for now, but needed to find safe harbor out of the moonlight that spotlighted them as though they were actors in the center of a darkened stage.

"Let me take a turn on the oars," Senior said.

"I'm okay. Just give me a second to catch my breath."

Kate asked, "How are your hands?"

"They're fine. Not as swollen as this morning."

Senior looked around the lake. "You know, I think we're on Beaver Dam Lake. When you were a kid, I brought you here a few times to fish for pike. If I'm right, the headlights we see up there are cars on Route 11. It's probably the road we came in on."

Matt looked at distant headlights as they traveled across the remote stretch of roadway. "I think you're right. Let's find a cove and get off the lake. We can hike back to Route 11 and flag down a car. We're sitting ducks out here, especially if they come after us in a boat." He splashed lake water on his face to rinse off the perspiration and remaining coal dust. The cool water reawakened his senses. They had escaped, but it was a long road yet to safety. The kidnappers were sure to pursue. "What do you think they meant when they yelled something about the Vendetti kid? Did you get the connection?"

Senior said, "No, Matt. I don't get it. Makes no sense to me, but we can't worry about that now. We need to get to a phone so we can call Detective Kelly."

Kate looked toward the distant southern lake shore and saw what appeared to be a house with its lights on. "Why don't we go there and see if there's a phone we can use?"

"Good idea. Let's do it. But from here on, we've got to be quiet. Sound travels forever over the lake." Matt set off in the direction of the light. Except for the sound of the oars cutting through the water, they crossed the lake in silence.

Matt rowed to what turned out to be a solitary two-story house. It was situated twenty-five yards from the tip of a small peninsula that jutted out from a thicket of pine trees. The lights they had seen from the lake were in two windows on the second floor.

"I see a car in the driveway," Kate observed. There were no other houses visible on that stretch of lake shore.

Matt crunched the boat onto the narrow sand and gravel beach. Senior jumped into the foot-deep water and pulled the boat onto shore to allow Kate and Matt to step out. "Follow me. Stay low," Matt whispered.

They snuck past a back wooden deck and hid behind some bushes at the side of the house. Matt looked through the windows to see if anyone was inside the darkened first floor. No one was visible. They continued working their way to the front of the house. Matt was about to knock on the front door when a dog inside the house started to bark. Floodlights immediately illuminated the outside of the house. Another light on the second floor was turned on. "Who is it?" shouted a man's voice from the bedroom window above the front doorway.

Matt stepped back to look up to where the voice was coming from, but was blinded by the light shining down. He shielded his eyes from the floodlights and said, "My name is Doctor Matthew Cortland. I'm with my wife and my father. We need your help."

"Please help us," Kate echoed. "We're in trouble."

"What kind of trouble? What's the problem? It's nearly midnight. What are you doing here this time of night?"

Matt said, "Please help us. We just escaped from some men who kidnapped us."

"Kidnapped?" The man was skeptical.

Matt continued to shield his eyes from the bright floodlight and raised his voice over the barking dog. "They held us in a farmhouse across the lake about a quarter mile off Route 11. We managed to free ourselves and found a rowboat on the lake. That's how we got here. We rowed to your house when we saw your lights. We think the kidnappers are still after us."

"That sounds like a crock! Listen, I have a mean-as-hell dog and a shotgun. I'll blow you away if you try to break into the house. You got it?"

Matt realized if roles were reversed, he wouldn't believe the tale either. "Listen, I know it's hard to believe, and you don't have to let us in. We're from Eaglesmount, south of here about half an hour."

"Yeah, go on. What do you want from us?"

"Would you please call the police in Eaglesmount for us and talk to a Detective Kelly? Tell him what we told you. He'll confirm what I said. We're not lying. The police are looking for us."

The man didn't acquiesce but his tone mellowed. "Tell me your names again."

"Cortland. Doctor Matthew Cortland. My father is Doctor Thomas Cortland and my wife is Kate Cortland. If you still don't believe us, you can call the Eaglesmount Hospital. They'll confirm we're doctors there."

The man ordered his dog to be quiet. "Hush, Reggie!" The three waiting outside looked at each other, hopeful the man believed them. After a minute's hesitation, the man announced, "Okay, I'll call. Stay where you are."

Five minutes later the door opened and the Cortlands were ushered into a large foyer. The walls of the foyer were lined with three generations of family photos. A tall, gray-haired man of about seventy stood at the foot of a nearby stairwell. He was dressed in blue jeans, slippers, and a dark blue pajama top, and cradled a single-shot twelve-gauge shotgun under his left arm.

"Stand over there," he ordered, and pointed with his shotgun where they were to wait. He was still uncertain what to make of the three. Their kidnapping story was farfetched. "I called Eaglesmount and tried to speak to your Detective Kelly, but he's off duty. I told the sergeant who answered—a Sergeant Madison—that I needed to talk to Kelly right away. I told him what you told me and gave him our address. Kelly's supposed to call me back. Sergeant Madison didn't confirm your account but said he would get hold of Kelly and that you should stay put until the detective got here."

At the top of the stairs, a woman said, "I'm Agnes, Irwin's wife." She held a border collie tightly by its collar to keep it from bounding toward the visitors. The brown and white collie strained against the woman's hold until she said, "It's okay, Reggie," and let go of him. The dog hesitated, then raced down the steps and went right to Kate, where it nipped playfully at her hand.

Agnes walked down the stairs to the foyer. She was in her bathrobe, her blue-gray hair still neatly curled even though she had been asleep.

Kate stroked the dog's head. "Hi, puppy. How're you doing, huh?" Reggie rolled onto his back and Kate rubbed his belly. The dog's legs twitched in rhythm to her scratches.

"He's a very good watch dog. Very protective of me. I know he sounded angry before, but now he senses you folks are friendly." She felt the need to offer a word of caution. "But if I say to him *S-I-C 'em*," she spelled out the word used to command an attack, "he would risk his life to protect me. He has no fear. He took on a black bear one day when I was gardening.

"I heard what you told Irwin, and I believe you." Agnes turned to her husband and said, "Irwin put the shotgun down and invite them into the living room."

Irwin obeyed dutifully by cracking his shotgun and leaning it against a wall.

"You've been through a lot, haven't you?" Agnes said. "Do you want to wash up? How about some coffee, or something to eat?"

"We hate to trouble you like this, but we haven't eaten all day. Food of any kind would be wonderful," Kate said.

"I'll be back in fifteen minutes," Agnes said, and disappeared into the kitchen.

Irwin turned off the floodlights by flicking a switch near the front door. He motioned everyone into a large living room and said, "Have a seat. If you want to wash up, the powder room is down the hall on the right."

The living room was filled with oversized furniture, knickknacks, paintings of birds, and shelves crammed with books. A cast iron pot-belly stove vented out through the ceiling highlighted one corner and, in front of the living room picture window, with the moonlit lake as a backdrop, a telescope stood pointed at the heavens. The room was comfortable and evoked warmth and hospitality.

Irwin said, "You said you were doctors?"

"Yes, my father and I are. We live in Eaglesmount and practice at the hospital there. It's a long story, but for some reason—and we don't know why—four men kidnapped us. We think they intend to kill us. After we escaped from the farmhouse and made it onto the lake, they shot at us, but we were able to row far enough away and across the lake to get away from them."

Irwin said, "I heard a shot a while ago. Woke me up. I thought it was poachers shooting deer. Sound travels a long way over the lake. If the wind is right, sometimes you can hear traffic noises from Route 11 clear to here."

Senior said, "So it is Route 11. And this is Beaver Dam Lake, right?"

"Yes."

"Do you know the farmhouse across the lake that we're talking about?"

"It's a huge lake, so I don't know which one it might be. There are a few farms around the lake and vacation houses too. This is our vacation home. We don't know many of the people who live here year-round. Actually, they don't like the fact that some of us have come out here to build vacation homes. They don't like all the development, and I guess you can't blame them. This is beautiful country, and they don't like to see outsiders coming in. Most of the local folk stay to themselves."

Agnes peeked out from the kitchen. "Give me a hand, will you, Irwin?"

"Be right there."

Kate jumped to her feet, "Let me help instead." Moments later the two women deposited a huge platter of scrambled eggs, bacon, toast, and coffee on the dining room table. The Cortlands ate voraciously. The smell of bacon was too enticing to Irwin who snuck a slice of bacon and got his hand slapped by his wife for his boldness.

Reggie had been hanging around the table waiting for a scrap of food when his ears perked up. He growled at a noise he alone could hear, then went to the front door and barked.

Irwin stood. "He hears something. And now I do too. It's a car coming up the driveway," he said. "Probably that Detective Kelly."

Everyone stopped eating and went to the foyer. "It's a police car," Irwin said and opened the door. When he did, Reggie scrambled out. Irwin yelled to him. "Hush, Reggie. It's okay." The collie sniffed the man who exited the police car then ran off to investigate other noises in the woods.

Matt stepped outside, then immediately wheeled around and darted back inside. "It's not Detective Kelly," he shouted. "It's them!" He slammed the door and locked it.

"What are you doing? It's the police," Irwin argued. "I saw the car."

"It's them, I'm telling you. Kelly drives an unmarked police car. He doesn't drive a black and white. The kidnappers were driving a stolen police car. We've got to get out of here."

"Go out the kitchen door," Irwin said. He retrieved his shotgun. "Agnes, you get upstairs."

"I will do no such thing." She turned to the others and said, "Come on. Follow me." She led them through the kitchen to the back door.

Kate said, "Thank you, Agnes. We won't forget your kindness. Will you be okay?"

"They won't harm an old man and woman. We're no danger to them."

The three Cortlands hurried across the deck, down to the beach, and piled back into the rowboat. Matt rowed parallel to the shoreline to a small cove a couple hundred yards from the Irwin's house then stopped rowing. The pine trees that stretched along the shoreline shielded them from view.

Five minutes went by when they heard a gunshot followed by a scream and then another revolver shot.

Matt, Kate, and Senior looked at each other in disbelief.

"Oh, no!" Kate cried. The thought that Agnes and Irwin might have been shot caused her to erupt in tears. She buried her face in her hands and her shoulders heaved from silent sobs. They sat on the still lake, beneath a sky so beautiful it begged of poets, but they were scared and uncertain about what to do next. Earlier, in the warmth and hospitality of the house, they thought they were nearly free of their nightmare. Now they realized all they had done was put Irwin and Agnes in jeopardy.

They heard the kitchen screen door squeak open, then slam shut. The men shouted at each other as they searched the back of the house down to the lake and along the shore.

Matt put his finger to his mouth. "Hunch down," he whispered. They slid low in the rowboat to reduce their profile as they bobbed about in the cove. Soon the shouting along the shore waned. Matt lifted his head and heard a car engine start followed by the sound of tires crunching over the gravel driveway. The cop car pulled away from the house and onto the dirt road that ran around the lake. The kidnappers used the police car's side-mounted spotlight to scan the pine forest. Matt saw the spotlight flicker through the woods. It traveled away from them to the north, back toward the farmhouse where the Cortlands had been held.

"They're leaving," Matt whispered.

Kate wiped away her tears. "Let's go back to the house," she said. "We've got to see if we can help them. Maybe they're okay."

Matt pointed to an area bereft of trees another hundred yards up the shore. "I'll head for that landing, and we can walk our way back to the house from there."

The rowboat skimmed along the lake toward the landing. A breeze drifted them into shore. On land, Kate whispered, "How did they find us so quickly?"

Matt answered, "They probably saw us docking here."

"From across the lake?"

"There aren't many houses around the lake. They probably checked each one and stumbled onto Agnes and Irwin's house."

"But, don't you think that if they searched all the houses on the lake, it would have taken them hours to find us? They found us right away—in less than an hour." She waited for Matt to respond.

"What are you saying—that Irwin didn't make the call after all?"

"No. He said he did, but I don't think Kelly ever got the message. If he had, he would have been here by now."

Matt turned to look at his father. "Kate's right. There's only one way to know if Kelly got Irwin's message. Let's get back to the house and call the police." He whispered to Kate and Senior to stay put while he worked his way to the house through a clump of pine trees. The lights were still on, but Matt saw no sign of anyone about. He circled the house and looked through the windows, then entered through the kitchen.

"I hope to God they're okay," Kate said under her breath.

A couple of minutes later, Matt came out of the house and signaled the "all clear." When Kate and Senior climbed onto the deck, Matt hugged Kate. He said, "Sweetheart, listen. They're in the kitchen. They're both dead. You don't want to see them this way. Wait out here. Let me call the police."

"No. Absolutely not. I'm going in," she said, and followed Matt inside. When she saw the sight of the murdered couple she broke down. "Oh, those poor people. Look what they've done to them." Matt put his arms around Kate to comfort her, but she was inconsolable. Blood was everywhere. Agnes was lying across Irwin's body, connected to him in death as she had been in life. She had been shot in the back of the head while kneeling to minister to him. "We did this to them. We did it."

Senior found a tablecloth and covered the two bodies. "Kate, we didn't do this. Don't think that. Those animals did, and they will pay for it."

"Where's Reggie?" Kate asked. "Do you think they killed him too?" She opened the basement door and shouted for the dog. "Reggie! Come here, boy."

Matt said, "Kate, I don't think he's in the house. I saw him run out when Irwin opened the door earlier. He's probably still outside."

Irwin's car keys were hanging on a hook near the pantry door. Matt saw them and said, "Let's use their car to drive back to Eaglesmount."

Senior said, "Let me call Kelly first." He picked up the phone and asked the operator to connect him to the Eaglesmount police. "This is an emergency."

"Sergeant Madison, Eaglesmount Police Department."

"Sergeant, this is Dr. Thomas Cortland—"

Behind Senior, a familiar voice bellowed, "Put the phone down or I'll blow your head off!"

CHAPTER 44

With his revolver drawn, Big Boy stepped around the two bodies and herded the shaken trio to a corner of the kitchen. "Remember me?" He grinned. "I've been waiting for you." He pulled a chair out from the kitchen table, turned it around to straddle it, and rested the wrist of his gun hand on the back of the chair. "My boss thought you might come back to see what happened to these two old farts. I guess you see they ain't havin' a good day. That old shit aimed his peashooter at me. I didn't have no choice but to waste him," Big Boy said with a grin.

Kate said, "Why did you have to kill her? She was no threat to you."

"Ah, it seemed like the right thing to do. She was a pain in the ass like you been."

"What are you going to do? Shoot us too?"

"You got it, sweetie. You first and then your asshole husband." He pointed to Senior and added, "Him too. We ain't gonna need none of you now. I'm gonna shoot you right between your eyes." He stood and aimed his revolver at Kate.

She didn't back down. "Yeah, go ahead. Shoot me. Bobby will be real happy with you. How are you going to explain that to him? First you shoot an old lady and then a girl. Wow, that's a great reputation you're going to have—Gianni is a real brave man, people will say."

"I don't care what people say."

"Bobby told us he wouldn't let anything happen to us."

"Yeah, maybe he said that. He says a lot of shit. That's because he's sweet on you. But he ain't tellin' me what to do. He keeps sayin' we need to keep you all alive, but I don't think so anymore."

254

Matt tried to intervene so Kate would stop antagonizing the giant. "Where is Bobby?"

"Out lookin' for you."

"Why don't you go find him and tell him you got us? Maybe he doesn't want you to kill us."

"Bobby ain't my boss. If I want to kill you, I'm gonna kill you. He ain't stoppin' me. You think Bobby is a saint. But he ain't what you think he is. He'd kill his own sweet mother if she was in his way."

"Who's your boss then, if it isn't Bobby?" Matt asked.

"I ain't sayin'."

Senior chimed in. His tone was that of a parent scolding a child. "If you kill us, and your boss didn't want you to, you're going to be in big trouble with him."

Big Boy scratched his ear, thinking what to do next. Senior had cast an element of doubt. "Nah. I'll tell him I didn't have any choice. I'll tell them you tried to fight me and I had to kill you so you wouldn't get away."

Senior said, "That's not a good plan, Gianni. Think about it. They're never going to believe you."

Kate said, "You are going to be in so much trouble."

Big Boy's addled brain was having difficulty processing what the Cortlands were saying. "Shut up! Do you hear me? All of you, shut up!"

Kate added to his confusion. "They know we couldn't beat you in a fight, Gianni. You're too strong."

"Don't give me that sweet-talkin' bullshit. Look at what you did to my face. What am I supposed to do—put up with all the shit you gave me and not give any back?"

"But the police from Eaglesmount will be here any minute," Senior said. "You'll be caught red-handed. And you know what—here's the funny thing—Bobby and the others will get away scot-free."

Matt piled on. "They set you up to do the dirty work, and then they get away. Pretty smart of them, wouldn't you say?"

Big Boy moved a step closer. "I don't think so. They ain't gonna do that. You can talk all you want. No one's gonna save your asses."

"I'm telling you, the police are on their way. We called them an hour ago."

"Shut up. Turn around and face the wall."

"Why? So you can shoot us in the back?" Matt said.

"Yeah. Back or front, sideways, or between your eyes, it don't make no difference to me."

They heard whimpering outside the kitchen door. The noise soon turned into frantic scratching. *Reggie!* thought Kate. The collie scraped and thumped at the door, rattling the frame. When Big Boy turned his head toward the racket, Matt hurled himself at the giant and drove him against the kitchen counter. Big Boy's revolver was knocked out of his hand.

The giant recovered quickly. He was stunned, but used his immense strength to fling Matt to the floor. He reached down to pick up his gun, but Senior heaved a kitchen chair at Big Boy, hitting him in the back.

Matt got back up and drove his shoulder into the bigger man's belly. The two tumbled to the floor with Big Boy on top. He cocked his fist to pummel Matt, but Matt rammed the palm of his hand into the ex-boxer's cartilage-eroded nose.

Big Boy shouted, "You sonofabitch," and stretched to retrieve his revolver, but Kate grabbed it first.

"That's it!" she shouted, and aimed the revolver at Big Boy. "Get off my husband." Big Boy eyed Kate, ready to lunge at her, but she stepped back. "You have three seconds, Gianni, to get off him or I'll shoot! Trust me, I will shoot you. One... two..."

Big Boy rolled onto his back. He lay on the floor, his chest rising and falling.

Reggie continued to bark and scratch at the door.

"Matt, here, take the gun. I'll let Reggie in." Kate handed the revolver to Matt and let Reggie into the kitchen. She got down on her knees to pet and hug the collie. "What a good boy. What a good boy."

Reggie wagged his tail, then wandered off to paw at the tablecloth that covered his dead owners. He sniffed the bodies, looked back at Kate, cocked his head, then lay down snug against the two, dropping his head between his paws.

Senior said to Matt, "I'll see if I can find some rope in the garage to tie up this oaf."

Breathing hard, Matt kept the gun pointed at Big Boy, "Okay, Dad. See what you can come up with." Then, with a wrath in his voice that Kate had never before heard, Matt said, "Listen to me, Gianni, you stupid shit. You've threatened us one last time. I've had as much as I can take from you. If you make one move, you're a dead man. Give me any reason to use this, and you'll end up piled next to those poor people over there." He jerked his chin to where Agnes and Irwin's bodies lay. "Understand, asshole?"

Big Boy did not acknowledge the threat.

"I said, do you understand?" This time, Matt fired a shot that thudded into the wooden floor six inches from Big Boy's head.

Big Boy flinched and jerked his head away, "Okay, I get it."

Senior ran back into the kitchen from the garage. "What happened?"

"Nothing. Gianni and I had a meeting of the minds. Right, Gianni?"

Big Boy didn't respond.

"I said, right, Gianni?" He aimed the gun at Big Boy's forehead.

"Yeah, okay."

Senior announced, "I found some rope."

"Good. Let's tie him up and get out of here."

Kate uttered an urgent "shh." When everyone quieted down, she said, "Do you hear that? I think it's a car." She hurried to the front window and peeled back the shade to look out. "There's a car coming down the driveway! It's them. We have to get out of here."

"Turn over," Matt demanded of Big Boy.

"Screw you. I ain't turning over. I told you they'd be back."

Senior bluffed, "Shoot him!"

Matt cocked the revolver and aimed it at Big Boy's head. The giant turned onto his belly. Matt kept the gun trained on him while Senior tied Big Boy's wrists and looped the rope around his ankle.

Kate shouted, "Hurry! They're getting out of the car."

Matt snatched Irwin's car keys from the hook on the wall. "Out the back. Quick, let's go! Get into Irwin's car."

Kate and Matt had run just a few steps from the house when Reggie barked and scratched at the door from inside the kitchen. Kate pulled her hand away from Matt's and ran back toward the house.

"What are you doing?" he whispered in disbelief.

Kate raced back and let Reggie out. She held tightly to the collie's collar with one hand and accepted Matt's hand with the other. They all sneaked low alongside the house to the front where Irwin's blue Chevy station wagon was parked. As soon as the gang went into the house through the front door, Matt climbed into the driver's seat. "Kate, get in the back."

Kate slapped her thigh to let Reggie know to jump in too. "Come on, Reggie." The dog jumped into the back seat. Kate hugged him to keep him from barking."

Senior slipped into the front passenger seat. "Matt, let's go. Quick."

The gang entered the house and shouted for Gianni.

"I'm in the kitchen. They tied me up."

"Man, can you not do *any*thing right? What the hell happened?" Felt Hat shouted.

"They jumped me. They're taking the old man's car. Untie me."

At that moment, they heard Irwin's car start up. Quiet Man and Driver ran out the front door and caught a glimpse of the old station wagon grinding down the driveway with its headlights off. Quiet Man raced back into the house. "They're in the old man's car. Let's go! We've got to get them."

The four kidnappers jumped into the stolen police car and spun down the gravel driveway in pursuit.

Matt stomped the accelerator down to the floorboard and navigated the lake road with the car headlights still off. The engine was loud and cumbersome. In his rearview mirror, he spotted the gang's car gaining on them. "We're not going to be able to outrun them. They're coming up behind us fast." Matt turned on the headlights and headed to Route 11. He noticed the gas indicator was below a quarter of a tank. "We don't have much gas. We might not have enough to get to Eaglesmount. What do you think? Should I take the first exit when we get on Route 11 and hope we can find a cop? We have to decide quickly."

Senior leaned over to check the gas gauge. "We'd only be chasing our tails. There's no guarantee we'd see a cop anywhere out here in the boondocks. I think we should head to Pigeon Mountain. We probably have enough gas to make it there."

Matt asked, "Pigeon? What can we do there?"

"If we can get to the mountain, maybe we can hold them off somehow, maybe get to our cabin. I don't know."

"Dad, that's a dead end. What would be the point?"

Senior twisted around and saw the headlights gaining behind them. "Hell, we don't have a whole hell of a lot of options. We've got Gianni's gun. If we stay on higher ground, we can try to fend them off—set booby traps, pelt them with rocks and, if worse comes to worse, one of us can try to climb over the top and down the other side."

"We'd have to be mountain goats to get over it."

"One of us is going to have to try if we get that far."

"Kate, what do you think?"

Kate agreed with Senior. "I think we ought to do what Dad suggests. You both know the mountain better than anyone. That gives us an advantage in fighting these guys."

Matt pushed the station wagon to its limit, but the gang was fast gaining on them.

Felt Hat leaned out the front passenger window and fired at the station wagon.

"Duck! Kate, get on the floor," Matt shouted.

Kate dropped to the floor, pulling Reggie down with her.

To keep the kidnappers from getting a clear shot at them, Matt zigzagged down the road. He pulled Big Boy's revolver from his belt. "Here, Dad, take this. See if you can lean out the window and fire a shot at them. That might slow them down. How many bullets are in it?"

Senior examined the revolver. "Only two more."

"Then fire once, and we'll save the other bullet."

Senior turned around and knelt on the front seat. He stuck his head out the window and, holding the gun in his left hand, fired once at the gang. He didn't know if he hit the car, but the shot had the desired effect. The police car slowed.

Matt rumbled south, got on Route 11, and took the exit for Mountain Road. He spun to a stop in the clearing at the foot of Pigeon Mountain. The three scrambled out of the car, and Matt led the way onto the mountain trail. They had only the moonlight to guide them. It was nearly four o'clock in the morning, still dark, but dawn would break within the hour. In the meantime, they would use the darkness as their shield. Reggie ran alongside Kate, enjoying the game he thought they were playing. Senior followed, trying to keep up with the pace Matt had set.

One minute later, the stolen police car screeched to a stop alongside Irwin's station wagon. The four gang members got out and debated what to do next.

Felt Hat squinted into the shadows of the dark mountain. "Anyone see where they went?"

Driver said, "I see them on the trail."

"Okay, let's go after them. They can't get away this time. I'm changing our plan. I want them dead now."

Quiet Man said, "You don't mean all of them."

"Yes, all of them."

CHAPTER 45

Kate had been to the cabin once before with Matt and remembered how difficult the trek had been—how cut-up her legs and hands had gotten from straddling obstacles of gray boulders and fallen pine trees, how she had to hug the mountain cliff overlooking a gorge to get around tight switchbacks.

After her sole overnight stay, she told Matt she found the mountain air pure and crisp, and the setting adjacent to Pigeon Creek tranquil, but getting there was too difficult for anyone to convince her to visit again. "It's peaceful, I'll give you that. But I'll leave it for you two to enjoy."

Now the events of the past two days were forcing her to climb Pigeon again—this time at an exhausting pace, in the dark and escaping kidnappers who wanted to kill them.

Senior took the lead, Kate and Reggie followed, and Matt was the sweeper. Matt and Senior knew the terrain like the backs of their hands and, because they had the advantage of knowing the obstacles they would encounter, were able to gain distance from their pursuers. They also knew Big Boy would be dogged. He had suffered so much punishment at their hands, he wouldn't give up and, if he caught them, would be brutal and vengeful.

The gang was well over a hundred yards behind and below the Cortlands, but a short, unobstructed section of the mountain gave the kidnappers a clear but brief view of the Cortlands as they passed over it.

Driver saw them first. "There they are! I see them." He took out his revolver and fired a shot, but the distance was too great and the light too dim for an accurate shot. The bullet ricocheted off the sheer granite wall below the Cortlands.

The cracking sound of the discharge echoed through the canyons like a drumroll—the noise loosening small rocks above the fleeing trio, creating a mini-slide as stone and debris tumbled down the mountainside.

Staying low, the Cortlands hurried through the open area and around a bend in the trail that took them out of sight of their pursuers. For now, they held the advantage. Senior still had Big Boy's revolver tucked in his belt—although only one bullet remained. What they didn't know was how they would keep the gang from pursuing them.

Matt stopped abruptly once he knew they were out of sight of the gang. "Let's hold up a second. I have an idea." From their countless other treks up the mountain, he knew several large boulders sat perched on a ledge of granite that jutted out over the path ahead of them. He had always marveled at how nature had stacked the boulders on top of each other and how they withstood the cycles of centuries of heaving weather systems without tumbling down the steep mountain. He looked up at the ledge, "If I can get up there and dislodge those boulders, I think I can start a rock slide. If the slide doesn't nail them, it might at least change their minds about following us."

Senior studied the fifteen-foot wall Matt would have to climb in virtual darkness. He realized they had to take dramatic actions to stop or delay the kidnappers. "How are you going to climb that? It's straight up."

"I can do it. If you give me a boost to get me going, I'm pretty sure I can make it to the ledge."

Kate had doubts. "And if you can't dislodge any of the boulders? Then what? They're huge."

"If I can't, I'll climb back down and meet you at the cabin. Come on. We're wasting time arguing over this. Let's get going. It's gotten light enough now for me to see what I'm doing."

Senior was convinced. "All right, Matt. Do it."

"If, for some reason I'm not at the cabin in half an hour, it means something happened to me. Cut the lines to the bridge over the gorge. They won't be able to get to the cabin if you do. And use Gianni's gun if you have to."

Kate said, "You worry about yourself. We're going to be fine. We'll wait until you climb to the top."

Matt managed a smile and a quick hug in response.

Senior boosted Matt up the first few feet but stayed below him to break his fall if he slipped off the wall.

Although his hands were still bruised from his fight with Big Boy, Matt's fingers were strong enough to pull himself onto the surface of the escarpment. He lay hidden behind the stack of boulders for a few seconds to catch his breath then peered over at his father and Kate. He cupped his hands over his mouth and whispered down to them, "I made it. I'm all right. You two go ahead. I'll meet you at the cabin. Wish me luck."

Kate and Senior gave Matt a quick wave and left. A confused Reggie trailed after them, turning around at one point to look up at Matt.

Matt got to his haunches, crouched behind the boulders and peered down at the men who continued their slow but relentless pursuit. Driver led the way. Big Boy was close behind him with Quiet Man some twenty yards behind them.

Felt Hat was falling farther and farther behind, pausing often to catch his breath. All four had discarded their jackets along the trail earlier and were down to their shirtsleeves rolled up to their elbows.

Matt sensed the toll that the rugged, inhospitable mountain was taking on the kidnappers. They were clearly at a disadvantage. He waited until Big Boy and Driver were fifty yards away before he rose and put his shoulder to the topmost of the stacked granite slabs. Big Boy saw him and yelled, "There's one of them."

Driver also saw Matt. He slid his revolver out of his shoulder holster and fired at him. The bullet missed and pinged off the wall well above Matt.

Matt dropped behind the boulders and took a series of short breaths. He lifted up and pushed with all his strength to dislodge the top boulder. Grunting through his clenched teeth, he managed to slide it only six inches. He dropped behind the boulders again, took a deep breath, and then, with a loud groan and all his power, shoved the boulder out and over the ledge. The huge rock rolled over once then teetered at the very edge of the cliff before its momentum carried it over the brink. It exploded when it hit the ground, pulling other rocks and boulders along with it. As the granite mass gathered momentum, it tumbled chaotically down the mountain and caused a crushing, frightful roar to the gang below.

Driver and Big Boy froze, terrified. There was no place to go, no time to seek cover. The growing landslide hurtled toward them. Driver turned to run down the trail but a curtain of stone, dirt, and debris hit him, throwing backward off the cliff. He bounced off the granite walls, his arms flailing as he clutched at air, and was dead before he hit the bottom of the gorge.

Big Boy, too, tried to run down the path and was hit by smaller rocks, one glancing off the top of his skull and knocking him to the ground. Blood flowed over his temple and down his cheek. He lay on the trail curled in a tight ball, his arms locked around his head as rocks and boulders spun by him.

Farther behind, Quiet Man and Felt Hat had more time to react to the avalanche hurtling toward them. They backtracked and crawled beneath a section of the wall that bulged out from the mountain. The rockslide slammed off the barreled wall and bounded harmlessly into the gorge.

When the dust cleared, a stunned Big Boy rose to his feet, shook his head, and staggered about in a boxer's defensive stance with his hands up to protect his face from illusory blows. He used his knuckles to wipe the blood from his head and threw several punches in the direction of Matt. Unbelievably, although concussed and bleeding, he was not seriously hurt.

Matt cursed when he saw the giant get to his feet. He had seen Driver being flung into the precipice and thought Big Boy had been killed too. "Sonofabitch." He put his shoulder to the second boulder to send it over the edge, but this one had a flat bottom and weighed twice the other. He wasn't able to budge it.

Driver's revolver had been knocked out of his hand during the slide and lay on the ground a few yards from the edge of the gorge. Big Boy retrieved it and loped up the trail, bellowing indecipherable threats of revenge.

Matt shot-putted several football-sized rocks toward the charging gangster and, although they missed him and bounced out of harm's way, Big Boy realized he was in a perilous position and retreated to join up with Felt Hat and Quiet Man.

CHAPTER 46

Felt Hat crawled from the underbelly of the cliff where he and Quiet Man had escaped the rock slide. He stepped to the edge of the gorge and looked over the precipice. When he spotted Driver's body partly covered under the remains of the rock slide, he was overcome with vertigo. Bobby saw Felt Hat about to reel and grabbed him by the elbow to yank him away from the edge.

Felt Hat was embarrassed by his swoon. "I'm okay. Got a little dizzy. I'm not too good with heights," he said with a nervous laugh. "Thanks, Bobby. Those sonsofbitches will pay for this."

Bobby had had enough. "Let's forget about them. Let's go home. Why do we have to chase them up this godforsaken mountain and risk our lives? We did what you said we had to do. Vincent will be in Italy by tomorrow. Let's forget about the Cortlands and let them go so they can operate on his son."

Felt Hat's gratitude at Bobby for saving his life turned to incredulity. "Are you shittin' me? We can't let them walk away now—they can identify us. I was gonna let the older doctor operate on the kid because he was the only one of the three who couldn't identify us. But now, they've all seen us. It's too late."

"Yes, thanks to Gianni," Bobby responded. "First he lets junior and his wife escape from their house, and then he lets them get away again last night after he shoots those two old people in the farm house. If not for him, we would not be out here risking our lives, climbing a mountain in the dark. And now the FBI is involved and the people who could put us in prison for life are killing us off one at a time. They know this mountain. We do not. They could set a trap at every turn. We

268

do not know where they are going. Can they get to the other side and somehow down into Eaglesmount?"

Big Boy returned, holding driver's gun in one hand and a handkerchief to his bleeding head with the other. "He almost got me."

Felt Hat said, "We saw. You were lucky."

Quiet Man said, "What we ought to do is shoot Gianni and forget about the Cortlands."

Felt Hat was stunned by Quiet Man's naiveté. "Get off that shit, Bobby. What are you thinking? We've gotta kill *them*." "Why do you care anyway?"

Big Boy said, "Because he's sweet on that girl. That's why."

Quiet Man reacted angrily. "What would you know, you cretin?"

Felt Hat shouted at Big Boy, "Shut up, Gianni. Let him talk."

Quiet Man continued. "I would not be able to live with my conscience if I let Vincent's son die. I am many things, but I do not kill children. And I do not kill women and old men, like Gianni likes to do."

"I don't give a shit what you think," Big Boy said. "That old bitch at the lake was a pain in my ass. She shoulda just stopped screaming."

"Maybe she didn't because you shot her hundred-year-old husband."

"Yeah, that was it. And you know what? It didn't bother me none to shoot either of 'em."

Bobby continued to argue with Felt Hat, "If you were going to kill them all, why did we hold onto them? Why didn't you kill them last night in the farmhouse to keep them from escaping?"

Felt Hat was surprised at Quiet Man's dogged arguments. "You were the one who came up with the idea to use Cortland's wife as bait. All three of them were our chips. But now we played our chips, and we're gonna cash in. Vincent is out of the country so we don't need them no more."

Bobby would not stop arguing. "I will say it again. I do not want that kid's life on my hands."

Felt Hat's patience snapped. "Enough! That's it! No more talking. You got no sense sometimes. Maybe you should've been a priest. Think, Bobby! What are we gonna do? Say it's fine, okay doctors, go ahead and operate on the kid? Make him better and then when you're through pick us out of a line-up? Now that don't make no sense, does it, Bobby? You're smart, but you scare me sometimes with how stupid you can be."

"Yes, I understand I am stupid all right. I was stupid to be part of this plan. But Vincent is not stupid. If he learns who has taken those doctors we are dead."

"I said, enough! I want the Cortlands dead, period. When Joey takes care of business in Italy, Vincent's not gonna find out who we are. So that's that." Felt Hat reiterated, "I want them all dead. I want you and Gianni to go after them. And don't come back unless they're dead or I'll send you both over the cliff. Now go. The more we talk about it, the more time they have to get away."

Blood continued to trickle down Big Boy's head, but he was impervious to pain. He showed a wide grin in support of Felt Hat's anger toward Bobby. "Okay with you if I toss Bobby over the edge now, boss?"

"Try me," Quiet Man challenged.

"Forget about it, Gianni. Bobby's gonna be a good boy. Right, Bobby?"

Quiet Man dropped his eyes. He knew he was in too deep to walk away now. There was no way out for him. He hated the idea of killing the Cortlands, but he knew Felt Hat was right.

* * *

From his perch on the ledge, Matt realized he did not have the strength to dislodge the larger boulders. He watched as Big Boy descended the trail to rejoin Felt Hat and Quiet Man, who were gesturing heatedly toward each other. He decided to take advantage of the time they spent arguing to climb down from the cliff and catch up to his father and Kate.

Matt had bought extra time to flee the gang and also sent one of the kidnappers over the cliff to his death. The other three would not rush up the mountain helter-skelter— another rock slide could be their reward for recklessness, so they would move with caution. Matt also knew they weren't going to quit.

He lowered himself over the ledge, found a toehold, and began to inch his way down the fifteen feet of sheer cliff. Halfway down, his boot slipped out of a small fissure in the wall and left him dangling. He struggled for a few desperate seconds to find another toehold, but his hands weakened and he was unable to hold on any longer.

Matt fell to the path, landing awkwardly on his heels and butt in a sitting position with his right leg twisted underneath. His head lurched forward and his nose smacked against his knee. He screamed a short, high-pitched cry of pain as blood shot from his nose.

He crawled an agonizing three feet to sit with his back against the wall, then leaned forward to keep from swallowing blood and applied pressure to his nostrils.

Matt had to catch up to his father and Kate, but was dazed and in crushing pain. He tried to stand, but let out another shout of agony so loud it echoed through the canyons. He fell back against the wall, certain he had fractured his tibia below his right knee. He looked around for something to use as a crutch and saw a limb from a pine tree lying across the trail a good distance ahead of him. He decided to crawl to the limb, using his elbows to propel himself one foot at a time. He was in terrible pain, breathing from his mouth and leaving a trail of blood.

Big Boy tilted his head in the direction of Matt's screams. "Did you hear that?" he asked Bobby.

Bobby pretended he hadn't heard. "Hear what?"

"Someone's hurt. Didn't you hear that? Twice I heard it."

"I did not hear anything," Quiet Man lied. "You are hallucinating, as usual."

"What are you, deef for Chrissake?"

"I heard it too," Felt Hat declared. "I think he's right. Someone's hurt."

Big Boy said, "I'm going. I know I heard it." Like a predatory animal sensing wounded prey, he would go in for the kill. He was eager to extract revenge. "You comin' or not?" he shouted at Quiet Man.

"Yeah, go ahead," Bobby said. "I'll be right behind you." He watched the giant lumber up the mountain.

"He'll take care of business," Felt Hat said. "He always does."

Quiet Man shook his head in disdain. "Yes, I know he does. I will let him do it himself."

Felt Hat glowered and erupted. "You go help him. I don't wanna hear any more shit about the kid. Go help him so we can get this over with." Bobby said nothing. "And listen to me," Felt Hat continued. "I'm goin' back to the farmhouse to pick up our car. I'll dump the black and white and come back for you and Gianni. I'll leave it up to the both of you to deal with the Cortlands. When you're done, wait for me at the bottom where we parked and I'll pick you up."

Bobby turned to walk up the trail without acknowledging Felt Hat's command.

Felt Hat worried about this change in Bobby. Maybe Gianni had been right about him all along.

CHAPTER 47

Matt had crawled twenty yards up the mountain trail when he heard a familiar cackle behind him. He lay helpless on his stomach as Big Boy's chortles got louder and closer. When the giant reached him, Matt craned his neck and looked up. Big Boy stood over him, pointing Driver's revolver at his back.

Matt was certain he was about to die and lowered his head to the ground.

"You don't look too good," Big Boy said. "I told them I heard someone screaming. Bobby didn't believe me."

"Where's Bobby?" Matt asked, his voice barely above a whisper.

"Bobby? Oh, he's coming. But he ain't gonna help you. The boss said we gotta kill you."

"Why?" Matt asked.

"Well, how about because you killed my friend? Why did you have to do that anyway?" he asked, almost childlike. "You'll pay for what you did to him." Big Boy kicked Matt in his side. "Where's your father and that pretty wife of yours? They leave you to die?"

Matt was able to utter, "They went down the mountain."

"I don't think so. Where are they?" Big Boy kicked Matt again. "That was for what your wife did to me." Matt was on the edge of shock, but Big Boy wasn't ready to kill him. He wanted to see Matt suffer. Big Boy held the gun across the top of Matt's head and fired a shot to crease his scalp—to hurt, but not to kill.

Felt Hat heard the gunshot echo through the canyon. *That's one down,* he said to himself. Gianni was taking care of business.

Quiet Man quickened his pace and continued up the trail to catch up with Gianni.

With his gun against Matt's temple, Big Boy cackled, "And now how about if I put you out of your misery? Yes or no? Please say yes. Do you want it in the back? How about the head? Let me see. Ah, what the hell. I know where."

Quiet Man, his gun drawn, rounded the bend in the trail to see Big Boy aiming his revolver at the doctor's head, ready for the kill shot.

"Gianni, drop it! Get away from him."

"Screw you, Bobby! He's going to be dead and you're next." Gianni turned his gun toward Quiet Man, but Bobby fired first.

Big Boy lurched toward him. "Bobby! You sonofabitch." He fell face down with a thud alongside Matt.

* * *

Felt Hat heard the second shot as he was climbing into the stolen police car to drive back to the farmhouse. "Two down. One to go."

* * *

Senior and Kate heard cries of pain, but they were uncertain if they had come from Matt. "I'm going back, Kate. It could be Matt."

"I'm coming with you."

Senior raced back down the trail ahead of Kate. At the sound of the first gunshot, he quickened his pace. He arrived in time to see Bobby shoot Big Boy. He didn't understand what he had just witnessed, but when he saw Matt writhing

275

on the ground, he ran to his son, unconcerned what Quiet Man might do to him.

Senior dropped to his knees to examine his son's injuries. Matt's face was swollen, his eyes and cheeks blackened, and his scalp and face caked with blood. Though his scalp wound was not serious, it was obvious to Senior that Matt's nose was broken. Matt drifted in and out of consciousness and was unable to tell his father that his tibia was fractured.

Quiet Man asked, "Dr. Cortland, what may I do to help?"

Senior cocked his head and was surprised to hear Bobby's offer of help. He stared at him for a few seconds and saw sincerity. "We've got to prop him up so he doesn't drown in his own blood. Help me move him up against the wall." Quiet Man crouched on one side of Matt while Senior crouched on the other. "On the count of three." They lifted Matt and propped him against the cliff wall.

"Thank you, Bobby. I don't understand why, but thank you for saving my son's life."

Kate burst onto the scene with Reggie beside her. When she saw the condition her husband was in, she gasped and knelt beside him. "What happened? What did you do to him, Bobby? Oh, my God, Matt. Matt!" she sobbed. "Will he be all right, Dad?"

"All I can tell right now is that he's bled quite a bit from his broken nose. He'll survive that, but I don't know where else he's hurt. And it was Bobby who saved his life. Bobby shot Gianni just as Gianni was about to shoot Matt."

Matt opened his eyes halfway and managed a slight nod of recognition to Kate and Senior. He sensed someone else nearby and lifted his head to see who it was. When he recognized Quiet Man, he moaned, "No... no..."

"Son, he's okay. Bobby saved your life."

Kate said, "Hi, honey." She held his hand in her own and stroked it gently. "Dad said you're going to be all right."

Reggie bared his teeth at Quiet Man and gave a deep growl, but Kate shushed him. The dog dropped to his haunches.

Matt slowly lifted his arm to touch his bullet-creased head wound, then examined his fingertips for blood. "I'm a mess, huh? What's the damage?"

Senior kept his emotions in check. "It looks like you broke your nose, and your head wound is superficial, but I don't know if you have internal injuries. Where else do you hurt?"

"Everywhere! I feel like I've been hit by a truck," he said, forcing a smile. "But mostly my right leg. I think I fractured my tibial plateau."

Senior examined Matt's leg to determine if the tibia had penetrated the skin. "Luckily it's not a compound fracture. It could be displaced, but I'm going to have to find a way to splint it. We've got to get it treated as soon as we can get off Pigeon. If you're up to it, tell us what happened."

Matt spoke slowly. "Started a rock slide then tried to come down from the cliff. Couldn't hang on. Fell. Then Gianni..."

"He's not a concern anymore, thanks to Bobby."

They all looked at Big Boy's body as it lay a few feet from where Matt was propped up. The front of the giant's tattered shirt was highlighted by an expanding circle of blood.

Matt uttered, "Thanks."

Kate extended her hand and said, "Thank you so much, Bobby."

Bobby took Kate's hand and accepted her thanks with a nod.

Senior asked Bobby, "Where are the other two men?"

Quiet Man calmed him, "Dr. Cortland, you do not have to worry about them. Our driver is dead. He was flung over the cliff by the rock slide started by your son. I wish that did not have to happen, but I do not hold it against him. I understand why he did it." Then Bobby added, "The other man has walked down the mountain."

"What's he going to do?"

"I cannot answer that, Doctor."

"I'm sorry about your friend," Matt said. "You understand, I had to try to stop—"

Bobby interrupted, "I understand."

Senior asked, "When we escaped from the farmhouse and were running along the lakefront, someone yelled that we needed to operate on Vincent Vendetti's son. What does our kidnapping have to do with him?"

Quiet Man shook his head. He was not going to explain the plot behind their kidnapping. He was having a difficult time rationalizing to himself why he had developed an emotional bond with the Cortlands. Perhaps because he had never been one to injure innocent people. He was different from Gianni, who had no regard for human life. Gianni had killed many men—and done so without remorse, including Officer Kuberski. Bobby did not know what he was going to do next or what was in store for him. But his loyalty to Felt Hat was unwavering—he would not do anything to put his boss in jeopardy. From his earliest years, he had been taught about loyalty to one's family.

Senior was apologetic. "I didn't mean to press you, Bobby. We're grateful, believe me. We know we wouldn't have made it without your help—and my son would be dead."

CHAPTER 48

A limb from a pine tree sat on the trail a dozen yards away from where Matt was propped up against the granite wall. Senior said, "I'll be right back. I want to get a couple of branches we can use as splints for Matt's broken leg." He struggled to snap off two branches but finally succeeded. He carried them back along with the four-foot main branch for Matt to use as a walking stick.

"Matt, I need to splint your leg before you injure it further." Matt knew it was going to hurt when Senior applied the splints, and prepared for the pain by digging the palms of his hands against his eyes. "Just do it, Dad!"

Senior positioned one branch along the inside of Matt's thigh and another on the outside of his leg. Quiet Man pulled off his necktie for Senior to use to tie the splints to Matt's leg. Then, without being asked, pulled off Gianni's tie too.

Senior nodded his thanks.

The splinting drew a muffled cry of pain from Matt.

"I'm sorry, son. I had to stabilize your leg. We're not that far from the cabin. I'd like to try to get you there. With Bobby's help, we can carry you."

Kate said, "Instead of that, why don't Matt and I stay here? That way, you can head down and find help, and the only person you have to worry about is that one guy Bobby said already walked down." She looked at Quiet Man and added, "He's the leader, isn't he?"

Quiet Man didn't answer.

Matt had become more lucid. "Kate's right. Just leave Gianni's gun with us.

"It's got only one bullet left."

280

"Hopefully, we won't need it." Matt pointed to Driver's gun on the ground next to Gianni. "You take that one. Check to see it's got some bullets in it."

"Are you sure you'll be okay?"

"Yes. Just go, Dad. The sooner the better."

Senior asked Quiet Man, "What do you want to do? Walk down with me?"

Bobby answered, "I will descend, yes, but then I will need to take my leave."

Kate asked him, "What will you do and where will you go?"

"I will have to think it through. I know I cannot go back— I can never go back. I may never be safe no matter what I decide to do."

Senior said, "But if you turn yourself in and tell the FBI what you know, they'll treat you with leniency. We will be witnesses to what you did for us."

"No. I would not survive two days if I did that. The people I associate with have long tentacles."

Kate said, "If that's the case, we won't identify you to the police. We promise." She rose to give him a hug.

Quiet Man was stunned. "Thank you. I sincerely apologize for my involvement in this affair."

"Let's get going," Senior urged. "I'll be back soon. Hang in, son, okay?"

Matt nodded. "I'll be okay. And, Bobby, thank you."

The two men left. Senior looked back and waved before they were out of sight.

"See if you can get some sleep," Kate said to Matt.

Exhausted from his pain, Matt closed his eyes and fell asleep instantly.

Kate sat beside her husband against the cliff wall. Reggie plopped down next to her, and rested his head on her lap. "You've been a good boy, Reggie. Are you going to help me take care of Matt?" She patted his head.

With her face open to the warmth of the rising sun, she, too, closed her eyes and allowed herself to fancy a long, hot bath safe in her own house. She continued to stroke Reggie with one hand and interlocked her other hand with her husband's. Big Boy's revolver lay on the ground beside her.

* * *

Reggie was the first to sense something. He lifted his head, stood, and growled. His low growl soon turned to a furious bark which woke Kate and Matt. Big Boy was standing over them.

"Oh my God!" Kate screamed.

"Oh no." Matt tried to stand, but his splinted leg caused him to fall back.

No one had ever checked to see if Big Boy was alive or dead. From the growing pattern of blood on his chest, everyone, including Senior and Quiet Man, had been convinced that Big Boy had been killed.

Kate recalled what Agnes had said about Reggie. "Sic him, Reggie! Sic him!" she shouted.

With his teeth bared, Reggie charged at Big Boy, then backed away, charged again, and backed away again. He nipped at Big Boy's ankles, pulled on his pants leg, backed away, and nipped again. Kate reached for the revolver, but Big Boy booted it aside. Reggie continued to attack. Big Boy ended it by kicking the collie in his side. Reggie barked a high pitch yelp of pain, then retreated and whimpered off to lick his side.

Kate tried to get up, but Big Boy grabbed her by the arm and dragged her to the edge of the cliff. She screamed and twisted her body as she tried to claw at his face, but he held her by the wrists. She dug her heels in, but her struggles were hopeless against Big Boy's power and strength.

Suddenly, Big Boy released her. A cry of pain emanated from deep within his belly. In his struggle with Kate, the bullet in his chest had moved and scraped against a nerve root from his spinal cord. He fell to his knees in agony, unable to move without suffering excruciating pain.

Kate clambered away.

Big Boy remained on his knees, his arms outstretched and blood trickling from the side of his mouth. His face contorted as he looked to Matt, imploring him to help. Kate feared and loathed Big Boy, but she looked away, unable to watch the sight of the giant in such agony.

Matt reached for the walking stick Senior had leaned against the wall. "Help me get up, Kate." He was going to try to help the wounded giant. He could not watch Big Boy die like an animal, but he was not willing to chance Big Boy turning on him if he got too close. He shouted, "I'll help you, Gianni, but get down on your stomach first."

Big Boy didn't move. He stayed on his knees making horrible, guttural noises. "I said I'll help you, but get down first. Get down."

Big Boy lifted his face to the sky as if in prayer. His eyes were wide open and rolled to white. He gurgled a deep-throated noise and fell hard to the ground on his back. He lay there immobile, the wide circle of blood on his chest now encompassing his entire shirt.

"Is he dead?"

"I don't know, Kate. It looks like he might be. But we thought he was dead before, so let's be careful. The gun's on the ground behind us. Get it—just in case."

Matt put one arm around Kate's shoulders and used the limb for further support. He hobbled to the prostrate hulk and leaned over to search Gianni's carotid artery for a pulse. At first, he thought he felt one, but then did not find it again. "He's gone," Matt said.

Kate was unsympathetic. "I'm not sorry he's dead. I hated him." She turned to help Matt move away from the chasm. Then, without warning, Big Boy reached out and clutched her ankle with a vise-like grip. He pulled her down to the ground. As she lost balance the revolver slipped from her grasp and bounced out of reach.

Big Boy held onto her ankle and lifted himself back to his knees. He pulled her toward him.

Without Kate to support him, Matt had fallen heavily on his shoulder. He struggled back up and hobbled onto his good leg. He swung the limb at Big Boy, hitting him in the back with a glancing blow. The giant groaned and released his hold on Kate. Matt balanced himself and stood poised to swing the limb again, but Big Boy snatched it away and used it to boost himself up.

Matt stumbled back to the ground, unable to defend himself, when all of a sudden Quiet Man rushed in with his revolver drawn, and shouted, "Get down, Gianni, or I will blow you away."

In one swift move, Big Boy dropped the limb, lunged, and grabbed Quiet Man's arm before he could use his gun.

Kate recognized Gianni could easily overwhelm Bobby, so she picked up the limb and swung as hard as she could, hitting the giant on his back. The force of the blow caused Big Boy to let go of Quiet Man.

Bobby yelled again. "Get down, Gianni!"

Big Boy smirked and took a step toward him, but Quiet Man fired his revolver, nicking his shoulder. The giant was oblivious to his wound and kept advancing. Quiet Man fired a second time. This bullet grazed the side of Big Boy's head. His hand flew up to his bleeding temple, but he continued toward Bobby, who fired again. Incredibly, the shot missed its mark. The giant knocked the gun out of Bobby's hand and kicked it into the ravine. "Say goodbye, Bobby. You're done."

The two grappled and fell to the ground, first one on top, then the other. Quiet Man showed surprising strength against the behemoth. But despite his injuries, Big Boy put Quiet Man in a bear hug and carried him to the edge of the cliff.

Quiet Man tried to brace himself, but was unable to gain a foothold on the granite surface. He resisted with chops to the giant's neck, but with a loud grunt, Gianni heaved his nemesis over the cliff.

Kate screamed, "No! No!"

Big Boy was breathing hard near the precipice. He yelled down. "Who's the smart one now? Who's the smart one? No more of your shit. I told you I was gonna throw you over the cliff."

Kate picked up the walking stick and again, using all her strength, hit Big Boy in the back with a swinging blow. She could not understand how he withstood such punishment. He put up his arm to defend himself, but she swung a second time and caught him hard on the side of the face, opening a deep wound on his temple. *Is he human? How can he still be standing?*

Big Boy took one more step toward Kate then thudded to the ground on his back.

* * *

Senior rushed up the trail to find Matt and Big Boy lying on the ground and Kate standing over both men. "Where's Bobby?" he asked, breathing hard.

"He wasn't dead," Kate shrieked.

"What are you talking about? Who wasn't dead?"

"Gianni!"

"So where's Bobby?"

"Gianni pushed him over the cliff."

"God, no. What happened?"

"We thought Gianni was dead. But he wasn't. He was covered with blood and convulsing and his eyes rolled up. He even stopped breathing."

Matt said, "I checked him for a pulse. There was none, so we were certain he was dead. But when we turned our backs to him, he grabbed Kate by the ankle. That's when Bobby showed up." Matt shook his head. "Gianni would have killed us both if it wasn't for Bobby. But Gianni was too big. He threw Bobby over the ledge like he was a rag doll." Matt pointed to the spot where Bobby went over.

Senior crouched next to Big Boy to check his pulse and found none. "Well, he's gone now."

"Finally," Kate exclaimed. "I'm not sorry I killed him. I'm not. I'm not."

Matt said, "If you hadn't done what you did, he would have killed us both."

Suddenly, a loud clatter shook the canyon walls. The wind kicked up and bent the pine trees on the side of the mountain above them. The three gaped at each other.

Kate shouted, "What's that?"

Reggie trembled from the intensity of the racket and held his tail tight against his belly. He sought refuge up against Kate.

"It's a helicopter," Senior yelled above the clamor. Kate grabbed Reggie by his collar and pulled him to the wall with her. "Maybe Detective Kelly sent it to look for us."

A shadow swooped past them, then reappeared. The Cortlands shielded their eyes from the swirling dust. The staccato din of the helicopter blades echoed so loud it hurt their ears. Senior waved frantically to get the pilot's attention. The helicopter moved away, then immediately looped back. The pilot gave Senior a thumbs-up.

CHAPTER 49

The helicopter hovered overhead, buffeted by updrafts created by the craft itself. The pilot struggled to hold it steady. The passenger door of the helicopter was open. A man holding a rifle was sitting on the floor with his legs outside the helicopter and his feet braced against the landing runners of the aircraft.

Kate shouted, "Thank God! We're finally going to be rescued."

Just as she said that, a rifle shot pinged off the wall above them, creating a spark and a puff of dust. A second and a third followed.

Matt yelled, "What the hell are they doing? They must think we're the bad guys."

Senior stepped away from the wall and waved his arms to get them to stop shooting, but was met by another rifle shot that struck to the right of him.

Kate pointed to where the cliff wall bowed out like the belly of a barrel and yelled to Senior, "We need to get Matt under that wall."

"Throw your arm around my neck, quick," Senior shouted to Matt. "Kate, I'll get Matt. You get under. Let go of Reggie. He'll be okay. Let him go."

She refused to release her hold on Reggie's collar and pulled him to the wall with her. Matt and Senior followed, tucking themselves into the fold at the base of the wall. Senior used his body to shield Matt while Kate shielded Reggie.

The rifleman had a slight angle to aim at them. With the helicopter bouncing about in the wind, only a remarkably lucky shot would hit any of them.

Senior aimed Driver's revolver at the helicopter and shouted above the din, "I'm going to see if I can hit the rotor." He held the butt of the revolver in both hands to steady his aim and fired two times in quick succession.

Bits of the rotor flew off and stopped whirring.

"You hit it!" Kate shouted.

The helicopter reeled to the right. The pilot struggled to pull it up and away from the face of the mountain, but he was unable to regain control of the craft.

The sharpshooter tried to maintain his hold on the reeling helicopter, his legs dangling in midair, but he lost his grip. He plummeted into the gorge with his rifle floating down in a wide circle behind him.

The helicopter was doomed. It careened from wall to wall, spraying off pieces of propeller and rotor. Seconds later, it dropped to the canyon floor and exploded with the force of a bomb on impact.

The Cortlands rolled out from under the wall and shook their heads in awe at the helicopter's flaming destruction.

Matt said, "If the kidnappers can send a helicopter after us, Dad, they can do anything. Lord knows what they'll do next. You have got to get back down Pigeon to contact Kelly and the FBI agents. They're our only chance."

"And what about you two?"

"I think we should get to the cabin and wait for Kelly to escort us down."

"Okay. I'll carry you."

"I'm not about to let you carry me. I can make it with Kate's help.

"I'm carrying you, and that's final."

"No, Dad. Come on. I'll be fine. The cabin's not that far from here. The splint helped. You just need to get going and find Kelly. Please, go."

Senior knew his son was right. "All right. I'll go and be back with help before you know it.

Kate handed Matt the pine walking stick. Senior studied his son's eyes. He knew Matt was in pain and needed medical attention for his fractured tibia, but he was strong and resilient and unwavering. The cabin would be a safe haven until Matt could be transported to the hospital.

* * *

Matt hobbled up the trail using the walking stick and Kate's shoulder for support. When they crossed the bridge over Pigeon Creek to the cabin, Kate shouted, "Hallelujah! I never thought I'd be happy to see this cabin again. Now we've got to pray that Dad can get hold of Detective Kelly."

"He'll get to him. You'll see. He's resourceful."

Reggie scampered to the edge of the fast-moving creek to drink of the sweet, cold mountain water. Matt and Kate drank too.

Before they entered the cabin, Matt explained to Kate how they would defend themselves if Felt Hat closed in on them. "We'll have to sever the ropes on the footbridge to prevent anyone from crossing the creek."

"Why don't we cut them now?"

"I don't think we should, yet. We need to be able to get back over the creek when Kelly gets here. And besides, Reggie will alert us if someone is getting close."

"Yes, you will, Reggie, won't you?" Kate petted the dog's head and chin.

The collie wagged his tail, appreciative of Kate's praise.

Kate and Matt hobbled into the cabin. While Kate opened the two shuttered wooden windows to air out the mustiness of the cabin, Matt collapsed onto one of the canvas cots. He folded his body awkwardly onto the cot, but left his feet planted on the floor.

Kate called for Reggie to come into the cabin. She put Gianni's revolver under the cot within easy reach and said to Matt, "Good idea to get some sleep." But he was already asleep. She lifted his splinted right leg onto the cot, causing him to moan in pain. When she was certain he was still asleep, she plopped down on the other cot and fell asleep too.

Reggie circled and explored inside the cabin until he found a spot to his liking on the floor alongside Kate's cot. He collapsed and rested his head on his outstretched front paws.

CHAPTER 50

Dawn had broken when Vincent's cab pulled up to Eaglesmount Hospital. Vincent had slept the entire ride back from LaGuardia Airport with his head tilted awkwardly against the side window.

The cabbie turned and said loudly, "Hey, buddy, we're here."

Vincent woke with a start and let out a wide, unrestrained yawn. He got out of the cab and rotated his neck from side to side then rolled his shoulders to work out the stiffness. On the sidewalk, he interlocked his fingers, clenched the back of his head and yawned again. Without a thank you, he pulled out his wallet and removed three one-hundred-dollar bills to pay the cabby—two hundred for the fare and one hundred for the promised tip. The cabby thanked Vincent profusely, but Vincent ignored the man and instead stood for a moment gazing at the mountains surrounding the hospital. The early morning sun bounced its rays off the high clouds, painting the sky a canvas of crimson and pink.

With a deep inhale of the crisp mountain air, he cleared his head then walked toward the hospital entrance. Before he reached the revolving door, he heard a familiar voice shout from behind. "Hey, Vincent!"

Vincent turned around and saw Frankie walking toward him. The two men embraced with back-thumping bear hugs. "Frankie, you're a sight for sore eyes. Did Concetta get hold of you last night?"

"She didn't call me, but I did talk to her. I thought you would've called and told me how my godson was doing. When I didn't hear from you, I called the hospital and they put her on the line. That's why I'm here now. She wasn't makin' no sense. I didn't understand her, with her talkin' Italian and crying so much. She said you had to leave, but she didn't know where you were goin'. I didn't know what she was sayin', so I got in the car and drove up here to see what the hell was goin' on. I said to myself, it don't take no genius to know somethin's not right, you know what I mean? I knew you wasn't gonna leave your boy unless someone had a gun to your head."

"Frankie, you gotta help me."

"You know I will, Vincent. Whatever you need we can do it together—anything. Now, tell me what's goin' on with your son. The hospital wouldn't tell me nothin'. They said I had to ask you or Concetta because I wasn't authorized. Authorized? I said 'I am authorized. I'm the boy's godfather.' They said that wasn't good enough."

Vincent's voice cracked. "I don't know if my son's alive or dead. When I left, he was gettin' worse. He's pretty bad, Frankie. I'm not sure he's gonna make it. Yesterday morning, two doctors were supposed to operate on his heart with this new machine they invented. But before they could operate, some guys took the doctors."

"What do you mean *took*? You mean kidnapped? Who would do that?"

"I don't know, but they did."

"Why don't you get some other doctors to operate?"

"Frankie, you don't understand. Those two doctors are the only two in the whole world who know how to use this machine they invented—they call it the heart-lung machine. No one knows nothin' about the damn thing except for them. We've gotta find those doctors or for sure my boy's gonna die. I'm gonna need your help. You gotta bring up some of our boys to help us find those two doctors. I should've done it myself. Come on. Walk with me. I'll fill you in on the way." Vincent explained the events of the previous two days—the kidnapping of the three Cortlands, the involvement of the FBI and Kelly, the death of Officer Kuberski, and the anonymous phone calls ordering him to fly to Rome. "Frankie, you're not gonna like this, but I gotta tell you the truth. As God is my witness, Pansie's in on this."

"My sister? No way. Stop it. I don't believe that."

"Believe it, Frankie. Pansie. And you know who else? Hammer."

"You gotta be shittin' me. Joey? Is he still alive? After all these years? Where's he been hiding?"

"He's been in Italy the whole time." Vincent told Frankie about the episode at the airport and how he escaped from Joey. "We shoulda killed him years ago when we had the chance."

Frankie shook his head in disbelief that their longtime nemesis had resurfaced after all these years. "Pansie—that whore! And Hammer! He's the one who planned the kidnappings?"

"No, he ain't got the brains. He's dumber than a rock. I think he's workin' for someone. I don't know for sure, but I think it's one of the New York families. You know it ain't no secret how much Anastasia and Lucchese want to horn in on our territory. They want it so bad they can taste it. Makes sense, don't it? They get rid of me, then try to get it for themselves."

"And what about me? Does New York think I'm just a piece of shit?"

"We'll deal with them later, Frankie. Right now, we gotta find the Cortlands."

"You know, Vincent, I'm pissed you didn't call me when all this shit started. You shoulda called me. I would've had a dozen men up here in a couple of hours to look for them."

"I wasn't thinkin' straight. I figured the cops would take care of this. How hard can it be to find someone in this hick town?"

Vincent opened the door to his son's room. He shushed Frankie when he saw Concetta dozing in a chair alongside the crib and wondered if his wife had left the baby's side at all in the many hours he had been gone.

Concetta woke with a start and looked at Vincent, who nodded to her. He leaned over and stroked his son's cheek. The boy didn't react. His condition was worsening.

Concetta lifted her hand and offered it limply to Frankie, but uttered no words of greeting. Frankie grasped her hand with both of his. He was struck by the drawn look on Concetta's face and the imperfect semi-circles of dark rings that bordered her swollen eyes.

"I can't believe this. You're right. It's gotta be New York— the sonsofbitches," Frankie said. "Who the hell else would even try somethin' like this? This is war, Vincent. This is war!"

There was a faint tap on the door before it swung open. Agents Dryer and Harris walked in. "We heard from Detective Kelly that you were back. Who's he?" Dryer asked, nodding to Frankie.

"A friend of mine."

The agent eyed Frankie. "Do I know you?"

Frankie said, "No, you don't know me. And who the hell are you?"

"Agents Dryer and Harris of the Federal Bureau of Investigation," Harris answered, and both men flipped their shields. "What happened, Mr. Vendetti? Why did you come back?"

Vincent said, "Keep it down."

Agent Dryer turned to Frankie and said, "We want to talk to Mr. Vendetti alone."

Vincent overruled the agent. "No. He stays. He's my friend. I don't keep nothin' from him."

"Okay, tell us what happened."

"The kidnappers told me that if I wanted the Cortlands released, I was supposed to catch a plane to Rome. They would free the doctors when I was on the plane. I drove to New York like they told me to do, and when I got to the airport they had people waitin' to go to Italy with me. But then I found out they double-crossed me."

"What do you mean?"

"They didn't let the Cortlands go, that's what I mean."

"Who was waiting for you at the airport?"

Vincent looked at Frankie, who shook his head that Vincent should not tell them.

"It's not important for you to know," Vincent said.

Agent Dryer offered a theory. "Listen to me, Mr. Vendetti. Maybe the Cortlands weren't released because they're dead."

"What are you talking about?"

"Let's look at this logically. The kidnappers succeeded in getting you to go to New York. Everything went like they planned. With you in the hands of their henchmen, they figured there was nothing to gain by letting the Cortlands go."

Frankie stared at Dryer. "You think they killed them?"

"Put yourself in their shoes. The Cortlands would be able to identify them. Wouldn't it make sense to get rid of them?"

Frankie shook his head.

Agent Dryer asked, "Why are you shaking your head no?"

"I don't agree. Sounds like the kidnappers didn't want the kid to die, so I don't think they would have killed them doctors."

"Then why do you think the Cortlands have not been released?"

"Maybe they found out Vincent was back here. What the hell do I know? I just got here. You're the experts. You find 'em. You should have people out there looking for them right now instead of bein' in here not doin' shit."

Agent Dryer got his back up. "Like you said, you just got here. There's not much more we can be doing. Along with every cop in the regional police force, we've been combing the entire four-county area and across the state into New York. Listen to me, Mr. Vendetti. Tell us what happened at the airport. Who met you there? The more you tell us, the better the odds we can help."

Vincent studied the FBI agent then turned to his friend. "Frankie, I think I should tell them what I know."

Frankie was shocked that Vincent was willing to discuss family matters. He motioned for Vincent to follow him away from the agents and into the corridor. Vincent had always been the stronger and more decisive of the two. But now, Frankie had to take on that role. "Vincent, what are you, crazy? What are you gonna tell them? That you think it's New

York who done this? How're you gonna do that without every family on the east coast gunning for you? You can't do it. You can't tell them nothin' about our family problems. You're dead if you do. There'd be a dozen contracts out on you in about three seconds—and on me, too."

"What am I supposed to do? Sit here and watch my son die?"

"Let me handle it from now on. You say there are no other doctors who can do this operation. I say there's got to be. I'll find some. The Cortlands ain't the only doctors in the world."

"Why ain't you listening to me? The Cortlands are the *only ones* who can fix my son's problem. I need them. There's nobody else."

Frankie faced Vincent and clutched him by the arms. "Okay, I understand. But, please, don't say nothin' to them about New York. Give me three days. We'll find the sonsofbitches."

"My son ain't got three days, Frankie."

Frankie inhaled deeply and said, "I don't know what to tell you. He's not my son, so I can't say what you should do. But if you go to San Bartolomeo, you can't think it's the end of you. We'll find the Cortlands. And when your kid gets better, you come back. You'll see."

"I don't know. The thought of leaving my kid... And you saw Concetta in there. I gotta be here."

"Don't worry. I'll take care of things until you get back. I'll make sure New York don't take over any part of our territory. I give you my word on that. If it means we go to war to protect what we've worked for, that's what we do. I promise—they ain't gonna take any real estate from us. Like the Professor used to say, what's ours is ours."

"Okay. You stay here and try to find the Cortlands. Bring some men up. I'll wait until the kidnappers call me again."

"What makes you think they'll call you again?"

"They will. I know they will. And when they do, I'll tell them I agree to go to Rome. Frankie, it's over for me." Vincent looked into Frankie's eyes and shook his head. "The next time Joey gets his claws in me, that'll be the end of it. He'll make sure of that. I won't be back. I gave him the slip last time, but he won't let me get away again. He'll finish me off once he gets me there."

"Nothin's gonna happen to you."

"Okay, look. I'm tired. I don't care anymore what happens to me."

Frankie kissed his friend on the cheek and said, "Vincent, just tell Concetta everything will be good. Tell her I'm here to take care of things. Maybe that'll make her feel better. Go ahead, talk to her, but don't tell the feds nothin'. My men and me, we'll find those doctors. You'll see."

CHAPTER 51

Senior had nearly climbed down to the bottom of Pigeon Mountain when he heard the sounds of a car door slam shut and people talking. He slipped behind a large boulder just off the trail and looked around it to see three vehicles in the clearing below—Irwin's station wagon, a dark blue sedan, and a black sedan.

Two men stood in front of the blue sedan talking and gesturing, but Senior was too far away to hear what was being said. One man wore a felt hat and pointed toward the mountain trail. Though Senior had never seen him before, the man fit the description Matt and Kate had given of the ringleader of the kidnap gang. Senior did not recognize the other man, who was dressed in jeans, a checkered shirt, and boots. *The ringleader probably sent for this guy to help find us. He doesn't know Gianni and Bobby are dead.*

After several minutes, the men appeared to agree on a course of action. Felt Hat lit a cigarette and watched as the second man drew his gun and started up the path.

Senior had nowhere to go. Pigeon Creek was to the right of the narrow trail and a cliff wall to the left. If he tried to go back up the path, the man would spot him. He had to remain hidden behind the boulder. He hunched down, taking long, measured breaths, and twisted around the boulder while the man in jeans passed by. He stayed low to the ground until the man was out of sight.

He would have to act fast now. Once Felt Hat's back was turned he would climb back up Pigeon to confront the man who had passed him. There was no time to get to Detective Kelly. Matt and Kate's lives were in jeopardy. Senior drew his revolver and was about to step out from behind the boulder when Felt Hat shouted, "Drop the gun or I'll blow your head off."

Felt Hat had seen Senior twisting around the boulder to avoid being detected by the man climbing the trail. Senior raised his hands. There was nothing he could do. Felt Hat jammed his revolver against the back of Senior's head. He grabbed Senior's gun, stuck it in his belt, and pushed Senior against the boulder.

"Where's your son?"

Senior looked at him but did not answer.

"How did you get down? What happened to Bobby and Gianni? I asked them to do one simple thing."

"Who are you talking about?"

"You know who I'm talking about. I should just shoot you here."

"What the hell do you want from us?"

"Shut up."

"You want to know about your men?"

"Yeah."

"My son's got them."

"Bullshit."

"Listen, my son knows these mountains like the back of his hand. He set a trap for your men to walk into and he's guarding them now."

"Keep talking."

"That's it. That's everything. Right now he's got Bobby and Gianni, and he's waiting for me to come back with the Eaglesmount police. We called them from the farmhouse."

CHAPTER 52

Matt willed himself to wake. Kate still was asleep, but Reggie was awake, watching Matt's every move, his tail tapping the floor. Matt prayed his father had reached Eaglesmount safely. The helicopter was evidence Felt Hat was able to muster any resource to recapture them.

Matt used both hands to lift his splinted leg off the cot, then picked up his pine walking stick and used it to stand. Careful not to wake Kate, he stood over her, watching her sleep. He was proud of her. She had been strong and resilient, and shown so much courage in the face of Big Boy's vengefulness.

Taking deep breaths to suppress his pain, he opened the cabin door and walked out into the cool mountain air. Reggie watched Matt but stayed behind with Kate. The sound of the flowing creek and the beauty of the mountain were elixirs to Matt's senses.

Several yards away stood a pine tree with a small mirror attached above an empty metal bucket that hung from a hook. Matt hobbled over, looked in the mirror, and was shocked at what he saw. His face and head were caked with blood. His hair was coated with residual coal dust. His right nostril was split. And both his eyes were black and swollen. He lifted the bucket from its hook and used the pine limb to make his way to the edge of the creek. He bent down awkwardly to fill the pail with water and heard shuffling behind him. He thought Kate had followed him outside. As he turned to greet her, he was surprised by a hard kick against his back that slung him face forward into the creek and sent the bucket clanging against the rocks on the bank. He thrashed about in the frigid water, struggling against the creek's rapid flow that wanted to pull him downstream. From the bank, the man who had kicked him into the water laughed a high-pitched laugh as he witnessed Matt's struggles.

Matt was able to pull himself onto the bank and rise to his feet with the help of his pine limb. He stood wide to maintain his balance, wiped the water from his face, and shouted, "Detective Kelly, what the hell is wrong with you? I almost drowned."

Kelly didn't answer. "Where's your wife and father?"

"Why are you pointing that gun at me?"

"You're a smart man. Guess."

"I can't. Why?"

"I'll ask you one more time. Where are your wife and father?"

Matt thought quickly. "They went down the mountain. They went back to Eaglesmount to find you and bring help back for me. I stayed behind because I hurt my leg."

"I don't believe you. I would have passed them on the trail." Kelly kept his eye on Matt as he moved toward the cabin to check for Senior and Kate. "They wouldn't be in the cabin by any chance now, would they, Doctor Cortland?"

Matt said, "I'm telling you they went to look for you. There's no one in the cabin."

Kate had been awakened by the commotion at the creek. She peeked outside to see what was happening and was shocked and confused to see Kelly aiming his revolver at Matt. *Oh my God. What's he doing?* She retrieved the revolver she had placed under the cot and held Reggie tightly by the collar to keep him from barking. They stood hidden from view just inside the cabin.

Kelly asked Matt, "Where are Gianni and Bobby?"

Matt was surprised the detective would know their names, but everything was starting to add up "How do you know their names?"

"Where are they?"

"They're both dead. Bobby fell into the ravine and we left Gianni dead on the trail."

"That's bullshit. I didn't see Gianni."

"I told you. They're dead."

"Yeah, right. So first your father and wife passed me on the trail and then Gianni did too?" He laughed. "What do you take me for—a rube?"

"I'm telling you, Gianni's dead. And so is Bobby."

"Well, if they are, that's too bad, because they were supposed to kill you. I guess now I'll have to do it."

"Why?"

"Because I was told you could identify everyone."

"I can't believe this. We trusted you to help us."

"You trusted the wrong person."

"Are you the mastermind?"

"Nope."

"Then who is?"

"That's not important to know, is it? What you really need to know is, since Gianni and Bobby didn't kill you, I'll have to do it."

Matt stalled. "We don't even know why we were kidnapped."

"You don't need to know."

"Why are you involved? Will you tell me that at least?"

"Sure. It's simple. Because some people gave me a lot of money and I do whatever they tell me to do."

"It's bad enough you helped them kidnap us, and now you're going to kill me. You're not going to get away with it."

"Oh, I beg your pardon. I'll get away with it. You see, what happened is, I came up Pigeon Mountain looking for you all, and I found everyone was shot dead. The kidnappers did it—those bastards. Ha! I'll announce that I'll pursue those killers and won't rest until I put them behind bars. Good story, huh?"

"No one's going to believe that."

"Oh, I beg to differ. They will."

"Detective Kelly, I told you my father and wife climbed down already, so concocting a story about all of us being shot is ridiculous."

"If that's the case, I'll just kill you. You won't mind if I check the cabin for them first, will you?"

"What happened to you, Detective? What made you turn? People had so much respect for you."

"Respect? I can't put respect in my wallet. You want to know what happened to me? I'm retiring in six months. And with what? A lousy pension, that's what. Do you think that's fair after thirty years of service? I don't think it is. So, along come some people who want to put money in my—let's call it my *pension fund*—in return for a little help with this plan of theirs. I said sure, what the hell. Why not?" He approached the open doorway of the cabin and yelled, "Come out, Cortlands! I'm not going to ask again."

Matt inched closer, hoping somehow to get close enough to wrestle Kelly down.

"Stay where you are, Doctor! Any closer and I'll shoot. Got it?"

Kelly was about to step into the cabin when Kate released her hold on Reggie. She shouted, "Sic him, Reggie! Sic him!"

The collie flew out of the cabin and clamped down on the back of Kelly's calf with his sharp teeth. Kelly screamed in pain. "Get that dog away from me. Get him away from me!"

Matt closed in and, with a powerful swing of his pine limb, dropped the detective to the ground. The blow knocked the detective's revolver out of his hand.

Reggie continued to growl and yank on Kelly's jeans. "Stop him! Stop him," Kelly yelled.

Kate stepped out of the cabin with her revolver aimed at the detective.

"That's enough, Reggie! That's enough! Good boy. Okay, good boy, Reggie."

Reggie let go of the detective's leg and plopped down alongside Kate. The collie was breathing hard and continued to growl deep from his throat as he looked at Kelly.

Kelly stood up and warily eyed both Reggie and Matt. "Mrs. Cortland, I'm going to get my gun." It was on the ground midway between him and Kate.

"No. Don't do that."

"But I have to get my gun. I need it to protect us from the kidnappers."

Matt shouted, "Kate, he's the kidnapper. Shoot him if he goes for it."

Kelly continued to edge toward the gun.

Kate warned him, "I said don't do that."

"I understand you've been a pain in the ass to everyone. But you're not going to shoot me, are you, Mrs. Cortland? You won't, will you? Let me get my gun."

"No. I said stop. I will shoot." She lifted the gun to eye level and looked down the barrel at him. She knew only one bullet remained. *I can't miss him.* Her hand shook but she tried to steady her aim.

Kelly saw her hand trembling. "You're not going to shoot. I know you won't. Why would you? I came up here to help you and your husband. Is this the thanks I get?" He kept an eye on her, slowly leaned down, and snatched the gun off the ground. In one swift motion, he raised it to fire at Kate.

But she pulled the trigger and shot him first, striking him in the chest. The force of the bullet drove Kelly back three yards and into Pigeon Creek.

"I told you I would shoot," she sobbed. "Why didn't you listen to me?"

Matt held his walking stick at the ready to strike another blow if Kelly tried to get out of the water, but the current pulled at the detective's body, bumped him against the bank a couple of times, then pulled him downstream.

Matt put his arm around Kate as they watched the body float down the first of Pigeon Creek's half dozen waterfalls.

CHAPTER 53

Felt Hat was surprised to see another car pull up alongside the three cars parked at the base of Pigeon. Senior lied to Felt Hat, "People come here early every day to hike."

"Shut up. You say one word to anyone who walks up here and not only do I shoot you, I shoot them too. Understand what I'm saying?"

Felt Hat put his gun in his pocket and waited as a man exited the car, looked inside the three parked cars for occupants and, seeing none, walked up the trail.

The man was Vincent Vendetti.

"Oh no," Felt Hat uttered.

Felt Hat pushed Senior ahead of him and walked down to intercept Vendetti. "Vincent, thank God you got here when you did. We found your doctor."

Vincent nodded and looked at Senior. "You okay, Cortland?"

Senior said, "Vendetti, tell me what the hell is going on."

Vincent removed his revolver from his shoulder harness and aimed it at Felt Hat. "Why don't we ask my friend that question? Tell us, *Frankie*."

Senior was puzzled to learn there was a connection between the two men. "You know this guy?"

"Yeah. I've known him my whole life. We go back a long way—back to when we were kids. He's like my own flesh and blood, like a brother."

"If he's like a brother, why did he kidnap us and keep us from operating on your son?"

"Come on, Frankie. Tell the doctor. I'd like to know myself. You kidnapped them doctors knowin' they were gonna operate on my son. Why? Explain it to us, *friend*."

Felt Hat twisted his face and shook his head. He looked at Vincent and appeared offended by his questions. "I don't know what you mean, Vincent. I never seen this guy before. Ever since I left you at the hospital a couple of hours ago, I been trying to find him so he could operate on your kid. I told you I was gonna find him for you. I sent a couple of my guys up the mountain to look for your doctors. I even got a helicopter looking for them. And that's when all of a sudden, this cop—Kelly, he said his name was—shows up and says he's looking for Cortland too. So he goes up the mountain. The next thing I know, this doctor comes walking down and here he is. I pulled a gun on him to make sure he wasn't gonna take off."

"Is that right? That's what happened, huh?"

"Yeah. Then you show up, so he's all yours."

Senior said, "He's lying. He's been holding us hostage—him and his friends."

Frankie turned to Senior and cursed, "What the hell are you talking about?" His eyes flitted back to Vincent. "I ain't done nothin' of the kind. He's the liar."

"No, Frankie. The doctor's right, ain't he? Don't insult me no more. I've known you too long. Why'd you do it? Why? When you knew this guy had to operate on my son? I don't get it."

"Now, Vincent, why don't you believe what I'm tellin' you? You believe this asshole doctor over me?"

"Ever since we were kids, you never lied too good. You want to know when I first knew you were the one who kidnapped the Cortlands?"

Frankie said nothing.

"When we were in the hospital and you said something about how I should go back to Italy, to San Bartolomeo. You said *San Bartolomeo*. How did you know Joey was gonna take me there? I didn't say nothin' to you about that. And I didn't tell the Feds either. How did you know that? Then I saw you and Kelly at the hospital, talkin' and shakin' hands like you were asshole buddies. That's when I put two and two together and followed you here."

"That ain't true. You told me Joey was gonna take you to San Bartolomeo."

"Nah, Frankie, I didn't. I never said nothin' about Joey takin' me there. So, tell me, Frankie, how did you get Joey and Pansie to play along? I gotta give you credit. How did you get them to do this with you? How did you even know where Joey was all this time?"

Confronted with the facts, Frankie finally changed his story. "Pansie told me about Joey. She's in love with the guy. She told me he'd been hiding in San Bartolomeo, and begged me not to say nothin' to you. She didn't want you to hurt him. She said they were gonna get married or some shit. She'd been goin' back and forth to Italy to see him all these years."

Vendetti nodded. "Is that right?"

"Listen, Vincent, we didn't want to hurt your kid. I was gonna let the doctors go so they could operate on him. You know I wouldn't let anyone hurt the kid. He's my godson, for Chrissake. I was gonna let them operate. Then, when I was gonna let them go, they ran off. I've been lookin' for them ever since. You can ask Bobby and Gianni. They'll tell you the truth."

Vincent was stunned. "No, not Bobby. Honest to God? And Gianni too? And here I'm thinkin' it's one of the New York families. Are you with them too, Frankie? With Anastasia or Lucchese?"

"You know I wouldn't do that."

"No, I don't know that anymore. Where are the boys now—Bobby and Gianni?"

Frankie said, "Cortland says they're up there." He pointed to the top of Pigeon. "He says his son's got them."

"Is that true?" Vincent asked Senior.

"No. I made that up so he wouldn't shoot me. They're both dead. And so is the driver—the other kidnapper."

Frankie glared at Senior. "They're dead? You lyin' sonofabitch..."

Vincent lowered his gun. "You are the lyin' sonofabitch, Frankie. You weren't gonna let those doctors go. You were lookin' for them so you could kill them. My kid's dyin' and you didn't give a shit. Why, Frankie? Don't lie to me no more and maybe I won't blow your brains out. Why?"

Frankie looked away from his friend. Like a child reacting to a scolding, he shuffled his feet and shook his head. "Vincent, all I wanted was a chance."

"A chance? For what? What are you talking about?"

"A chance to show what I could do. You've always been better than me. I ain't never done nothin' on my own. You've always done it for me. You always took care of me—even when we were kids. Shit, if it wasn't for you, the Professor would never have hired me. But you know what? I'm good too. I'm more than just a pisshead. I want to prove I can run the family. I don't want to follow you no more. Nobody has ever respected me like they respect you. I want some respect myself. Remember we always said it was important to have respect?"

"I've always respected you, Frankie."

"The hell you have. I've always been your errand boy. Frankie, do this. Frankie, do that. Everybody always calls me your errand boy behind my back. That's all I ever was, your errand boy. I knew that and everybody else did too."

"Why didn't you kill me and leave my kid alone?"

"I would never kill you, Vincent. You're the best friend I ever had in the whole world. I would never think of doin' that."

"I still don't get it. What were you plannin' on doin'?"

"I figured if I got you to go to Italy, maybe you could be happy there. You could retire. You know what I mean? Like Salvatore Sabella when he retired to Florida back in '41. You've got a shitload of money—enough to live like a king— and could retire no problem. Your wife and son could be there with you. I'd be in charge of the family and everything would be okay. That's all I wanted. Then that asshole Joey screwed it all up by lettin' you get away. He's always been a piece of shit. Remember when we worked for the Professor and how we'd plan what we'd do to him? Those were the good old days, eh, Vincent? Remember Nunzio and Angelo? Remember?"

"Yeah, I remember. That's why this hurts me so much."

"Listen, why don't we forget all this. I screwed up. I made a mistake, okay? I made a bad mistake. But it ain't too late. We'll get the doctor here to operate on your son. Let's do it. Come on. You're still my best friend. We'll take Cortland down to the hospital. We still got time. Let's say this never happened. I promise I'll do anything you want me to do. Anything, okay?"

"What about Kelly? He was on the take? How much did you have to pay him?"

"Ten grand. But I was gonna get rid of him. He opened his mouth to another cop to get him to help him. I couldn't trust him to keep his mouth shut."

"So what did you do—send Kelly to kill the other doctor and his wife?"

Frankie looked at Senior before answering. "Yeah. I ain't proud of that but, yeah, that's what I did."

Vincent looked Senior over. He was bruised, his clothes were dirty, and his face showed a two-day stubble. "Doctor Cortland, you think you can you still operate on my son?"

Senior looked at the mobster and said, "Detective Kelly went up the mountain to kill my son and daughter-in-law. That means they're in grave danger. Here's my deal for you. You help me make sure they come down alive and I'll try to help your son. You help my son, and I'll help yours. That's the way it's got to be. We've got to keep Kelly from getting to them. Then, my son needs transport to the hospital. You help me do that and I'll operate on your son. But no promises. No guarantees. All I can do is give it my best shot with your son. Understand?"

"I trust you, Doctor Cortland. I never say that to anybody. Maybe you can see why," Vincent said. He nodded toward Frankie and added, "I trusted my best friend, and I shouldn't ever have done that."

"I'll give it my very best shot. That's a promise."

Vincent agreed to Senior's terms. "Let's go find your son before that asshole Kelly gets there first. Start walkin'. You too, Frankie."

"Me?"

"That's right. You come with us. I'll decide what to do with you later."

"What are you gonna tell the Feds about me, Vincent?"

"I ain't gonna tell them nothin'. This is between you and me."

"What about the Cortlands? Don't you think they're gonna tell the Feds what happened? Shit, if they do that, I'm dead. They'll have me on a kidnapping rap and for killin' that cop and who knows what else."

"What do you want me to do, Frankie? Kill them for you?"

"No, just let me go. I won't bother you no more. I promise. Give me a couple of days to get my act together, then I'll go over to Italy. You'll never see me again. What do you think? Nothin' but bad will come if the FBI gets me. Give me one more chance. For old times' sake. I'll flat out disappear."

"Yeah, you'll disappear until you can pull another one of these stunts on me."

"I don't blame you for thinkin' that, Vincent. But as God is my witness, I'll never do nothin' to you or your family again. Never! Trust me."

Vincent stared at Frankie, seething at his friend's betrayal. He wanted to kill him in revenge, but the pull of their years of friendship kept him from acting. "You turn my stomach, you pitiful bastard. I'll think about it."

The trio turned to climb up the trail but stopped when they heard a car speed into the parking area and fishtail to a stop. Agents Dryer and Harris jumped out of the car, saw the three men on the trail, and, with guns drawn, headed toward them.

Vincent said, "It's the Feds."

"Don't say nothin' to them, okay, Vincent?"

Vincent disregarded his friend's urging. "Up here," he shouted.

"No!" Frankie panicked. He threw his felt hat at Vincent to divert his attention, then barreled into him. The two fell to the ground with Frankie on top trying to pull Vincent's gun from his grasp. But Vincent was able to turn his revolver toward Frankie's chest and pull the trigger.

The two men stopped wrestling. "Get off me, you crumb," Vincent shouted. He rolled his old friend onto the ground, then stood looking down at him. Blood rushed from Frankie's chest, but Vincent felt no pang of guilt or pity. He turned to Senior and shrugged.

Senior dropped to his knees and ripped open Frankie's shirt. He immediately thrust his palm into the gaping chest wound in an effort to stem the flow of blood.

Agents Dryer and Harris raced the short distance up the trail to Vincent and Senior. "Get on your stomach. Now!" they yelled.

"I'm Doctor Cortland," Senior shouted back.

"I said get on your stomach. Now!"

"I'm Doctor Cortland. That man kidnapped me."

Vincent said, "He really is Doctor Cortland. My so-called friend here is the guy who kidnapped the doctors."

"Vincent," Frankie said in a barely audible voice.

"What?" Vincent knelt down beside him and leaned in closer. "What are you saying, Frankie?"

"Vincent, you know, I didn't want to kill you. I love you like a brother."

"Like a brother, Frankie? Like a brother?" Vincent scooped up Frankie's felt hat and ground it into his face. "Screw you, brother."

CHAPTER 54

Senior entered the waiting room. He was still wearing his green surgical gown and his mask hung loosely around his neck. Concetta looked up from her rosary and knew from the look on the doctor's face that her son did not survive the surgery. She let out a high-pitched, quivering wail and pounded her hands against her chest. Vincent had been dozing, but Concetta's wail snapped him awake. Senior approached them and said, "I'm sorry. I tried everything."

Vincent sobbed, beseeching Senior, "Don't tell me that! No! No! No! Not my son! Not him! You said the machine was gonna make him live."

"The machine did its job, but your son was too sick. It was simply too late. If we had been able to operate on him earlier, perhaps..."

Senior squeezed Vincent's shoulder in sympathy, then reached for Concetta's hand, covering it with both of his. "I'm so sorry, Mrs. Vendetti." He was at a loss for words. He had never dealt well with this part of being a surgeon.

A priest had been alerted and was waiting in the doorway to offer his assistance. Senior turned to the priest, nodded for him to step forward, then walked out of the room.

After taking a few steps down the corridor, Senior heard Vincent shout, "Someone's gonna die for this. Remember what I say. Someone's gonna die for this."

Senior stopped short and dropped his head to his chest. *Not again. Who will die this time?* Would he have to live in fear that Vendetti would seek revenge against Matt and Kate? Senior had warned Vincent time and again about the risks of the complicated surgery, the experimental use of the heart-lung machine, the boy's weakened state, and the delay in operating on him as a result of the kidnappings. All those factors made the operation extremely high risk. But it would be fruitless to try to reason with Vendetti now. He heaved a deep sigh before walking up the flight of stairs to check on Matt.

CHAPTER 55

Matt lay in his hospital bed with his leg elevated and his head propped up by a couple of pillows. He and Kate were talking about the kidnapping when Senior entered the room. Matt read his father's body language and knew immediately that the operation on Vincent Vendetti's son had failed. "Dad?"

Senior shook his head. "He didn't make it. He was too ill. The heart-lung machine worked well, but the boy was just too weak."

"You did everything you could."

"I know I did."

"Where is Vendetti now?"

"Downstairs with his wife. They're taking it badly."

Kate gave Senior a hug. "You did your best, Dad. There's nothing else you could have done."

"If we'd been able to get to him earlier, maybe—"

Matt interrupted. "That's not your fault. He can thank his best friend for the delay."

"Nice friend, huh?" Senior remarked. "Not only was Impolito plotting to take over the mob from Vendetti, but in the end, he didn't care if his friend's son lived or died. I don't think he ever planned to release you and Kate. But they were going to let me go to perform the operation. That's why they kept me blindfolded. They didn't want me to be able to identify them. But you could, so they were going to kill you both."

Matt asked, "Why the hell didn't Impolito kill Vendetti to begin with and get it over with? Why the elaborate kidnapping plot? Why sacrifice the boy?"

Senior shrugged. "He said he didn't want to hurt his friend. They had been best pals since they were kids. You know the saying—honor among thieves."

"Some honor."

There was a knock on the door. Agents Dryer and Harris walked in.

Agent Dryer spoke to Matt. "I understand the surgery on your leg was successful. That's good, Doctor Cortland. Happy to hear that."

"Thanks. I appreciate that, and I appreciate your help. I know I didn't make things easy for you."

"You did what you thought you had to do, Doctor," Agent Dryer said. "In the end, it all worked out—except for the Vendetti kid. We heard about him—and we also heard about your heart-lung pump."

Senior said, "Yes, the pump worked fine."

Matt asked, "We were talking before you got here, trying to fill in some of the details about what happened. Can you tell us what you know about all the characters?"

"Sure, as much as we can. We've learned most of what we know from Pansie Impolito, Frankie's sister. Her real name is Elaine. We agreed to drop all charges against her and put her in a witness protection program if she gave us a full confession about the players in the scheme."

Senior said, "Would you first explain how you knew where to find Vendetti and Impolito? You were a sight for sore eyes when you showed up at the Pigeon trail, but, how did you know to go there?"

Agent Dryer answered, "We followed Vendetti. We thought he knew more about what was happening than he let on. And even though Vendetti and Impolito were pals, we suspected Impolito was involved somehow."

"What about their driver?"

"The guy who was killed in your rockslide was a street-level mobster—no one of importance, a small-time player by the name of Albert Marcase."

"And Bobby?" Kate asked. "Who was he?"

"His real name was Robert Cardone. Ten years ago, his father Danny Cardone—a.k.a. the Professor—was head of the Philadelphia mob. Danny Cardone was killed by his nephew, Joey Caitano, with Pansie's involvement. But Vendetti and Impolito masterminded the murder so Vendetti could take over leadership of the family."

Kate said, "Frankie Impolito put together the plan to kidnap us, right? So how did he get Bobby to help him? Bobby must've known Frankie was involved in the killing of his father."

Agent Harris said, "That's a good question. Frankie probably convinced Bobby that Vendetti came up with the plan on his own. Of course, Pansie knew what really happened, but Frankie had sworn his sister to secrecy."

Agent Dryer added, "Our guess is Bobby got involved in the plan to take revenge against Vendetti. As it turns out, though, Bobby was close to Vendetti as a kid—considered him the older brother he never had—and didn't want to kill him. He just wanted Vendetti punished for killing his father by having him exiled to Italy. That way, Vendetti would lose everything he had worked for."

"What happened to Joey after he killed the Professor?" asked Matt.

"According to Pansie, he fled to a small village in Italy— San Bartolomeo. Joey hated Vendetti, so Frankie had Pansie talk Joey into joining the scheme to get Vendetti out of the country. No one seems to know where Joey is now, but I don't think we've heard the last of him."

"And Detective Kelly?"

Agent Harris explained, "Interestingly, Kelly was going to retire in a few months. Pansie said she learned from her brother that Kelly held a grudge for not being selected as chief of the regional police force in Eaglesmount. He felt underappreciated and was ripe for a bribe, so Impolito had no trouble recruiting him. Kelly, in turn, enlisted another cop to help him do his dirty work. He was the pilot killed in the helicopter crash. The shooter in the helicopter was a mobster Impolito had brought up to Eaglesmount from Philly."

"And Gianni? Who was he?"

Agent Dryer answered, "Gianni DeCarlo—an ex-boxer, a thug, and a killer."

Agent Harris interjected, "He's the one who killed Officer Kuberski."

"He fought under the name of Johnny One Punch. Had a big right hand. From what we know about him, he was never knocked down in the ring. That says a lot, because he fought against some top heavyweights like Marciano and Charles."

"I can certainly believe he was never knocked down," Matt said. "He kept coming at us no matter what we hit him with. We thought he was dead at least three times. Where is he now?"

"We're still looking for him. We don't have a plausible explanation for where his body could be. You said he was dead, but we couldn't find him on the trail."

"He couldn't still be alive, could he?" Matt asked.
Kate said, "Anything's possible with that guy."

EPILOGUE

MOB BOSS VENDETTI ESCAPES HIT! DRIVER KILLED!

January 2, 1954: Another attempt has been made on the life of Vincent Vendetti, reputed head of the Philadelphia crime syndicate. Vendetti and his driver were sitting in a car in front of Vendetti's Catherine Street home at approximately 10 p.m. on Friday night when shots were fired. Vendetti escaped unharmed, but his driver was killed.

A neighbor who did not want to be identified said she was out walking her dog when she heard three shots. She initially thought neighborhood kids were setting off firecrackers, but when she saw two men flee the scene, she suspected gunfire. She described the men as follows: One was a very big man who ran with a limp and the other was tall with dark hair.

Residents in the area describe Vendetti and his wife as nice neighbors who keep to themselves.

Last August, Frankie Impolito, former underboss of the Philadelphia mob, was shot and killed by Vendetti during a failed kidnapping scheme intended to force Vendetti out of power. The killing was ruled self-defense.

Lead investigator Detective Robert O'Hara said the police have no suspects at present but they believe the shooting may be a revenge incident in the ongoing gang warfare to wrest control of the syndicate from Vendetti.

The End

ABOUT THE AUTHOR

Tony Spallone is a retired executive who, when not traveling with his wife Patti or clocking miles on his bike, devotes his time to writing. He has a graduate degree in psychology, served as an officer in the U.S. Army, and has held various executive positions in business. His first two novels *Murder at Breeze Canyon* and *Murders in the High Desert* have received high praise. He and Patti live in Chester Springs, Pennsylvania. You can reach Tony on his website www.tonyspallone.com.

Your review is valued.

Tony welcomes feedback via email at:
tony@tonyspallone.com

www.ingramcontent.com/pod-product-compliance
Lightning Source LLC
Chambersburg PA
CBHW072126250626

47159CB00007B/2572